BE NOT AFRAID

Recent Titles by Christopher Nicole from Severn House

The Russian Sagas

THE SEEDS OF POWER
THE MASTERS
THE RED TIDE
THE RED GODS
THE SCARLET GENERATION
DEATH OF A TYRANT

The Arms of War Series

THE TRADE
SHADOWS IN THE SUN
GUNS IN THE DESERT
PRELUDE TO WAR

The To All Eternity Series

TO ALL ETERNITY
THE QUEST
BE NOT AFRAID

WOO

WWOK	
WWOO	
WLOW	
WMAI	12.01
WSPE	6/01
WTWY	3/01 12/02
WCON	9/02
WWAR	3/02
WMOB	10/01
WMSS	6/02

16. JUN 01
16. JUN 01
16. APR 01

BE NOT AFRAID

Christopher Nicole

This first world edition published in Great Britain 2000 by
SEVERN HOUSE PUBLISHERS LTD of
9–15 High Street, Sutton, Surrey SM1 1DF.
This first world edition published in the USA 2001 by
SEVERN HOUSE PUBLISHERS INC of
595 Madison Avenue, New York, N.Y. 10022.

Copyright © 2000 by Christopher Nicole

All rights reserved.
The moral right of the author has been asserted.

British Library Cataloguing in Publication Data

Nicole, Christopher, 1930-
Be not afraid
1. Townsend, Berkeley (Fictitious character) - Fiction
2. Secret service - Great Britain - Fiction
3. Adventure stories
I. Title
823.9'14 [F]

ISBN 0-7278-5644-8

This is a novel. Except where they can be historically identified, the characters are invented and are not intended to portray actual persons, living or dead.

Typeset by Palimpsest Book Production Ltd.,
Polmont, Stirlingshire, Scotland.
Printed and bound in Great Britain by
MPG Books Ltd., Bodmin, Cornwall.

Contents

Prologue: Berlin, 1928 1

Part One: The Feud

The First Attempt 13
The Second Attempt 26
The Lawyer 45
A Visit from the Past 66

Part Two: The Avenger

The Trial 89
The Visitor 109
The Wound 130
The Avenger 142

Part Three: The Pursuit

The Police 165
The Adventure 186
The Prisoner 205
The End of the Journey 223

"Be not afraid to do thine office."
Sir Thomas More

Prologue

Berlin, 1928

The mob bayed. Then it moved forward, up the entire breadth of the street, like a wave in a high-banked river, seeming more powerful than it was because of its confinement.

"Drive through them," Commissioner Schuler snapped, as his chauffeur instinctively braked.

"It would be better to wait, Herr Commissioner," the chauffeur suggested. "If we were to hit one of them . . ."

Schuler snorted, but allowed himself to be persuaded. A man ran past the stopped automobile, panting, hair wild, tie halfway down his shirt.

"Why are they chasing him?" Eva asked.

Schuler squeezed her knee. He did this often, as well as various other bits of her body; she was a pretty little thing, very blonde but also very buxom. It had never occurred to him to consider whether or not she enjoyed being squeezed – she knew who buttered her bread.

"He is probably a communist," he said. "Or a Jew."

The mob flowed up to the car and round it. They made no effort to damage it, intent on chasing the man.

"But if they catch him," Eva said.

"They will beat him up. Serves him right."

Eva shuddered. "Shouldn't they be stopped?"

"I would need an army, not a police force," Schuler pointed out. "Drive on."

But he was glad to gain the security of his desk, having despatched Eva to the security of her office.

"There has been another riot," he told his secretary.

Studt nodded. "We heard." He frowned. "You were not involved, Herr Commissioner?"

"I saw it," Schuler said.

"Nazis?"

"How should I know?"

"They are becoming a problem."

"It is a political, not a criminal matter," Schuler said. And grinned. "Unless they actually kill somebody. Now what is this?" He gazed at his appointments diary.

"He wishes to see you, Herr Commissioner."

Commissioner Schuler frowned at his secretary. "Who is this man?"

"I believe he is a chicken farmer, Herr Commissioner," Studt said.

"And what on earth does he wish to see me for? Someone has been stealing his chickens, eh? Send him to the charge desk."

"He says it is very important. It concerns that gun battle a couple of years ago. When that man Grippenheimer was killed, along with several of his bodyguards."

"And damned good riddance," Schuler remarked. "The fellow was a scoundrel."

"Nevertheless, Herr Commissioner, it was murder."

"It was a gun battle," Schuler pointed out. "Between two sets of thugs."

"One of which got away," Studt objected.

"Ah," Schuler said, "but one was killed, as I remember."

"We never identified the body, Herr Commissioner. And whatever our personal feelings, the fact is it remains an unsolved crime. This man . . ." he glanced at his notebook, "Himmler is his name, claims to have information. It would be better for us to hear what he has to say than for him to take it to some newspaper editor who might accuse the Berlin police of not doing its job."

"A chicken farmer," Schuler said contemptuously. "Very well, Studt, show him in. And be prepared to show him out again, very rapidly."

Commissioner Schuler leaned back in his chair and stroked his moustache. Combined with his square head and close haircut he thought it made him look like Field Marshal Hindenburg, whose portrait hung on the wall behind the desk. Schuler was a good German who had been decorated in the war – he wore the Iron Cross Second Class – and worshipped the ground on which the Field Marshal walked. Having successfully survived the past few years, the quite horrifying inflation of 1923 and the internecine strife between the various political parties, to all intents and purposes civil war, while slowly making his way up the ladder of the Berlin police force, he had learned both his business and the limitations of power that went with it. In this autumn of 1928 he thought Germany, or certainly Berlin, was on the up. The war was behind them. If he was prepared, privately, to apportion blame, none was due to the Field Marshal, elected to the presidency of the country three years ago. As for the future, now that Germany had been allowed to enter the League of Nations, he was perfectly prepared to leave that too to the old man. For the time being, all was well. As winter approached, Berlin was an irresponsibly happy place, save for the odd social and political outcast. It was as if the trauma of the previous dozen years had been entirely forgotten. Some critics complained that the crime rate was too high, but Hermann Schuler was a practical man who saw his job in Benthamite terms: as preserving the peace and well-being of the greatest number of citizens that he could with his limited resources. That meant cracking down with the fullest rigour of the law on murderers, rapists, burglars and the like. But there was very little he could do about organised gangs, except when his men actually caught them on the job, principally because they were nearly all involved with and protected by various political bosses; so when rival gangs decided to kill each other he was inclined to clap his hands. The same went for political antagonism. If this chicken farmer intended to be a nuisance . . .

He bent a baleful gaze on the door as it opened to admit a man in a trench coat and carrying a slouch hat. Schuler snorted. The man was somewhat young – only in his middle twenties, Schuler estimated – of medium height, and wore rimless glasses. His dark hair was carefully brushed, his suit was neat as was his tie knot, and his shoes were polished. There was nothing the least bit remarkable about him. Even his face was totally unremarkable; the glasses made him look like a schoolmaster. It was impossible to imagine him wrestling with a rebellious cockerel.

He was also very nervous. "Herr Commissioner."

"Well?" Schuler barked.

"In the matter of the assassination of Herr von Grippenheimer . . ." Himmler said tentatively.

"Yes?"

"It is nearly two years now, Herr Commissioner, and I do not believe there has been an arrest."

"That is quite true," Schuler conceded.

"And you have no leads? There were something like a hundred people present."

"My dear Herr Himmler, those hundred people were busy getting out of the house as soon as the violence began. The evidence we have is that four people entered Herr Grippenheimer's house, apparently as guests at a large party he was throwing, and suddenly started shooting. As I say, the other, legitimate, guests made themselves scarce as rapidly as possible. When the police arrived, they found Grippenheimer and five of his bodyguards dead, and also one of the assailants. This man carried no identification. The other three disappeared into the night. We have no names, and not even adequate descriptions. We know there were two men and a woman. Our informers in the Berlin underworld have been able to give us nothing. Whoever these people were, they came, they killed and they disappeared."

"And perhaps you did not look for them as vigorously as you might have done," Himmler suggested, mildly.

Schuler pointed. "You had better get out of here before I lose my temper. What business is it of yours, anyway?"

"Herr von Grippenheimer was a friend of mine."

"Of yours?" Schuler gave another snort, this time of disbelief. Grippenheimer had been a millionaire, which this chicken farmer certainly was not.

"We were also political associates."

"Ah!" Schuler said. "You mean you are a member of the National Socialist Workers' Party. Grippenheimer certainly was. He helped finance it."

"I am a member of the Nazi Party, yes," Himmler agreed. "I am not ashamed of it."

"I think I saw some of your people at work this morning."

"You cannot prove they were our people," Himmler riposted.

"That is true. And your Herr Hitler has renounced violence, has he not? It is a pity that he and his organisation seem to attract it. Well, I am sorry, but I cannot help you. I regard the Grippenheimer affair as closed."

"Suppose I told you that I know who the assassins were. One of them, anyway."

"Oh, yes?"

"He is an Englishman named Berkeley Townsend. He holds, or held until his retirement, the rank of colonel in the British army."

"Oh, yes?"

"I assume you still have the guest list for that party," Himmler said. "You will find his name on it."

"There were several English people at that party."

"Berkeley Townsend was one of them. His associates were named Harry Lockwood, Alexandros Savos and Martina Savos. These last two were husband and wife."

"And you are saying they are English? With a name like Savos?"

"No, they are Serbs, but resident in England and old friends of Townsend."

"Who are now dead."

"Only one man was killed. I would say it was probably Lockwood."

"I see. Now tell me, Herr Himmler, what possible reason could a colonel in the British army, together with an itinerant Serb and his wife, have for killing Herr Grippenheimer?"

"We have spent the last year investigating this man Townsend," Himmler said. "What we have found out is quite devastating: he is a professional assassin for the British government."

"Oh, come now."

"Here are some facts. We have discovered that he was involved in Serbian politics before the war; that he married the daughter of a leading member of the Black Hand secret society, and indeed took part in their activities; that he was commissioned a brigadier general in the Serbian army during the Balkan wars."

"And this makes him a British agent, instead of a renegade?"

"We have evidence that throughout this period he was taking his orders from London and corresponding with them through the embassy in Athens. Since the war he has been prowling about Europe, eliminating people considered to be hostile to Britain."

"How come I have never heard of this?"

"Well . . ." Himmler took off his glasses to polish them. "Most of his victims appear to have been common thugs. We have not established any link. But there has to be one. The point at issue, Herr Commissioner, is that we know Berkeley Townsend and his gang attended Herr Grippenheimer's party on the twelfth of November 1926. We also know that he left the country immediately, that same night, with his surviving associates and perhaps one or two other people, and that he was back in England two days later. That is a man travelling in haste."

"November the twelfth," Schuler mused. "That is the night your Führer nearly got himself blown up, is it not?"

"That is true."

"You'll be claiming next that this man Townsend had a hand in that."

"We do believe that. We know he was in Munich only a couple of days before the explosion. But it is very difficult to prove he actually planted the bomb because he was in Berlin when it went off. However, and for that very reason, his connection with the Grippenheimer killing is established."

"To your satisfaction," Schuler pointed out. "Not to mine. You have yet to provide me with a motive."

"He is opposed to the Nazi Party and all it stands for. Hence the bomb in Munich and the killing of Grippenheimer in Berlin. We believe he was sent by the British government."

Schuler gave a shout of laughter. "Do you really think anyone in the world, much less the British government, believes any of your people important enough to be murdered? Tell me, Herr Himmler, how many votes did your party gain in the last election."

"Well . . ." Himmler flushed. "Eighty-five."

"Out of thirty million. One assumes you are about to take power."

"We will one day; that election was three years ago. Next year you may find things have changed. And you cannot deny that the beer cellar in Munich was blown up, only half an hour before Herr Hitler was due to arrive."

"Munich is not my jurisdiction," Schuler told him. "There is some suggestion that the explosion was the result of a leaking gas main."

"That is absurd. Herr Commissioner, I have supplied you with sufficient evidence to apply for the extradition of Berkeley Townsend on a charge of murder."

"You have supplied me with nothing beyond a collection of wild and unrelated facts, Herr Himmler. I will bid you good day."

Himmler stared at him. "You refuse to act?" He stood up, then raised his right hand. "Heil Hitler!"

"And the same to you," Schuler said.

"The swine will do nothing." Heinrich Himmler crouched over his cup of coffee, seated at a corner table in the crowded café. "What are we to tell the Führer?"

"I think we should tell him nothing, at the moment," the other man said. Somewhat older than Himmler although still a young man – he was twenty-nine – he had compelling if somewhat ugly features with burning eyes and lank dark hair. Of small build, he sat awkwardly, trying to conceal his club foot from the other customers in the restaurant. "The Führer does not know all that we know. He only wishes Grippenheimer's assassin brought to justice, one way or the other; he does not know who the man is. If he remembers Townsend at all – they only met once, you know – it is simply as a man he tried to use and failed. Well, one way, what might be called the legitimate way, has failed. We shall have to take matters into our own hands. And inform the Führer when it is done."

Himmler licked his lips. "You mean . . ."

His companion smiled. "Have you not wrung sufficient chickens' necks?"

"Yes, but – I have never killed a man. And this man . . . he is a professional assassin."

"You mean he might shoot first," the lame man said contemptuously. "I am quite sure he would, Heinrich. In any event, the party cannot afford to be involved. It is, as you know, the decision of the Führer that our rise to power must be entirely legitimate and by the democratic process. Until then, officially, we keep our noses clean. So, for a job like this, we need someone who has a reason to kill Townsend but can in no way be linked to us."

"Do we know of such a person?"

"I think we do. Before poor Frederika Lipschuetz got blown up in Munich, she gave me a file she had compiled on Townsend. You know she used to work for an English newspaper and had access to a lot of material which is not generally known. I would like you to make a journey to Nish, in Serbia. There I think you will find the person, or people, who will fill the bill. I will give you all the information and anything else that you require."

"I do not understand."

Josef Goebbels sighed. His own brain being as sharp as a razor, he found it sometimes hard not to become impatient with these thick-headed louts he was forced to employ.

"Then listen. You know that Townsend rode with the Black Hand before the war. He was second in command to the famous Anna Slovitza, whose daughter he married. But next in command was a man named Karlovy. After Anna Slovitza was killed, Townsend and Karlovy fell out and Townsend shot Karlovy. What he did not realise was that Karlovy had three children who took on the burden of the blood feud – they are like that in the Balkans. After the war, when Townsend returned to Serbia to wind up his wife's affairs, the eldest Karlovy child, a girl named Irene, attempted to avenge her father. She failed. Townsend either killed her himself, or had her killed by his friends in the Serbian police; it is not clear what exactly happened. However, there are still two children left, now adults. It is their sworn duty to avenge their father and sister."

"But . . . our information is that it is some years since Townsend was in Serbia. They have done nothing in that time. Does that not mean they have decided to bury the feud?"

"A Serb," Goebbels pointed out, "never buries a feud. That these two people have not yet fulfilled their duty is because they have lacked the money to leave Serbia and travel to England, and because they do not know where Townsend is to be found. You will supply them with both the money and the documentation – passports and the like – as well as all the information they need."

"But – do we know where this man Townsend is to be found?"

"We do. We have several agents in England. One of them, a man named Green, has been working on this for us and is in fact keeping Townsend under constant surveillance. It will be your business to send these Karlovy people to Green."

"We have an agent in England named Green?"

"His real name is Gerber. But he has been living in England since just after the war and is an accepted part of the community. He will take care of everything when the Karlovys get to England but of course he must not be involved in any action they undertake."

"And you want me to get in touch with the Karlovys," Himmler said, slowly.

"That will not be difficult. I have the address of their home in Nish."

Himmler swallowed. He had never left Germany. "But what about my chickens?"

"We will find someone to look after your chickens, Heinrich. And you will only be gone a few weeks. This is party business. Carry it out successfully and I will see that your name is brought before the Führer. Then your feet will be on the ladder of success."

Himmler licked his lips. Josef Goebbels had just been chosen, by Hitler himself, to head the Berlin branch of the Nazi Party. Anyone with his recommendation could go far.

"Tell me what I must do," he said.

Part One

The Feud

"Be absolute for death; either death or life
Shall thereby be the sweeter."
William Shakespeare

The First Attempt

Berkeley Townsend drew rein and brought his panting mount to a halt on the rise overlooking his family home. A cavalryman in his army days he never felt happier than when in the saddle, and he always ended his morning ride with a gallop, which was good for both Hannibal and himself. Now he could allow himself a few minutes to enjoy the view and to contemplate the possibility of snow. It was already a cold winter, even at the beginning of December.

The house was isolated, a mile from the next dwelling. No longer a farm, it retained its outbuildings, and Maria Lockwood, the Serb-born maid and housekeeper, had a run full of clucking chickens. Chickens apart, it was a peaceful place; the ideal retreat for a man with a past.

Tall and powerfully built, with greying black hair and aquiline features relieved by a ready smile, just as his somewhat stern personality was alleviated by his equally ready wit, Berkeley Townsend was trying to get used to the idea that he was retired. This was partly because he was not yet fifty and felt as vigorous as at any time in his life. It was also because he could not be certain that he *was* retired. At the end of the war the British government had determined that they could no longer employ a man like him in this brave new world. He had accepted that, having personal matters to attend to. But then Whitehall had discovered that they could not do without him. So they had called him back into service. For one last assignment, they had said.

When one is recalled for one last assignment, there is always the likelihood of another last assignment.

He wondered what they really thought of him. But then, he often wondered what he thought of himself. It had all been wildly romantic in the beginning. As a subaltern desperately wounded by a Dervish spear at the Battle of Omdurman in 1898, he had assumed his military career was over. But his talents had been noticed, in particular by Colonel Gorman, an officer on Kitchener's staff. Gorman it was who had persuaded him to remain in the army, when his wound was finally healed, as a riding instructor and draughtsman; he was brilliant at delineating fortresses and military establishments with pencil and paper.

Just happy to be able to stay in uniform, Berkeley had never suspected where Gorman was going, and more personally important, what this would mean to him. Promoted general, Gorman had been placed in charge of military intelligence and felt he possessed the very man to head his team in the field.

Spying in those far-off days had been fairly genteel, Berkeley recalled with some nostalgia. He had travelled the length and breadth of Europe – part of the training on which Gorman had insisted had been languages, and Berkeley spoke German, French, Italian and Serbo-Croat fluently – apparently an English gentleman on a perpetual grand tour. In reality he was observing the armed forces with which he came into contact and making sketches of their establishments and fortifications. Until that day in 1908 – in the Hungarian Carpathians as they had then been – when he and his faithful servant Harry Lockwood had gone to the rescue of a beautiful woman being maltreated by Austrian soldiers, and, as he had often reflected since, launched themselves into space.

He had had no idea that Anna Slovitza had been an anarchist and a terrorist, a member of the Black Hand, a secret organisation dedicated to opposing Austria's ambitions in the Balkans. When he had learned the truth it had been too late; he had already fallen in love with both Anna and her even more beautiful daughter Caterina.

Gorman, always the pragmatist, had decided to take advantage of the emotional and legal morass into which his protégé had fallen. With the Balkans clearly approaching a crisis, he had wanted a man with his finger on the pulse. Accepting a commission in the Serbian army as the Balkan wars started but suspected of being a terrorist in his spare time, Berkeley had spent several years feeding London all the information he could obtain. He had known all along that his triple existence had to end in tragedy, but the deaths of both Anna and Caterina and his blood feud with the Karlovys had become submerged in the far greater tragedy of the war. It was only when he returned to Serbia in 1920 to sell the old Slovitza house, that he discovered the feud was still very much in existence.

He had supposed that with the help of his friend Colonel Savos of the Belgrade police he had coped with the situation, but he had underestimated the opposition. The Karlovys had become affiliated to another terrorist group, the Internal Macedonian Revolutionary Organisation, far more powerful and widespread than ever the Black Hand had been. They had kidnapped his eldest daughter Anna, meaning to draw him back into their orbit. Well, they had done that, but without truly understanding the nature of the beast they had in their turn aroused. His career, as a soldier and as a government assassin, had required him to kill, coldly and dispassionately, people he had not known and who therefore had no real existence for him. But in his pursuit of Anna, which had taken him four years, he had been angry. He had laid a trail of blood across Europe which had terminated in Grippenheimer's vicious harem.

He regretted none of it, even if it had cost the life of his oldest and closest friend. But Lockwood would not have had it any other way, and it had brought Anna home.

And then the difficult part had begun. A girl who has for four years, beginning when she was just twelve, been shunted from brothel to brothel, man to man, cannot be rehabilitated overnight. There had been so many difficulties to be overcome, not least the cocaine habit which had been induced by her various masters to keep her in subservience. It had taken several months, but slowly she had been weaned off the drug. Even so she had not been able to go back to school; Berkeley did not suppose it would ever be practical for her to have a job or live a normal life.

But at least she was happy, he thought. And Lucy was proving a treasure.

He reached the head of the drive which led off the main road – on a ridge above the farmhouse – and was startled by the sound of a car engine. He hadn't noticed the vehicle before; the road was tree-lined and it had been parked in the shadows. But it had definitely been overlooking the house and was now driving away at speed.

Possessing as he did a past which he had no desire to intrude into his present, Berkeley frowned as he walked the horse down the hill.

Lucy was waiting for him as he dismounted in the yard. "There's coffee in the house," she said.

He kissed her. Theirs was a strange relationship. Lucy was only half his age, a tall, slender young woman with black hair which she had allowed to grow out from a fashionable bob when she had discovered that was what he would like. They had married because, having retired, he wished a wife, and because she had found him a romantic figure. Of course, she did not know the truth and never could; she supposed he had been merely a roving military attaché. He had wondered from the beginning if he would be able to carry it off, if he might not talk in his sleep, if it was possible for a husband to keep such a secret from a wife. The problem had become acute when he had been called out of retirement for that last job. But Lucy had accepted it was simply to regain Anna, particularly when he had come home with the girl and, like everyone else, she had put down Anna's kidnapping to masculine perversion.

Now they walked up to the house hand in hand. When they had first married, they had bought a place of their own, but on the death of his father early this year, she had willingly agreed to sell the new house and move into the old, isolated farmhouse to be with Berkeley's mother. The children, having lived almost all their lives there, had been happy about that. Lucy's baby, and his own fourth child, had been born just after Anna's return, and was now crawling; they had named him Howard after his other grandfather. Berkeley thought that Lucy was happy but Anna's problems hung like a low cloud over them both. And now this strange car . . .

"You didn't have a visitor while I was out?" he asked.

"No. Were you expecting one?"

"No," he said.

He had no intention of alarming Lucy, but the waiting car, so anxious not to be identified, coming on top of another incident a week ago, definitely indicated that they were being watched.

By whom?

The house was quiet in the middle of the morning; Berkeley missed the sound of barking dogs. He kept meaning to replace his two old friends, both recently died, but had not yet got around to it. Both John junior and Alicia junior were away at school and would not be home for the Christmas holidays for another fortnight. Maria Lockwood, Harry's widow, waited to take Berkeley's hat and whip. Like her erstwhile mistress, Caterina, Maria was Serbian, but hers had been a happy life, both before and after her marriage to Berkeley's servant – until last November. She bore no grudge for Harry's death but her face was masked by tragedy. Her children also were out at school; they were day pupils in Northampton, riding in and out on their bicycles . . .

All three of them cocked their heads as the morning peace was broken by a short, flat explosion, followed immediately by another. Maria offered no comment and hurried back into the kitchen. "Will she ever stop?" Lucy asked.

"It makes her feel better," Berkeley said.

"You mean she imagines she's shooting at a man? One of *the* men?"

"I should think that's very likely."

She shuddered. "Young girls, playing with guns . . . *owning* a gun . . . it terrifies me."

"She's never going to shoot at you, my love," Berkeley pointed out and followed her through the drawing room to the conservatory, where his mother sat. She had aged enormously since the death of her husband and looked every day of her seventy-two years.

Berkeley leaned over and kissed her cheek as he squeezed her hand.

"She's out there," Alicia Townsend said. "Firing her gun."

Berkeley went to the door and opened it, watched his daughter coming towards him. He enjoyed looking at her; any man would. Anna was now nineteen, fully grown. Her long hair was the magnificent auburn he remembered from her mother and grandmother, her body was perfectly shaped for her below average height.

Her face was exquisite, or should have been with its perfect features and lustrous dark eyes, but the lips were usually tight and the eyes fathomless. It was impossible to gauge what might be going on behind that beautiful mask but he knew that her ghastly experience had been laid on top of a personality that had always been both enigmatic and disturbing. She was half Serbian and, unlike her younger brother and sister, she could remember that country and the mother who had died so tragically, a death she had long refused to accept. Berkeley had never probed into her experiences during the four years she had been a plaything for so many men; imagination was grim enough. He could not blame her if she hated his entire sex, or perhaps the entire world. That she had asked him if she could own a gun – he had licensed it in his own name, along with his Browning automatic – and spent hours firing the Smith and Wesson revolver to become a crack shot would be regarded by most people as a deplorable hobby for a young girl, but Berkeley believed it was helping her to overcome the nightmares in her mind. He could only rely on time, kindness and utter normality . . . and on the fact that, however kind Lucy was, Anna only smiled when she looked at him.

As now. She threw her arms round his neck, still holding the hot gun, and hugged and kissed him. "May I go into town this afternoon, Papa?"

"Don't tell me you have a date?"

Oh, that one day she should have a date.

"I have my Christmas shopping to do," she said seriously, "and no money."

"You shall have money," he assured her. "We'll go into town together." He looked at his wife. "Will you come?"

Lucy hesitated for just a moment, then shook her head. "I have the menus to see to."

She felt it beneficial for father and daughter to spend as much time as possible together.

"This time next year you are going to be twenty years old," Berkeley remarked as he drove the Austin Seven into Northampton.

"Does that make me an adult?" Anna watched the streets unfolding in front of them.

"Not in the eyes of the law, I'm afraid."

"But old enough to be doing something with my life," she suggested.

"That's up to you."

"What would you like me to do, Papa?"

"I can't possibly tell you what you should do with your life." Berkeley parked the car.

"You told me once that your ambition for me was to grow up and marry an English gentleman. That was before . . . I went away."

"And, as I remember, you weren't very keen on the idea, even then."

"Even then," she said, half to herself. "Papa . . . please tell me how Mama died. The truth."

Berkeley sighed. But his attempts to shield her in the past had turned out disastrously. "She was captured by the Austrians after the assassination of the Archduke Franz Ferdinand, and tortured. When they left her alone in her cell, she hanged herself."

"And you?"

"I was very close. But I could not get to her in time."

"Did she assassinate the archduke?"

"No. She tried, but failed. It was one of her associates who fired the fatal shots."

"Did she and her associates do wrong, Papa?"

"Well . . . as a result of that murder, something like twenty million people died. On the other hand, it is possible to say that the war was coming anyway. The Black Hand merely precipitated events."

"Were not the Austrians hateful people?"

"They were the masters in the Balkans before the war. All masters are hateful to those they rule."

Anna smiled. "You are a philosopher, Papa. You have become a philosopher."

"Meaning that I wasn't always?"

"I would have said there was a time when you would have shot first and asked questions afterwards."

"Not a lot changes," he remarked. "Let's go shopping."

He followed her through the department stores, picking up the bills. With his pension and the golden handshake from the government, together with his large fee for that last assignment and the proceeds from the sale of the houses in Sabac and Northampton, he was well off if not wealthy, and it was a pleasure to indulge her. She had been back in England for the two previous Christmases, but she had not wished to go out and be seen. This was another step in her general rehabilitation and he was delighted.

They had accumulated a large collection of parcels and boxes and were leaving the last store when Berkeley experienced an uneasy feeling. Years of living on a knife-edge had made him peculiarly sensitive to stares or unwanted attention, and he had been alerted by the watching motor car that morning. Now he turned his head sharply and saw a young man observing him from a little way along the street. This was the same boy he had seen on his last visit to town but at that time he had not thought too much of it. And now there was no reason to suppose he had been watching *him*; far more likely that he had been gazing at Anna and was embarrassed to be caught out. But there had been something familiar about his face.

In any event, it was growing dark, and he had disappeared into the gloom and the crowd. Berkeley was escorting Anna down the side street leading to where the car was parked, when he suddenly heard a rush of movement behind him.

"Run," he snapped and swung round, dropping the parcels he was carrying. In the lane there was no street lighting and the figure approaching him at speed was not really distinguishable, but even in the gloom Berkeley could make out the gleam of steel in his hand.

He whipped off his hat and struck it downwards as the knife was thrust at him. The bowler caught the blade and deflected it, and Berkeley swung his fist, connecting with the side of his assailant's head who tumbled to his hands and knees. Berkeley kicked the hand holding the knife. The would-be murderer gasped as the knife flew away into the darkness, then he had rolled over and gained his feet, and was running away as hard as he could.

"Papa!" Anna was only a few feet away.

"I told you to get out of it," Berkeley said.

"That man tried to kill you."

"If it *was* a man," Berkeley said thoughtfully.

"Are we going to call the police?"

"Not right this minute; let's go home." He gathered up the scattered parcels, took her to the car and unlocked it.

They drove out of Northampton. Anna was silent for some minutes, then she asked, "Do you have a lot of enemies, Papa?"

Berkeley grinned. "Ever heard of a chap called Richelieu?"

"He was a cardinal, who ruled France in the seventeenth century."

"That's right. He was a pretty tough egg. There is a legend that when he was on his deathbed his confessor asked him if he would forgive his enemies. And Richelieu replied, 'I have no enemies; I have killed them all.'"

Anna glanced at him. "But you have not killed all yours."

"I suppose I'm not as tough as Richelieu. But I'm getting a little old for that sort of thing."

"You're not old," she said. "I don't want you ever to be old. And the way you handled that thug was magnificent."

"He was an amateur. Meanwhile . . . let's not mention him to anyone."

"Not even Lucy?"

"Especially not Lucy."

Who on earth would have sneaked out of the darkness to kill him, here in England? Had it been that boy? The disconcerting thing was that although his assailant had been wearing male clothes, Berkeley had a strong suspicion that it had been a female. In which case the two could be working together, and that could be a problem. Oh, to have Lockwood standing at his shoulder.

He was not the least afraid for himself but his children were so vulnerable, Anna most of all. The thought of her ever having to undergo another such experience was unbearable. But that was impossible. He had killed everyone who had been involved in her kidnapping and rape. There was no one . . . He sat up in bed.

Lucy, just nodding off, looked up. "Is there something the matter?"

Berkeley lay down again. "No. I was having a nightmare."

"That cheese at dinner," she suggested. "It was a bit high."

"More likely that second glass of port."

"Would you like something?"

"I'll be all right," he said.

He closed his eyes and saw Irene Karlovy's face in front of him. A haunting face, by no means pretty but attractive in its intensity. She had tried to kill him and, when that had failed, she had engineered the kidnapping of Anna. For that she had paid with her life, cut down by the bullets of Serb policemen. But she had had a brother and a sister. He had never met the brother but he could still remember Helen Karlovy, Irene's sister, saying, very simply and without rancour, "We have to kill you. It is our duty for the sake of our father." She had been his prisoner at the time and then he had handed her over to the police and had supposed she was gone from his life for ever, as long as he did not return to Serbia – or the kingdom of the Serbo-Croats, Bosnians and Herzegovinians, as he supposed it should now be called. Many people were starting to replace that mouthful with the simple term Jugo-slavia.

But if that boy had not been Helen and Irene's brother he would eat his hat. And if his actual assailant had been a woman, then she had been Helen, a girl he had once held captive for two days, hoping to exchange her for Anna. A girl, now a woman, who was still hell-bent on revenge.

After five years? And in England? That did not seem practical, unless their financial and social situation had vastly improved.

Well, then . . . IMRO again? But IMRO had collapsed, as far as he knew, assisted by himself.

Yet someone had been watching his house, and the boy had been there, watching him. And the girl had been there, waiting to strike. And perhaps even at Anna. The thought made his skin crawl.

He felt so helpless in England. Had this been the Balkans, he would have loaded his Browning automatic and gone hunting. In England one had to wait for the blow to fall before one was permitted to take action. And even then one could not take the law into one's own hands. One was required to go to the police . . .

Next morning he again drove into Northampton, but this time went to see Inspector Watt, now Chief Inspector Watt. Peter Watt and Berkeley Townsend were old friends and business acquaintances. Watt had investigated the attempted murder of

Berkeley back in 1908 – by Karlovy as it had turned out, although nothing had ever been proved. Watt had also investigated the strange disappearance of Caterina Townsend, and then, more recently, the abduction of Anna, equally without success. He regarded his visitor somewhat apprehensively. "No problems, I hope, Colonel."

"I always seem to have problems," Berkeley said. "You remember that Karlovy business."

Watt remembered it only too well. "The gentleman you had to kill. In self-defence. And whose family you suspected of having kidnapped Miss Anna."

"Spot on."

"But Miss Anna is back with us," Watt said enthusiastically. "So the matter is closed . . . surely."

"Unfortunately, it does not appear so. I did not manage to kill all the Karlovys."

Watt swallowed. This was not the sort of talk any English police officer liked to hear.

"Frankly," Berkeley said, "I did not think it necessary. The only surviving members of the family were an elderly uncle and two teenage children. They had very little money and almost no prospects. Like you, I considered the matter closed. However, during the past week I have been aware of being followed."

"You didn't report this?"

"I didn't think it particularly important, to begin with. But yesterday afternoon I saw Stefan Karlovy here in Northampton."

Watt looked suitably outraged but also sceptical. "A teenage boy, you say?"

"That was five years ago, Chief Inspector. Teenage boys grow up. So do their sisters. Soon after I saw the boy, I was attacked by someone with a knife. I think it was the sister."

"But . . . you haven't reported *that*? Really, Colonel, a knife attack on the streets of Northampton . . . we can't have that sort of thing."

"I'm reporting it now. But I do not wish a song and dance made of it."

"The law is the law, Colonel. Could you identify this woman?"

"I can identify Helen Karlovy but I cannot identify her as my attacker. It was dark, and everything happened rather quickly."

"But you are quite sure it was the same boy? Er, man?"

"Yes. Anna was with me. She saw him too."

"She recognised him?"

"Of course she didn't, Peter. She never saw him before. But she saw the man watching us."

"You don't suppose they're after her again?"

"I don't, actually. I think I taught them a lesson five years ago. Anyway, there's no way it can happen; Anna never goes anywhere unaccompanied. I would say it's more likely they have murder in mind. My murder. It was me they attacked."

"Do you require protection?"

"Wouldn't it be simpler just to arrest them and have them deported?"

"I can't do that, Colonel. Presuming they each have a passport and a visa, I can't touch them until and unless they commit a crime."

"You mean you don't consider attempting to stick a knife into me committing a crime."

"Of course I do. But you have just said that you cannot identify your assailant. The fact that you saw the boy watching you does not link him and the knife attack. Nothing that would stand up in court, anyway."

"However, if they try again and succeed, you will arrest them."

Sarcasm was lost on Peter Watt. "Oh, come now, Colonel, I'm sure it won't come to that. You'll have protection."

"How?"

"Well, a constable . . ."

"Mounting guard outside my house? Following me wherever I go? Will he be armed?"

"Well, no, sir, I couldn't permit that."

"Then he'd be on a hiding to nothing. Anyway, if they get too close I'll deal with them myself."

Watt was beginning to look agitated. "Colonel, do please be careful. You simply can't go about shooting people.

"Even in self-defence?"

"That would have to be proved, sir. Your victim would have to have a weapon in his hand. And to have fired it." He gave Berkeley a quizzical look.

"Point taken, Chief Inspector."

Watt sighed. "I tell you what I'll do, Colonel. I'll see if I can locate these people. It shouldn't be too difficult. Two Serb nationals . . . they have to be lodging somewhere. I'll find them and I'll give them a good talking to. Warn them off, like." He paused. "Don't you think that's the best way of handling this?"

"Oh, I do. I think that's an excellent plan. However, I'd be grateful if, when you find them, you let me have the address."

"Now, Colonel . . ."

"I'll be good, Chief Inspector."

The Second Attempt

"I wish you'd tell me what's going on," Lucy complained.

"What makes you think something is going on?" Berkeley asked.

They were sitting on the bench in the orchard, Baby Howard in his pram in front of them.

"Well," she said, "you've been odd the last couple of days. And now you tell me I mustn't take baby for a walk . . ." She gazed at him from under arched eyebrows.

"I didn't want to bother you," Berkeley said. "But it seems there is an escaped convict in the district, a man guilty of violent crimes, and I feel we should be careful."

She frowned. "There's been nothing in the papers."

"Well, no, they're keeping it very quiet. I only know because Peter Watt told me."

When, he wondered, would he be able to stop lying?

And it was easier to lie to some people than to others. Lucy was still frowning. "You say Inspector Watt told you? Why you? I mean, if this man is a menace, surely he's a menace to everyone, not just us."

"I'm sure that's right. I imagine Watt told me because he and I are old friends. He knows we're a bit isolated out here, and he knows about Anna and how fragile she is."

He suspected she didn't believe him.

"What about your hat?"

"Eh?"

"Your bowler. It is quite ruined. It has a great big tear in it."

"Ah," he said. "Yes. It blew off in the wind, and got stuck on a railing. Would you believe it?"

She obviously didn't, but she decided not to press the matter.

* * *

Anna was also concerned. "Please tell me the truth, Papa," she asked.

He could, to her. "Remember that this is our secret," he said.

"It's to do with me, isn't it?"

"Indirectly. That boy we saw is the brother of the woman who arranged your kidnapping. She's dead now . . ."

Anna's mouth made an O. "You killed her?"

"As a matter of fact, I didn't. She was shot by the Serbian police. But this whole thing began because I killed their father, oh, more than ten years ago now."

"And you think they are coming after me again?"

"No. I think this time they're coming after me. What I would really like to find out is where they got the money to come all the way to England, where they got the passports and visas. They're clearly being financed by someone."

"And you can't just go out and get them."

"No, I can't." Berkeley gave one of his savage grins. "It's against the law. We have to wait for them to come to us."

"Papa, I will help you. You know that."

"Of course. But you'll help me best by just keeping your head down. If I need you, believe me, I'll shout."

Yet he was acutely aware that he did need help. John junior, who with Anna was the only member of the family who knew what he had really done for most of his life, would be invaluable. But the holidays were still several days off. The Lockwood children went to school in Northampton and cycled out every afternoon. But they were still young teenagers, and he didn't want them involved.

Savos? The old Serbian police chief could be trusted absolutely. Equally, he knew all about both the Karlovys and the feud. The operative word here was "old", Alexandros had to be nearly seventy. But he remained forever in Berkeley's debt for having made it possible for him to take refuge in England following his retirement, safe from the vengeance of the relatives of the many people he had tortured and executed when in charge of Belgrade. And, as he and his wife Martina had proved only two years previously when they had accompanied Berkeley to Germany to regain Anna, they could be deadly.

But there were other drawbacks to calling on them for help.

Most important was that by the terms of Savos's permission to live in England, he could be deported if he ever broke the law in the slightest fashion. Then there was the fact that Martina, beautiful, high-spirited and only slightly more than a third of her husband's age, also had a cocaine habit, picked up in her girlhood in Serbia, which she seemed able to keep serviced in her new country.

But they remained his best chance of obtaining adequate help.

He telephoned the next day; the Savoses lived at Hastings on the south coast.

"Berkeley!" Martina shrieked. "But it is so good to hear from you."

Too late Berkeley recalled that she had a distinct weakness for him, as her fertile brain made plans for when Savos should be no more, but perhaps seeing him at home, in the company of his wife, might cool her off.

"It's nice to speak to you, too. I'm calling to ask if you and Alexandros would like to come and visit us, for a week or so."

"Oooh!" she squealed. "We would like that very much. It is to do a job, eh?"

"No, no," Berkeley said. "I would just like to see you. So would Anna."

"But you would like us to bring our revolvers."

"Do you ever go anywhere without them?"

She giggled. "It is not safe for us to do so. We will come tomorrow."

"Shouldn't you ask Alexandros?"

"Alexandros does whatever I tell him," she explained.

"Ah. Right. Then I'll expect you tomorrow. Take the train to Northampton and I'll meet you at the station."

"I can hardly wait," she said. "I will pack now."

Berkeley hung up thoughtfully. He didn't suppose it would have done any good to remind her that he was married. Such moral issues did not interest her, and she was not, in fact, married to Savos, whatever forged documents she possessed; the old villain had abandoned his wife to spend his retirement with his beautiful secretary.

But it was necessary to tell Lucy.

"We've some people coming to stay, tomorrow," he said.

"People? Just like that? Do I know them?"

"I'm afraid you don't, yet. They're old friends of mine. Serbians. You remember I served in the Serbian army during the Balkan wars."

"Yes," she said doubtfully.

"I made their acquaintance then. He was a police chief and a great help to me. Now he and his wife happen to be in England and they would like to come and visit."

"I see," she said. "For how long?"

"Well, I don't really know. You'll like them." He could only hope he was right.

"I'm sure I shall," she agreed. "I was merely thinking that we don't really have a spare room when the children are at home. I can put them in Anna's room, and put Anna in Johnnie's, but when Alicia comes home she and Anna will need to share their room again."

"That's not for another ten days," Berkeley said. "I imagine the Savoses will have gone by then."

"Savos," Lucy said thoughtfully. "I hope Anna won't be upset at having to move out."

"Anna will love to," Berkeley assured her. "They're old friends of hers as well."

Anna frowned. "I think I remember them, just," she said. "It was all so confused."

Because she had still been on the habit when held captive by Grippenheimer.

"Do you ever feel the urge now?" he asked.

She shuddered. "Not after that rehabilitation centre."

"Well, remember that Martina is probably still indulging."

"What do I do if she offers me some?"

"Tell me."

"What will you do?" She giggled. "Spank her?"

"No. I think she'd enjoy that too much. I'll just confiscate her supply. She'll find that much more difficult to accept."

He didn't like leaving anyone alone at home but his car was only a four-seater.

"I'll stay," Lucy volunteered. "Don't worry. Maria is with me."

Berkeley was still uncertain. "You'll keep every door and every downstairs window locked until I return. And you'll admit no one. No one at all."

"All right," she said. "I really don't see why you are so agitated. The odds on this criminal choosing our house to attempt a break-in must be a thousand to one."

"We happen to be very isolated," Berkeley reminded her. "Please just do as I ask."

She kissed him on the nose. "You worry too much. We'll all be safe and sound when you return. There's a promise."

Berkeley and Anna drove into Northampton and parked in the station yard. They waited on the platform, sheltering beneath the roof as it had begun to drizzle.

"Do you think we'll have a white Christmas?" Anna asked.

"I wouldn't doubt it."

"I'm so looking forward to it. I don't think I was very much use last Christmas."

"No one expected you to be," Berkeley said. "This winter you've been just great. Here's the train."

The engine puffed to a halt and the passengers disembarked.

"There they are," Berkeley said and went forward, Anna at his shoulder.

"Berkeley!" Martina screamed, throwing herself into his arms, long curling black hair flowing out from beneath her hat and streaming in the breeze. Berkeley reckoned she might have put on weight, which merely made her more voluptuous than ever; her features retained the same crisply attractive contours that he remembered, and her legs, revealed by the fashionably short skirt, were as shapely as ever . . .

He gave her a hug and kissed both cheeks, while reaching past her to shake Savos's hand. The retired policeman had not changed at all; his hatchet face might have been carved from granite and for all his age he stood absolutely straight. Only his white hair, revealed as he raised his hat, indicated that he might be past middle age.

"Berkeley, my old friend," he said, squeezing Berkeley's

fingers. "How good to see you again. And how well you are looking. And Anna!" He stepped past Berkeley to embrace the girl. "Even more beautiful!"

Anna waggled her eyebrows at her father over Savos's shoulder and Martina giggled. "He cannot keep his hands off a pretty girl," she said.

"I feel I know her so well," Savos said. "Do you remember me, Anna?"

"Very well," Anna lied, and was embraced in turn by Martina.

"I am so looking forward to meeting your wife," Martina said to Berkeley.

She was a past mistress at the art of lying.

"And your children," she added.

"Well, my older children are away at school," he explained. "But there's Baby."

"Oooh, I adore babies."

"He makes a lot of noise," Anna commented.

"Even when they cry," Martina asserted.

Berkeley put her in the back of the little car with Anna and had Savos sit beside him in the front; he reckoned that was safer for all concerned.

"Now tell us what the trouble is," Savos said as they drove out of town. "I know you did not bring us up here just for a visit."

"Karlovy," Berkeley said.

"But . . . are they not all dead?"

"Not the young ones, now grown up, who have both their father and their sister to avenge."

"But surely they are in Serbia," Martina said.

"They are right here in Northampton, when last I saw them." He told them about the attack.

"Cannot the police handle it?" Savos asked.

"We don't go in for preventive detention in this country; even supposing we knew where to find them."

"And that is what you wish us to do?" Martina asked. "Find them?"

"I think we should leave that to the police," Berkeley said.

"But you say they will not act until a crime has been committed."

"That's right. But I am also pretty sure that the Karlovys cannot afford to hang about. They'll have another go."

"Ah," said Savos. "We are to be your bodyguards."

"In a manner of speaking. My problem is that with poor Lockwood gone I don't have any back-up. And while those two kids are at large, I don't like leaving the house."

"Of course. We will be there, always."

"Well, until this business is sorted out. I should be very grateful. And I shall, of course, make it worth your while."

"We should not dream of taking payment," Martina declared. "We owe you too much already. It is enough that we can help you."

She squeezed Anna's hand.

"Well, then . . ." They were out in the country now; he topped the rise and slowed the car. "There it is."

"It is beautiful," Martina said. "And you keep chickens. I do like chickens."

"But I see what you mean. It is very isolated," Savos observed.

"Yes," Berkeley agreed, frowning as he drove slowly down the hill to the yard.

"What is the matter?" Savos asked, noting the change of expression.

"The front door is open," Berkeley said.

"Is that unusual? Of course, it is drizzling."

"And cold," Martina observed.

Anna made no comment.

"My wife promised to keep it closed and locked," Berkeley said.

"What do you wish to do?" Savos asked.

Berkeley was now driving very slowly indeed while he tried to think. But every thought was unthinkable. On the other hand, he had only survived as long as he had by looking facts squarely in the face.

"We must assume that the house is in the hands of the Karlovys," he said. "Lucy must have allowed herself to be taken in."

"But if that is the case . . ." Savos said.

"Yes," Berkeley agreed through gritted teeth. "We can only hope for the best. It is me they want. If they are inside the house, waiting for me to return, they may not know you are with me. We might be able to surprise them. However, remember that inside that house, hopefully alive, are my wife and my mother, my son and a maidservant. So there can be no indiscriminate shooting. In fact there should be no shooting at all, unless they begin it. As far as we know, they do not have firearms."

"I have always believed in shooting first," Savos remarked.

"This time restrain yourself. Where are your weapons?"

"Here." Martina took her small .38 from her handbag.

"And here." Savos took a similar weapon from his pocket. "And yours?"

"In the house. It is not customary to carry guns in England."

Savos blew through his teeth.

"Now here's what we do," Berkeley said. The car was just entering the yard. "I will stop at the foot of the steps and we will go in at the double. As I said, they will only be expecting me and perhaps Anna. Hopefully the sight of you two, armed, will make them stop to think. I will go up the stairs; Alexandros, you will go to the right, into the drawing room. Beyond that is the conservatory. You will hold anyone in there at gunpoint until I join you."

"And if someone shoots at me?"

"Then you may return fire. Martina, you will go through the door on the left, into the dining room and beyond, the pantry and kitchen. You will do the same."

"I am ready," Martina said.

"What can I do, Papa?" Anna asked.

"You stay in the car, on the floor in the back, until I call you. Until then, you don't move."

"Oh, Papa, let me come with you!"

"Definitely not. Please obey me, Anna. Let's go!"

The car was at the steps. Berkeley ran up them, throwing the half-open front door wide to rush into the hall, and tripped over the body that lay on the parquet. For a moment he was absolutely paralysed, afraid to look. But it was definitely Lucy. His heart surged with horror and anger. Two wives, both violently killed. But she was breathing, for all the blood that had spread around her like a shroud.

There was a shout, and he looked up to see Stefan Karlovy

coming down the stairs, a long-bladed bloodstained knife in his hand. Berkeley reared back on his heels. But Savos was immediately behind him and brought the young man down with a single shot. Stefan tumbled down the last two steps, rolling over as he struck the floor.

"You said there would be two," Savos panted.

"The other's around." Berkeley cradled Lucy in his arms.

"You said there'd be a man," she whispered. "But there was a girl, such a pretty girl. I did not see the man, until . . ." Her head drooped.

"We must stop the bleeding," Martina said, kneeling beside him.

"Too late," he muttered. He had seen enough dead bodies in his time.

"Is this your wife?"

"Was." Berkeley laid Lucy's head on the floor and slowly stood up. The sense of loss, of outrage, had been overtaken, at least temporarily, by the white hot anger that had driven him through so many crises.

"She will be upstairs," Savos said, standing at the foot of the staircase and looking up.

"Check the kitchen anyway, Martina," Berkeley said. "And be careful."

Martina got up and stepped over Lucy's body. She paused at the dining room door, drew a deep breath and then threw it open, leaping through in a flutter of skirt.

Savos still waited at the foot of the stairs.

"There is a dead woman here," Martina called.

Berkeley ran to join her. She was in the kitchen, looking at Maria sprawled on the floor on her back. She too had been knifed in the chest.

"They are swine," Martina said.

"Yes," Berkeley agreed. He was convulsed with fear for his mother and son. He ran back into the hall.

"Up?" Savos asked.

Berkeley nodded and Savos climbed the stairs, slowly, revolver thrust forward. Berkeley followed, aware that Martina was immediately behind him.

At the top Savos hesitated, looking over his shoulder. Berkeley pointed to the nursery and Savos nodded, but as he turned in the indicated direction Howard began to wail.

Berkeley gave a sigh of relief and pointed instead to his mother's bedroom. Savos threw this door open, while Berkeley dashed into the nursery. Howard was very wet and moving restlessly, and the nursery window was open. And as he reached the cot there came a shout from Anna.

"Damnation!" Berkeley leaned out of the window. There was a sloping roof over the hall which shut out any view of the car by the steps. "Keep down!" he bellowed.

For reply there came a shriek.

"Oh, shit!" He ran for the door.

"Take this." Martina threw him her gun. "I'll look after Baby."

Berkeley dashed into the corridor and encountered Savos who looked absolutely devastated. "Berkeley . . ."

Berkeley stepped past him and ran down the stairs. No father should have favourites but Anna was more precious to him than any living creature. He reached the hall, jumped over Stefan Karlovy, checked again at the sight of Lucy's body, then leapt over it and ran on to the porch. And gazed at Anna and Helen Karlovy, wrestling on the tarmac beside the car.

He ran up to them. Helen Karlovy was on top at the moment, one hand on Anna's throat; but she had lost the knife long ago. Berkeley put the muzzle of the revolver on the back of her neck. "Get up," he said. "Before I blow your head off." He spoke Serbo-Croat.

She hesitated, drawing deep breaths, then turned on him, teeth bared. But he had anticipated her lunge and kicked her in the belly. She dropped to her hands and knees, forehead on the ground, and retched, both hands pressed to her stomach.

"Are you all right?" Berkeley asked Anna, reverting to English and keeping Helen covered.

"Yes," she panted. "Just a bump on the head."

Her dress was torn, and he reckoned she had more bruises than that.

"I thought I told you to stay in the car."

"I couldn't let her get away, Papa."

"You could have been killed. Everyone else has."

Anna gulped.

He went back to Serbo-Croat. "You," Berkeley said. "Get up."

Helen Karlovy slowly got to her feet. She was a slight young woman, with pertly attractive features and straggly brown hair; Berkeley remembered her from their brief encounter six years before. She was wearing trousers, but her clothes were thoroughly disordered, and she attempted to straighten them.

"You are a swine," she said in the same language. "I hate you."

"The feeling is entirely mutual," he said. "Get inside."

She hesitated, glanced at Anna, and then went into the house, checking at the sight of her dead brother. "Stefan!" she screamed, ignoring Lucy as she stepped over her and knelt beside the boy.

Anna, beside her father, stared at Lucy. "Oh, my God!" There was only six years between them and they had become like sisters over the past year. "Is she . . ."

"Yes," Berkeley said.

"And . . ."

"Maria certainly." He looked up as Savos came down the stairs.

"Your mother . . ." Savos said.

"Her too?"

"She was not stabbed," Savos said. "I think it must have been a heart attack."

"That's still murder, in my book," Berkeley said.

"What are we going to do? You will have to call the police."

"In due course. Keep an eye on her."

"What about Baby?" Anna asked.

"I think he's all right," Berkeley said, and at that moment Martina appeared at the head of the stairs, cradling Howard in her arms.

At least he was too young to understand what was going on, Berkeley reflected.

He went up the stairs and into his mother's room. She sat in her rocking chair, where she had spent so much of her time in the last year, her head slumped to one side. As Savos had indicated, there was no blood, no sign of any wound. But she was definitely dead. There was no pulse and she was quite cold.

Anna stood in the doorway.

"Did I cause this, Papa?" she asked, her voice trembling.

"No," he said. "I caused it."

"Oh, Papa!" She ran to him, threw both arms round him. "That woman . . ."

"Will hang for murder," he said. "But not until she's answered one or two questions."

He returned down the stairs to where Savos and Martina waited, Martina still carrying Howard.

"Let's get organised," he said. "Anna, take Howard and go into the drawing room. Stay there until the police arrive."

Anna took the baby into the drawing room and Berkeley closed the door.

"Martina," he said, "keep an eye on Miss Karlovy. Alexandros, step into the dining room."

Savos raised his eyebrows but obeyed. Berkeley followed him and closed the door.

"Give me your gun."

Savos was still holding it. "Do you not have one of your own?"

"Yes, but it hasn't been fired. This has."

"Well, of course. I shot that crazy man."

"That's it. When that comes out, you'll be deported."

"But it was in defence of you."

"You'll still be putting your head on the block. Have you a licence for it?"

"Well, no. Your people would not allow me to have a gun, legally."

"So you'll have broken the terms of your residence here. We can't risk that. Our story will be that I shot him. In self-defence."

"But why should you do this?"

"Simply because there is no risk of anyone deporting me. It will have been justifiable manslaughter."

"But what about the girl? She will say differently."

"She can't, because she wasn't there when her brother was shot. She didn't even know he had been shot until I brought her back into the house."

Savos handed over the weapon. Berkeley used his handkerchief to wipe the gun clean of fingerprints, then held it in his right hand, making sure his prints were on the trigger and the guard as well as on the butt. Then he put it in his pocket.

"Right. Let's talk to Helen."

They returned to the hall, where Helen still knelt beside her brother's body. Martina continued to watch her, gun in hand. Lucy lay as still as Stefan. There was enormous grief in Berkeley but for the moment it was overlaid by a combination of guilt and anger. *He* had caused this to happen, by the simple fact of shooting Karlovy, in self-defence, fourteen years before. Now . . .

"We need to know who sent you," he said, in Serbo-Croat. "Or who financed you."

"You are a murdering swine," Helen said. "I will tell you nothing."

"You will," Berkeley said. "Or I will allow Colonel Savos to question you. You have heard of Colonel Savos?"

She gazed at the colonel and licked her lips.

Savos smiled at her.

"I am sure you have," Berkeley said. "Irene will have told you of him. He once questioned her."

"He tortured her," Helen said.

"That's one way of putting it."

"I did not torture Irene Karlovy," Savos said. "I merely whipped her, and then let my men have her."

"Bastard!" Helen snarled.

"Well, I am sure you can think of something interesting to do to this young woman," Berkeley said.

"You cannot permit this," Helen protested.

Berkeley pointed. "That is my wife lying dead, and you presume to tell me what I can and cannot do?"

"I did not kill her."

"Your brother did, with you at his side."

"I did not want to do it," she shouted. "I swear it. I did not wish to kill anybody, except you. That was our mission. To kill you. Nobody else. Stefan . . ." She sighed, and her shoulders slumped.

Berkeley knelt beside her. "Listen to me, Helen. You have admitted, before witnesses, that you came here to kill me. That it was your brother who killed two other people and caused the death of a third does not absolve you of guilt. You are going to be tried for murder and hanged by the neck until you are dead."

Her eyes were enormous and filled with tears.

"Your only hope," Berkeley told her, "is for us to tell the police you did not know what your brother was planning to do. We will do that, if you cooperate. If you do not, we will let justice take its course. But I will find out who is behind this. Even if it means letting Colonel Savos have you for half an hour before calling the police."

Helen looked at Savos.

"We are wasting time," Savos said. "I will not take long."

Berkeley stood up. "So be it."

"In there." Savos pointed to the dining room. "I will need some cord to tie her to a chair."

"Get up," Berkeley said.

"No. Wait," Helen said. "He said if we ever revealed his identity we would be killed."

"Well, as your brother is already dead, and at the very best you are going to spend a long time in prison, he's going to have a problem carrying out his threat. In any event, this is your only chance of avoiding the gallows."

She licked her lips, glanced from face to face, and drew a deep breath. Whoever her motivator was, he had clearly terrified her. "It was a man called Himmler. Heinrich Himmler."

"Himmler?" Berkeley frowned.

"Heinrich?" Martina asked. "That is a German name."

"What about this man?" Berkeley asked.

"He came to Nish. Came to our house. He knew all about you, and us. He asked us if we still intended to do our duty by our dead father and our dead sister. Well, we said yes. But we did not know how it could be done unless you returned to Serbia. Then he said he knew how it could be done. He gave us money and arranged for us to obtain passports and passages to England."

"And your instructions?"

"Were to kill you."

"And then?"

"To leave the country and return home."

"Did you seriously believe you could do that?"

"Herr Himmler said it would be quite easy. He said no one

would know who we were. With you dead, no one would know we even had a motive."

"So you tried the other night. And when that failed, you came out here. Did you suppose I would be that easy to kill? You have seen me at work, when I kidnapped you and took on those IMRO people."

"Well," she said sulkily, "we did not know you had these people with you."

"Quite. You were careless. Did this man Himmler tell you why he wanted me dead?"

"He said he was helping us to avenge our father and sister."

"A man appears, out of nowhere, and tells you he will pay you to avenge your father and sister and you were not suspicious? Or at least curious?"

"It was what we wanted to do. It was our duty."

"I see. All right, tell me what he looked like?"

Helen shrugged. "He was a very ordinary man. He wore rimless glasses."

"Rimless glasses. Did he give you any instructions as to what to do, or say, if you were caught?"

"He said we would not be caught."

"And you believed him. I almost feel sorry for you." Berkeley went to the telephone and asked for 999.

"What a miserable business." Peter Watt stood in the centre of the drawing room and surveyed the four people in front of him. Howard had been placed in his pram and had gone back to sleep. The rest had waited, listening to the tramp of feet as ambulance men had removed the four bodies, and the police had placed Helen Karlovy under arrest; she was being held in the dining room. Savos and Martina had each had a brandy. Anna sat silently, her face closed. But Berkeley knew her brain was alert and as active as his own.

They had each written out a statement and signed it. Now Watt surveyed the revolver that had been laid on the coffee table. "I'll have to take this for ballistic tests," he said. "But you say you shot that fellow, Colonel."

"He was charging me with a knife in his hand," Berkeley said. "What would you have done?"

"Probably the same, sir. If I had happened to be carrying a loaded revolver. But that is not something I normally do."

"Neither do I, Chief Inspector. But I have done since I was attacked in Northampton the other night."

"You do realise that it is an offence to carry a concealed weapon?"

"I have a licence, Peter. You know that."

"With respect, sir, you have a licence for a Browning nine-millimetre automatic pistol, and for a point three two Smith and Wesson revolver. This is a point three eight."

"I had intended to obtain a licence, but with all this happening I didn't get around to it. Are you going to charge me with possessing an unlicensed weapon?"

"Well, I don't know about that, sir. It will have to be reported. But in the circumstances, with your mother and Mrs Townsend both dead . . ." He turned the pages of his notebook "I can only offer you my deepest sympathy, and I am sure that will be echoed by my superiors. Now, just to recapitulate: you and Miss Anna went to the station to pick up, ah . . ." he read his notes, "Colonel and Mrs Savos . . ." he looked at Alexandros and Martina, "leaving both Mrs Townsends in the house with the maidservant and the baby. You had seen nothing suspicious before you left?"

"Nothing," Berkeley said.

"But you will agree that these two people must have already been in the neighbourhood?"

"You'll have to ask the woman that."

Watt made a face. "That will be difficult, as her English appears to be limited. We haven't even been able to take a statement."

"I will translate for you," Martina volunteered.

"That would be very helpful, Mrs . . . ah . . . Savos." He looked hard at her. "You had no knowledge of what might be going to happen?"

"Well, of course we did not. We came here to spend a holiday with our old friend Berkeley."

"You had never seen or heard of these people before?"

"We had never seen them. But . . ." Martina looked at her husband.

"I know the name," Savos said. "I was a police officer in

Belgrade before I retired, and I remember there were some people named Karlovy, anarchists, who we had to arrest."

"And what happened to them?"

"I cannot say. I have not heard of them since the war."

"But you think these may be members of the same family?"

Savos shrugged. "It is possible."

"And did Colonel Townsend mention them to you when he met you at the station?"

"No, he did not," Savos said, with careful exactitude. The mention had been in the car.

"I did not wish to alarm my friends," Berkeley explained. "They were coming here for a holiday. I would probably have told them what was going on once they were settled in, but there was no time for that. It simply did not occur to me that those two thugs would attack me in the house."

"I'm sure." Watt closed his notebook. "You will be remaining here for a few days, Mr Savos? Mrs Savos?"

Alexandros and Martina looked at Berkeley.

"I sincerely hope so," Berkeley said.

"We will be happy to stay," Martina said.

"Very good. You will be required to give evidence at the inquest, you see. I imagine that will be next week."

"And my mother and wife? And Maria?" Berkeley asked.

"Well, sir, there will have to be autopsies. Unnatural deaths, you see. I know it's hard to think of, but it's the law. But those will be carried out right away, and the bodies will be released for burial."

Berkeley nodded. It *was* hard to think of, Lucy's fine body being cut open by a surgeon's knife to no purpose. "Thank you. There is just one thing, Chief Inspector."

"Yes, sir."

"As I am sure Miss Karlovy will put in her statement, before you arrived she told us that it was not her intention that anyone should be killed except me."

"And you believe that?"

"I do, yes. It was her brother who ran wild. I will have to testify to that in court."

"You must do as you think best, sir. I don't think it will make a lot of difference. She came here intending to commit murder.

That the wrong persons got killed does not alleviate her guilt. Now, madam . . ." Watt looked at the Savoses. "You were going to help me with this statement."

"Of course." Martina stood up, as did Alexandros.

Anna watched the door close. "Won't he find out the truth?"

"Not unless one of the four of us tells him."

"Is it always like this?"

Berkeley sat beside her and put his arm round her shoulders. "It's never been like this before."

"Not even when mother died?"

"That was bad. As it was when your grandmother was killed. But they were both doing something for the cause, for Serbia. Lucy and Grandma, and Maria, were just trying to live their lives, at peace. Can you understand that?"

"I think so. Will they hang that woman? I hope they do," she said with sudden anger. "Why did you attempt to defend her?"

"I promised I would, if she would tell me who sent them."

"And did she tell you?"

"She said it was someone called Himmler. First name Heinrich. Martina thinks that sounds German."

"Do you have enemies in Germany?"

"Certainly I do. Friends or associates of Grippenheimer. I don't want to remind you of those days, Anna, but does the name ring any sort of bell?"

Anna shook her head.

"He is apparently a rather ordinary looking man who wears rimless glasses. Do you remember anyone looking like that coming to Grippenheimer's?"

"I do not remember. We tried not to look at the men. They had only to be endured."

He gave her another hug.

"What are you going to do?" she asked.

"There's not a lot I can do, unless I can find out something about him."

"Do you think he will try again?"

"That's quite likely. But not until he learns that this attempt has failed, and that can't be for a while yet."

Anna shivered. "Are we going to tell Johnnie and Ally?"

"I think we will have to. And . . ." He bit his lip.

"Yes," she said. "Harry and Mary. They'll be home from school, soon."

He nodded. "And Maria really was their mother."

"And you will tell them about this Himmler and the German connection?"

"Not right now. It'll have to come out, sooner or later. But, for the time being, there is just us and Baby." He squeezed her hand. "You will have to be his mother."

"Yes," she said, and then added fiercely, "But when you find out who this man Himmler is, I want to help you avenge Lucy. And Maria and Grandma."

"We'll talk about it," he said. "When I find out who he is."

The Lawyer

As Berkeley's only hostile contacts in Germany had been with the Nazi Party and Grippenheimer, he had no doubts as to whence the man Himmler had emanated. What he did not know was whether Himmler had been acting on behalf of the party, or whether he was just a friend or employee of Grippenheimer who had somehow discovered the identity of the millionaire's executioner and was out for personal revenge.

But whether or not Himmler was working for the party, he was certainly not working on his own. There was also the business of the car, and whoever had been driving it. There was no evidence of how the Karlovys had got out to the farmhouse; it was too far for them to have walked from Northampton, and they had to have made some plans for getting away once they had killed him. He wondered if and when Watt would start to wonder about that. He didn't want to introduce the probability of a third person being involved until he had had the opportunity to find out more about Himmler, and finding the car might be the quickest way to do that.

Watt joined him half an hour later, intimating that he would like a private word. Anna took Howard out to be with the Savoses.

"I have the young woman's statement here." Watt laid it on the table. "Copied out in English by my sergeant as translated by Mrs Savos. You'll see Miss Karlovy has signed it, after it was read back to her in that language of theirs, by Mrs Savos. I can't pretend I'm too happy about this standing up in court, as we only have Mrs Savos's word that it's a faithful translation and that she correctly read it back to the accused." He glanced at Berkeley. "May I ask how well you know the young lady? Mrs Savos, I mean."

"I have known Mrs Savos for several years, Chief Inspector. And her husband for even longer. I trust them both absolutely, and I am quite sure you will find the translation is both faithful and accurate."

"Well, if that is the case, it is an open and shut confession to murder, even if, as you suggested, Miss Karlovy claims that she did not know her brother intended to murder anyone else and would not have accompanied him if she had. But the fact is that she was armed with the knife with which she assaulted Miss Anna, and in the context of what happened here today that must be considered a deadly weapon. She will be very lucky to get away with her neck."

"I would not like her to be hanged, Peter," Berkeley said.

Watt sighed. "I'm afraid, sir, her fate is now in the hands of a jury. And a good defence lawyer, of course, if she can afford one. But there remain several intriguing and unexplained points about the case. Such as, how did her brother and herself obtain the necessary documentation to get into this country in the first place."

"Wouldn't she tell you that?"

"No, sir. On my behalf, Mrs Savos asked her several times, but she refused to say. But they must have had some outside assistance. Judging by the quality of their clothes and, well, I suppose you might say, cultural appearance, I would not suppose they were well-to-do. You say you knew the family; were they well off?"

"Not to my knowledge. Their father was an anarchist and their elder sister was a prostitute."

"Well, then, you see what I mean. To obtain a passport one must have acceptable references. To obtain a passage from Serbia to England one must have ample funds. To live in England without arousing suspicion, for some time, one must have ample *English* funds. You'll forgive me, but one does not obtain these things by, shall I say, walking the streets. And then we have the question of where they have been staying during the weeks they have been here; obviously in or around Northampton, but our inquiries have turned nothing up."

"No doubt you will be questioning the young woman again?"

"Well, yes, sir, we will, using a proper interpreter. However, it did occur to me . . . You say you know these people, and the reason they came after you. Surely you must have some idea who might have backed them? Some relative, or . . ." He paused.

"I'm afraid I have no idea whatsoever, Peter," Berkeley lied, gazing into his eyes.

"Well, we'll just have to see what we can get out of her."

"Will it help the case in any way?" Berkeley asked. "You have her confession."

"Loose ends, sir. Loose ends. No policeman likes loose ends. Now, Colonel, we need to talk about you."

"I don't think I need protection any more," Berkeley said. "That would be rather like shutting the stable door after the horse has bolted."

"Yes, sir. Believe me, I feel most terribly guilty about the death of your dear wife and your mother, not to mention the maid. I hope you understand that my hands were tied, until . . ."

"I do understand that, Chief Inspector. The guilt is mine for leaving them alone, even for an hour."

"You weren't to know, sir. What we really need to discuss is the shooting of the brother."

"The man attacked me with a knife, Chief Inspector, having recently stabbed my wife. You agreed that I was perfectly justified."

"I certainly feel you were justified. But still, a man is dead, without, shall I say, benefit of judge and jury. The matter will have to be dealt with. As for your wife, while we are all deeply sorry about such a tragedy, may I recommend that you do not bring her into your defence."

"My defence?"

"You have killed a man, sir. A charge will have to be made. I have no doubt at all that if it is properly handled by your barrister it will turn out to be justifiable homicide, that is, self-defence. As for the gun, well, I will certainly testify on your behalf that you felt you were in some danger well before the murders, and although I could not possibly condone your carrying a weapon, I certainly cannot blame you for doing so.

"But as I say," Watt went on, "I consider it would be a grave mistake to allow any suggestion of revenge for your wife's death to have played a part in your decision to shoot the young man.

That is coming very close to malice aforethought, even if the aforethought was a matter of a second. Self-defence, Colonel. That's the ticket."

"Thank you for the advice," Berkeley said.

"I take it you have a good solicitor, sir?"

"I think I'll give the case to my father-in-law," Berkeley said.

The Horsfalls drove down from Northampton the moment they heard the news the following morning, their distress at the death of their only daughter aggravated by the circumstances and by the delay in informing them; Berkeley had simply not thought of it.

Howard Horsfall, a successful solicitor, was only a couple of years older than his son-in-law, and neither he nor his wife had entirely approved of their daughter marrying a man more than twice her age. Equally, they remained suspicious of Berkeley's background, always officially described as that of military attaché but fairly widely known to have included some unsavoury incidents. That Lucy had found it all very romantic, had appeared to be utterly happy and had presented them with a grandchild had been reassuring, but now . . .

It was ten o'clock when they arrived; by then, the police had taken all the necessary photographs. Anna, Martina and the Lockwoods – Berkeley had decided the children should not go back to school this term – had cleaned up the blood in the front hall, on the stairs and in the kitchen. The house looked perfectly normal and the Horsfalls entered with an air of almost incredulous apprehension.

Berkeley met them in the hall.

"Where is she?" Howard demanded.

"Lucy is in the morgue," Berkeley said. "Along with my mother, Maria and the murderer. There will have to be autopsies."

"Oh, my poor baby!" Joan Horsfall moaned and burst into tears.

"Where is Baby Howard?" Horsfall demanded.

"Upstairs in his playpen. He is perfectly unharmed."

"Thank God for that. But what happened?"

Berkeley had already determined that as all the facts would have to come out at Helen's trial, nothing would be gained by prevaricating.

"I'm sorry to say that the assassins were after me," he said.

The Horsfalls stared at him.

"It's a blood feud which goes back to when I served in the Balkans before the war," Berkeley explained. "I found it necessary to kill a man, and his family undertook to avenge him. I had supposed that at this distance in time and space it was over and done with, but apparently I was wrong."

"You . . . caused this to happen?" Horsfall demanded.

"I suppose you could say that, yes."

"You caused the death of our daughter, and you stand there, cool as a cucumber—"

"I think you should remember that my mother also died in the attack," Berkeley said. "As for being cool, I shot and killed Lucy's murderer, and arrested his accomplice."

"But Lucy is still dead!"

He and his wife gazed at Anna and the Savoses who, hearing the raised voices, had appeared in the drawing room doorway.

"Colonel and Mrs Savos," Berkeley introduced. "Anna, you know. Mr and Mrs Horsfall, Lucy's parents."

"Oh, madame, what a tragedy," Martina said.

"You were here?"

"We had just arrived, to stay with Lucy and Berkeley."

"You saw it happen?"

"We came home just after it happened," Berkeley explained. "Anna and I had picked Alexandros and Martina up from the station. The murderers were still in the house."

"And Berkeley shot one of them," Savos said.

"I wish to see Baby Howard," Joan Horsfall declared.

"Of course. Anna?"

Anna led her step-grandmother up the stairs.

"You shot the fellow?" Horsfall enquired. "Just like that?"

"It was him or me. I gather I will have to be charged, but according to Peter Watt if my case is properly presented I will be acquitted on the grounds of justifiable manslaughter, that is, self-defence. However, I will need a capable barrister. I'd be very happy if you'd find one and handle the case for me."

"I'm afraid that will not be possible," Horsfall said coldly, and followed his wife up the stairs.

* * *

Johnnie and Alicia came home from school for the funerals. The Horsfalls wanted Lucy to be buried in their family plot, and Berkeley saw no reason to increase the estrangement by objecting; he was too aware of his own guilt, if only by association. He and the children attended, of course; the Savoses remained at the house to look after Baby Howard; they had never actually met Lucy.

"What's our next step?" Johnnie asked.

Coming up to eighteen, as tall and powerfully built as his father with the same lank black hair and strong features, he was in his last term at school; he was bound for Sandhurst in the autumn and a career in the army. He knew what his father had done during his career and dreamed of emulating him. Berkeley had confided in the boy three years previously, when the trauma of Anna's disappearance had been weighing heavily on all of their minds; he had been desperate to share, and John Townsend had been desperate to be shared with.

"There's not a lot I can do," Berkeley told him. "Until after the court cases."

"But that could take months."

Berkeley nodded. "It probably will. But there is not a lot I can do until I find out something about this man Himmler."

"How can you do that?"

"I have some friends in Berlin who may be able to help us."

"Of course," Martina exclaimed. "That woman who escaped with us: Julia somebody."

"Julia Hudson," Berkeley said.

"I remember her," Anna said. "Not on the night of the escape, but . . ."

"Before you ever went away," Berkeley said. "She had her eye on me at the time. In fact, she's had her eye on me several times but we always seem to marry someone else."

"You're not going to marry her now, Papa?" Alicia asked anxiously. She was a little bewildered about everything; she did not know her father's profession and she had never before met the Savoses, who seemed to be on such intimate relations with both Anna and Berkeley. At sixteen, Alicia was very nearly a carbon copy of Anna. Her features were softer, her hair titian rather than auburn, but they were very obviously sisters.

"Fortunately, as I said, she is married to someone else. This fellow Hudson. But he is, or was a couple of years ago, an official in the British embassy in Berlin. He should be able to find out something for us."

"Do you suppose he will help us?" Martina asked. "After we involved his wife in that shoot-out at Grippenheimer's?"

"We did not involve her, if you remember," Berkeley said. "She got herself involved. And I think her husband will help us for that very reason. Because, unless Julia has been very stupid and broadcast what happened, we are the only people who know she *was* involved. Then there are the Cohns."

"The catering manager and his wife!" Martina cried. "They showed us the way out."

"Because we are old friends. Harry Lockwood and I managed to rescue them from a very sticky situation back in 1921."

"They were Jewish," Savos remarked.

"Still are, I imagine. They were about to be beaten up by a gang of thugs when Harry and I happened upon the incident and saw the louts off. They will certainly help us find out about this fellow."

"However," Savos said, "whether this British envoy and these caterers help you or not, with the court cases we are talking about several months, as you say, before we can take action. Is it not likely that this man Himmler will try again?"

"I'm afraid that is extremely likely," Harry said. "We shall have to take precautions."

"The only precaution you can take is to have adequate support. You had no problems when poor Lockwood was here. Now . . ."

Savos looked at Martina.

"I could not possibly ask you to give up your home and come to live here," Berkeley protested.

"It would be our pleasure," Martina said, "if you would like us to." She looked at each of the children in turn. "And if there is room."

"Well, there is room now," Berkeley said. "My parents' bedroom is vacant. But . . ."

"It would only be until you have sorted out this Himmler fellow," Savos said.

"And I could help with Baby," Martina suggested.

Berkeley looked at Anna.

"I think it would be ideal," Anna said. "I really would like someone in the house all the time, and Johnnie and Ally will be going back to school in a couple of weeks."

"That's true," Berkeley agreed, and cocked an ear. "I hear Baby now. Why don't all three of you take him for a walk in his pram."

The children knew their father well enough to understand that they had just been dismissed so that he could talk with the Savoses.

"Of course, Papa," Anna said, and got up. "Come along, you two."

Savos waited for the door to close. "Is that safe?" he asked.

"At this moment, safer than at any other time," Berkeley pointed out. "The Karlovys are either dead or in police custody, and their employers do not yet know what has happened. Now, I want you to know that I am most awfully grateful for your suggestion, Alexandros, Martina, and I don't wish to sound like a Dutch uncle, but there is something I need to say."

"Of course," Savos said.

"There are two things, actually. The first is about guns. You may keep them handy inside the house, although there can be no shooting except in defence of yourselves or my children."

"That gives the opposition a great advantage," Savos remarked.

"Yes, it does, but that is the way we do things in England. Equally, there can be no carrying of weapons when you leave the house. That is illegal."

Savos shrugged. "As you wish. But you are emasculating us as bodyguards."

"You cannot possibly be a bodyguard if you're in prison," Berkeley pointed out. "The second point is that there must be no visible drugs. If you feel the absolute necessity, Martina, kindly do it in your bedroom and nowhere else, particularly nowhere my children can see you."

Martina pouted then gave her flashing smile. "But of course. I would not dream of upsetting you or your children, Berkeley. We only wish to help."

"I know that, and I appreciate it," Berkeley said. "Well then, we'll have to make arrangements for you to bring some more of your gear up."

"Who are those people?" Alicia asked, as Anna pushed the pram along the lane behind the house.

"They're old friends of Papa's," Anna explained. "Colonel Savos was chief of police in Belgrade before the war, when we lived there."

"Do you remember Sabac?" Johnnie asked.

"Well . . . not really. I can't even remember Mama," Alicia confessed. "Was she very beautiful?"

"Very," Anna said reverently.

"Papa says you look like her."

"So do you."

Alicia considered this. Then she asked, "Were those people, the Savoses, the reason Lucy and Grandma were killed?"

"No, no," Johnnie said. "Those people were trying to kill Papa. Grandma and Lucy and Maria just got in the way."

"But . . . just to kill people for being there . . . and why should anyone wish to kill Papa?"

Anna and Johnnie looked at each other across the pram.

"Because Papa killed their father," Anna said. "That's why they kidnapped me, seven years ago."

Alicia was aghast. "Papa killed somebody?"

"Papa has killed lots of people," Johnnie asserted.

Alicia looked at Anna in disbelief.

"Well," Anna said, "he fought in three wars. Both the Balkan wars and the Great War."

"Four," Johnnie pointed out. "There was that war in the Sudan before any of the others. That's where he got his first wound. But I meant he's killed lots of people outside of wars."

"But why?"

"Because he was told to do so, by the government."

Alicia looked from one to the other. "The government? I don't believe you."

"He also killed the people who kidnapped me. Well, most of them, anyway."

"You are saying that Papa is a murderer?"

"No," Anna said. "He is an executioner. He never killed anybody who did not deserve to die."

"And you approve of what he's done."

"Yes," Anna said. "I do."

Alicia swallowed, then quickened her pace and walked away from them, in front of the pram, hands thrust into the pockets of her coat.

"You've upset her," Johnnie remarked.

"It had to happen some time."

"Suppose she tells her school friends."

"We must make her promise not to. But even if she does, they won't believe her. They'll think she's making it up."

Johnnie glanced at her. "Sometimes I don't believe it myself."

"Well, you can. I've seen Papa at work."

"I know." Johnnie hesitated. In the more than two years since Anna had been back, they had never had an intimate conversation. This was partly because of what had happened; he had no idea how one could possibly ask a girl what it felt like to be raped, to be absolutely at the mercy of whichever man happened to have paid for her. But there was also the fact that he had always been vaguely afraid of her. This went back to when they had been children. Like Alicia, he could remember very little of Serbia. He had no clear idea of what his mother had looked like, although he did have a vague memory of the house in Sabac, tall and heavy-shuttered and forbidding. Memory really began after they had all reached England and security; he had never thought of himself as anything but English, and he knew that Alicia felt that even more so.

Anna was different. Although she had only been five when their world had exploded with the murder of the Archduke Franz Ferdinand, she could remember what both her mother and grandmother had told her of the struggle between tiny Serbia and mighty Austria-Hungary. In those days, ambush, robbery and murder had been normal events, and Mama had taken her part in them just as much as Papa. Anna had always considered herself a Serb, or more accurately a Bosnian rather than English, and when they had been small she had endeavoured to make her siblings think the same way.

Then she had disappeared. As Johnnie had still been very

small, it had been some time before he had learned the truth of the matter. He remembered being just as horrified as Alicia now was but his reaction had been different. He had wanted to join in the search for her and to kill the wretches who had carried out such a crime. Papa had not permitted that, of course; he had gone off and done it all himself. And after five years, miraculously, he had brought Anna home, alive and apparently unharmed . . . but that was impossible, at least psychologically.

This was a rare opportunity.

"Those men," he ventured. "Do you hate them?"

"Yes," she said.

"Does that mean you hate all men?"

"I don't hate Papa," she said. "But there were women, too."

Johnnie gulped; something else he had never quite believed.

"So . . . I mean . . . well, will you ever marry?"

"Papa would like me to marry."

"It's what most girls do," Johnnie pointed out, ingenuously. "And it would, well . . . enable you to . . ."

"I don't think that is possible," she said.

"Yes, but if you were to fall in love . . ."

"I don't think that is possible, either. Besides, any man, even if I found him . . . acceptable, would want to have sex."

"Well," he said.

"Have you ever had sex with anyone?"

He flushed. "No."

"But you've wanted to. And I imagine you know what happens?"

"Well . . . yes."

"Well, try to imagine being tied to a bed and having a woman of perhaps fifty or sixty, fat and greasy and stinking, pawing you all over, making you put your fingers into her . . . Making you suck them, feeling them inside you, being beaten just because they feel like beating you . . ." She paused, flushing herself now anger flashing from her eyes at the memories.

"Oh, my dearest Anna."

Anna had stopped pushing the pram, and Johnnie took her into his arms to hug her close.

"I had no idea. Or perhaps I did, but it never sort of became real."

"You won't tell anyone what I said."

"Of course not. It will be our secret. Yours and mine."

"And Papa's," she said. "He knows." She looked past him. "Someone's watching us."

"Eh?" Johnnie turned, watched the car drive away. "Who was that?"

"I have no idea. Some peeping Tom. Let's go home."

Berkeley stood at his bedroom window. The room was at the back of the house; he could look out over open country and see his children coming back along the lane. He felt a sense of momentary relief. For all his confident words to the Savoses he did not really wish them out of his sight.

Then he heard another sound, and half turned his head. The clip-clop of hooves on the front drive could only mean one visitor. And he would actually be glad to see her, on this occasion.

He went down the stairs, paused on the landing. Martina was just opening the door.

The two women gazed at each other. "Who are you?" Julia Hudson demanded.

Not to be put out, Martina replied, "Who are *you*?"

"I remember you," Julia said. "You are that woman who was with Berkeley when he created all that mayhem in Berlin."

"And I remember you," Martina agreed. "You are that woman who was also with Berkeley when he created that mayhem in Berlin."

"I see," Julia said. "So now you have moved in here."

"For a while," Martina said.

"Within twenty-four hours of his wife's death."

"No, no," Martina said. "I was here before his wife's death. Well, nearly."

Berkeley continued down the stairs, before they actually got to scratching.

"Why Julia," he said, "I had no idea you were in England."

"I've been home for a week," Julia said. "Daddy isn't very well."

"I'm sorry to hear that. You must give him my regards."

Not that there was any love lost between himself and Julia's parents; they considered that he had stood Julia up many years before. It had been a marriage hoped for by both halves of the family but it would never have worked – they were utterly incompatible. Julia, tall and increasingly gaunt as she grew older – she was the same age as himself, fifty-nine – had always regarded life as a very orderly business; her sole ambition had been to get him out of the army and into farming, something he would never have considered.

"I will do so," she said. "I actually rode over to offer you my sincere condolences, but this person—"

"Martina is looking after me for the time being."

Julia gave Martina a glance that would have shrivelled most people, but Martina merely smiled.

"Why don't you come in," Berkeley invited. "I'm actually very pleased to see you."

"Are you?" Julia asked suspiciously. But she entered the hall, drawing off her gloves and removing her hard hat.

Berkeley escorted her into the drawing room, while Martina tactfully retreated into the kitchen.

"I assume that woman is your housekeeper? If she isn't . . . I mean, with poor Lucy hardly cold . . ."

"It would be the height of bad taste for me already to have acquired a mistress. But then, in some people's eyes, everything I do is in the height of bad taste, even taking you to bed. Do sit down."

Julia flushed but sat on the settee, boots pressed together, "Why must we always quarrel?"

"Simply because you insist on criticising other people's arrangements. Martina happens to be my bodyguard."

"Your . . ."

"With her husband. Who is also in the house somewhere. Now, would you like a cup of tea."

"Well, that would be very nice."

"Excellent." He opened the door. "Martina, do you think you could make some tea?"

"Of course," Martina said. "I have studied this. I will bring it in."

"Thank you." Berkeley closed the door and sat down. "She is actually domesticated. I think."

"I really did come over to say how sorry I am about the

tragedy. There are all sorts of rumours flying about, of it being some foreign madman . . ." She paused, expectantly.

"There are wheels within wheels," Berkeley said.

"Oh. You mean it's something to do with, well . . ."

"My murky past? I'm afraid it is."

"But your wife? And poor Mrs Townsend . . ."

"And my maidservant. They were after me, but I wasn't here."

"But who?"

"Now here is where you can be helpful. Is your husband still stationed in Berlin?"

"Yes, he is."

"Does he know anything of what happened on the night Grippenheimer was killed?"

"No, he doesn't. No more than anyone else. I mean, he knows the place was suddenly invaded by a bunch of thugs who shot it up, including Grippenheimer. But as they have never been identified . . ."

"How did you explain your part in it?"

"I told him I was trying to leave, like everyone else, and we became separated. He was very worried."

"But no doubt relieved to see you alive and well."

"Well, of course. You mean this has something to do with that? You killed Grippenheimer, didn't you?"

"He stopped a bullet, certainly. I would like to think it came from my gun. You know he had Anna in that harem of his."

"I sort of gathered that. How is she, by the way?"

"Mending. She'll be home in a minute. You can see for yourself."

"Tea," Martina announced, opening the door and placing the tray on the table. "You wish me to go?"

Berkeley observed there were three cups.

"No, no, you stay. What about Alexandros?"

"He is having a nap."

"Ah, right. Well, you can be mother."

Julia looked apprehensive.

"And you think this attack has to do with that evening?" she asked.

"I think so. I have the name of the man who set it up: Himmler."

"Heinrich Himmler," Martina added, passing out cups of tea. "You know this man?"

"Me?" Julia squawked. "How should I know him?"

"Martina means, have you ever heard of him. You see, it would seem obvious that he is either a friend of Grippenheimer's or works for the Nazi Party."

"You think the Nazi Party wants you dead? Why?"

"Well, Grippenheimer is one reason. He was one of their financial backers. But there are also other reasons. Now, I imagine your husband keeps his ear very close to the ground about what is happening in Germany, and especially Berlin. That's what he's there for, right?"

"Well, I suppose so."

"So it's possible that he may have heard of this fellow Himmler. I mean, he seems able to command quite considerable resources, to have sent two assassins clear across Europe to get at me. Do you think you could ask Dick to let me, or you, have any information he may possess?"

"Any information Dick possesses will be confidential," Julia pointed out, "certainly if you intend to go after this man in your well-known murdering fashion."

"I'm sure you mean executing," Berkeley said. "That I don't believe in waiting for the verdicts of judges and juries is because they are both tardy and usually wrong."

"Well, I'll try," Julia said.

"I'm sure you will. Remembering always that when it comes to confidentiality you and I have some skeletons we would prefer to keep in the closet. Or you would, I am sure."

She glared at him. "You are trying to blackmail me."

"I never *try* to do anything," he reminded her. "Here are the children."

They flooded into the house, Howard wailing.

"He's wet himself," Anna explained.

"This is Mrs Hudson," Berkeley said. "I'm sure you remember her, Anna. But I don't think you've met John and Alicia, Julia."

Julia was on her feet. "My pleasure. They're lovely children,

Berkeley. You are to be congratulated. Now I must rush. I'd like to be home by dark."

She hurried for the door. Berkeley accompanied her. "I'll look forward to hearing from you," he said.

Geoffrey Walton arrived the next day, accompanied by one of his juniors, a young man named Harry Druce. Berkeley entertained them in the dining room, where they could use the table as a large desk.

Walton took various papers from his briefcase and spread them out. "I have copies of all the statements here," he said, "and it seems very straightforward. You will appear in the Magistrate's Court on Friday morning. I shall of course ask for the case to be dismissed, but even if it is not, you will be released on bail. Your ultimate acquittal is just a matter of form."

Berkeley nodded. "Just supposing it goes to Crown Court, do you have a good man in mind?"

"Oh, yes, indeed. Tom Bullard. There's no better barrister in the Midlands. I've put him in the picture, but he doubts very much whether you will need him."

"But if he's prepared to take my case, should it come to that, I assume he would be prepared to take the girl's case as well."

"The girl?"

"Helen Karlovy. I'd like you to act on her behalf as well."

Walton scratched his ear and glanced at Druce. "I'm afraid I don't understand, Colonel. This young woman and her brother set out to kill you. She has admitted this in her statement. And you want me to defend her?"

"I want you to brief Bullard, yes. I'll meet the fee."

"But why, in the name of God?"

"I have destroyed just about her entire family."

"You shot her brother in self-defence."

Berkeley nodded. "I also shot her father, in self-defence. I did not personally kill her older sister but I was responsible for her death."

"And you think that puts you in their debt. Were they not a family of international gangsters, anarchists, terrorists?"

"Absolutely. But for a while I was one of them."

Walton frowned. "Is this widely known?"

"No, it is not. I was acting on behalf of the government. Thus *I* would not like it to be widely known now. I am just putting you in the picture."

"I see. Well, if you wish me to, I will undertake the defence of the girl and brief Bullard. However, I must tell you that, having studied her statement and all of the facts, I'm not sure what even Bullard will be able to do with it. And please don't start on the business of her not intending to kill any of the three victims. She admits she came here to kill you. If Druce and I had come here to kill you and Druce here draws and fires first but misses you and kills someone coming through that doorway, we are both guilty of murder, no matter how vehemently I may swear that I did not mean that to happen. Oh, I beg your pardon."

Because someone had at that moment opened the door. Anna, checking in embarrassment.

"I'm sorry, Papa. I did not know you had guests."

"Come in," Berkeley said. "This is my daughter Anna."

The lawyers stood up to shake hands, both obviously attracted to the girl.

"I didn't mean to intrude," Anna said.

"You haven't," Berkeley said. "Mr Walton wanted to have a word with you, anyway. Have a seat."

Cautiously, Anna sat next to Druce.

"You understand that you will be called as a witness, Miss Anna," Walton said. "In the murder case. As a witness for the prosecution."

Anna looked at her father.

"I'm afraid that will be necessary," Berkeley said. "You were attacked by Helen Karlovy and you helped me capture her."

"But the defence lawyer . . ."

"Will neither pry himself, nor permit any prying by other counsel, into your background," Walton said. "I will see to that. All you must do is state the exact truth, as you remember it, of what happened on the day."

"And about seeing them in town, and the first attack?" Anna asked.

"Certainly, if asked by the prosecutor, as I am sure you will be. You understand, Colonel, that your daughter's testimony will be another nail in Helen Karlovy's coffin."

Berkeley nodded. "However, you must get Bullard to do the best he can. A plea for mercy, perhaps, in view of the fact that she is now orphaned. An assertion that she was led astray by her brother . . ."

"And no reference to the fact that her family was responsible for the kidnapping of Miss Anna."

"You said that wouldn't be brought up."

"Quite. I am merely illustrating the problem we will have in attempting to save her neck."

"However," Berkeley said, "while I would like to avoid anyone going into the details of Anna's kidnapping," he squeezed her hand, "I think it would help Miss Karlovy's case if certain aspects of my relations both with her father and her elder sister were brought out in cross-examination. I will write you a letter, in strictest confidence, stating the various facts which Bullard may wish to raise."

Walton frowned. "You are sure this will not be awkward for you?"

"I'm sure it will be. But it should go a long way to obtaining that recommendation to mercy I'm after."

"Well, it's your funeral, if you'll pardon the expression." Walton gathered up his papers and replaced them in his briefcase. "We'll see you in court on Friday, Colonel."

"Why are we trying to save Helen Karlovy's neck, Papa?" Anna asked.

"Just say that I feel responsible for the deaths of too many of her family already," Berkeley said.

"Her brother killed Grandma and Lucy, and Maria," Anna said. "I hate her."

"I'm sure you do," Walton agreed. "But I would try to keep your emotions under control when you appear in court. Good day."

Walton led Druce out to the car. Druce drove. "Rum do, isn't it," he remarked. "You're virtually appearing for the defence and the prosecution."

"Not obviously," Walton said. "I'm appearing for the defence in both cases. As regards Colonel Townsend, the young man he shot was admittedly one of the would-be assassins but the sister was nowhere in evidence when the shooting occurred. In defending her, a quite hopeless task in my opinion, I may be seen as changing sides, but that is an entirely different matter."

"Hm," Druce commented. "What an extraordinarily beautiful girl."

Walton glanced at him, "Yes, she is. She also has a somewhat chequered background. You've read the file."

"It's not very complete. Merely says she was once abducted. I gather it was to do with this ongoing feud."

"Yes, it was. However, when friend Townsend got going, the abductors decided to unload the girl just as rapidly as possible."

"Is he that tough an egg?" Druce was sceptical. "He's the perfect picture of a retired army officer. All he lacks is the moustache."

"Appearances can be deceptive. There was a time, only a few years ago, when he was regarded as the most dangerous man in Europe."

"Oh, come now, sir."

"That is fact, Harry. I have a brother in the FO, and he has heard of some quite hair-raising tasks Townsend carried out for HM Government."

"And the government was engaged in following up the abduction of his daughter?"

"Not directly. But they virtually gave him *carte blanche* to find her, as he eventually did. Leaving a trail of corpses across Central Europe."

"Then I take back all I said and lift my hat to him. I would probably have done the same thing if that girl had been my daughter."

Another glance. "It took him five years, and Anna Townsend spent those five years in various brothels."

"That lovely girl?"

"That lovely girl. Do keep your eye on the road."

"Sorry, sir." Druce concentrated. "But that ended a couple of years ago, didn't it?"

"I don't think something like that ever ends," Walton observed.

"Oh, quite. A dreadful experience. What I meant was, if . . . ah, she had been diseased, it would have come out by now, surely."

"Not necessarily," Walton said. "If it was syphilis. It could be lying dormant in her body, waiting to manifest itself as she grows older, either in various unpleasant physical ailments or to be transmitted to her children."

"That's a somewhat gloomy prognosis," Druce observed.

"It happens to be true. The truth is often a bit gloomy."

"Couldn't the possibility be diagnosed?"

"Certainly, by means of a blood test. They're mandatory in the States, before anyone can get married."

"Well, then . . ."

"This isn't the States, Harry. It is not a legal requirement in England. And I hope you are not thinking of taking up with this girl."

"Well . . . is there anything unethical in asking her out, as we're representing the defence?"

"Nothing at all, although I will have to inform Bullard. But why do you wish to take her out?"

Druce flushed. "She has to be about the most beautiful girl I have ever seen."

"So all you wish to do is look at her. In my experience, young men who take young women out generally have a further idea in mind. And if they are honourable young men, as I know you are, Harry, the further idea is supposed to end in marriage."

"Well . . ."

"So I would like to hear your plan of campaign. You will, after taking Anna Townsend out a few times and determining that you love her, ask her to marry you. But, you will say, do you mind awfully if we trot along to your doctor and have him take a blood test, just to make sure you do not have syphilis? If she doesn't slap your face, Berkeley will probably blow your head off. He's very sensitive where his children are concerned, and especially Anna."

"I would put the matter to him first," Druce said.

"Very proper. Well, then, let's look on the bright side. Berkeley doesn't hit you over the head but welcomes you as a prospective son-in-law. He agrees to Anna having a blood test and she is found to be all clear. You marry. Can you guarantee that when you, ah, consummate the event, you will not find yourself thinking of all the men who have been that way before you, wondering if she is mentally comparing you with them, whether every endearment, every gasp of passion that she emits is not part of the responses she was trained to make to keep her clients happy?"

"If you weren't my senior in the firm, Mr Walton," Druce said. "I'd stop this car and punch you on the nose."

"Which would be an entirely honourable thing to do, if I had raised the point *after* you had proposed and been accepted. I am merely trying to point out that you need to be very, very sure before you take an irrevocable step. Or you could be ruining both your life and hers."

"Well," Druce said. "It seems to me we're putting the cart a long way before the horse. All I want to do is take her out to dinner."

A Visit from the Past

"Well," Berkeley said, throwing his hat at the stand, "I think this calls for a drink. Champagne. There's some in the cellar."

"I will get it," Martina said. She seemed to be thoroughly enjoying her temporary role as cook-housekeeper and was, in fact, an excellent cook, if somewhat heavy-handed with the spices.

"Was there ever any doubt?" Anna asked.

"Not according to Walton," Berkeley said. "Do you know, that is the first time I have ever been put on trial for killing someone?"

"When do I get my gun back?" Savos asked.

"I imagine, now the case is over, that the police will release it in a day or two," Berkeley said.

"And then?"

Berkeley went to the window and looked out at the snow-covered drive and fields. Christmas had come and gone, a very sombre Christmas, and the children had returned to school, reluctantly. But life had to be resumed, even if normality remained some distance in the future. If his own court appearance was out of the way, Helen Karlovy's trial was still some months away; there was nothing any of them could do until after that. And then? He had heard nothing from either Julia Hudson or the Cohns to whom he had written before the holiday.

And he had Helen Karlovy on his conscience. He had attended the magistrate's court where she had been committed for trial and never had he seen so despondent a figure. For all the harm she had done him, on reflection he could understand that she had been driven by a force deep in her subconscious so that, as if hypnotised, she had felt obliged to carry on the blood feud once presented with the opportunity to do so. In the blood-soaked jungle in which he had spent most of his life, he could not hate her for that; he could only feel sympathy. And unless Walton or his friend Bullard could produce a miracle, she was going to hang.

He turned back to face the room as Martina brought in the tray of champagne and glasses.

"You must go home," he said.

Both the Savoses gazed at him with arched eyebrows.

"You've been here more than a month," he pointed out. "I can't ask you to devote the rest of your lives to me."

"But who will protect you?" Savos asked. "You still have not found out who this man Himmler is."

"Well, until I do, Anna and I will have to protect ourselves. We can do that, can we not, Anna?"

"Oh, yes," she said.

Martina filled the glasses and handed them out. "We have to be here to give evidence at that Karlovy woman's trial," she said.

"That is unlikely to happen before the summer. I can't ask you to stay here for several months."

"We would like to," she said. "Wouldn't we, Alexandros?"

"Oh, yes," Savos said. "It would be a great pleasure. And then, when this Himmler character tries again, we will be waiting for him."

Berkeley looked at Anna. She appeared perfectly happy; she liked both Alexandros and Martina. More important, she trusted them.

"Well," he said, "I can't pretend I'm not grateful, although I still feel it's an imposition. Hello, who's that?"

A car was slithering to a stop on the snow-covered forecourt.

"And I have no gun," Savos said. "You will have to lend me your pistol, Berkeley."

"I'll get it," Anna volunteered, as the doorbell rang.

"No," Berkeley said, "I'll get it."

"I still have *my* gun," Martina said, picking up her handbag.

"You didn't take that thing to court?" Berkeley was aghast,

"Of course, I have it with me at all times."

"You and I are going to have to have a serious chat," Berkeley said, as he went into the hall. He unlocked the front door. "Hello. Druce, isn't it? Did I forget something in court? Or have you an account for me already?"

"No, no, sir," Druce said. "And I do apologise for this intrusion . . ."

Berkeley had observed that the young solicitor was carrying a bouquet of flowers.

"Ah," he said, "I suspect that you haven't actually come to see me at all."

"Well, sir . . ." Now he was flushing. "Have you any objections?"

Think, goddamit, Berkeley told himself. To have some well-mannered and probably well-to-do young man come courting Anna was what he had dreamed of over the past year . . . while all the time dreading it. His fears were far greater than mere fatherly possessiveness. This was the only possible way Anna was ever going to regain normality and perhaps even happiness. But it was also the situation which might prove she would never be able to do that, which was too terrible to contemplate.

While the difficulties of detail were stupendous.

"Of course I have no objection," he said. "Come in."

Druce took off his hat as he entered the hall and Berkeley indicated the stand. "In here." He waited at the drawing-room door and Druce, pausing a moment to check his tie knot, stepped past him.

"You remember Mr Druce," Berkeley said. "Walton's junior. He was in court."

"I'm afraid I didn't have much to do," Druce said. "Colonel Savos. Mrs Savos. Miss Townsend."

"Mr Druce has something for you, Anna," Berkeley said.

Druce was blushing again as he presented the flowers.

"Oh, how beautiful," Martina said.

Anna took the flowers, slowly, and Berkeley realised this was the first time in her life she had ever received such a gift; something he had sorely neglected, but it had simply not occurred to him. And perhaps this was better.

Now she was flushing also. "Thank you," she said.

They gazed at each other, and it was Martina who grasped the initiative. "Berkeley," she said. "There is something in the kitchen I wish to show you."

"Ah . . ." Berkeley hesitated.

"Come along," she insisted. "You too, Alexandros. It is man's business." She smiled at Druce and Anna. "We shall not be long. Pour Mr Druce some champagne, Anna."

They left the room.

"Would you like some champagne, Mr Druce?" Anna asked.

"If that is what you are drinking. Is there a celebration?"

Anna poured. "Only Papa's acquittal."

"There was never any doubt about that."

"There speaks the legal mind," she said. "When one is the accused, there must always be an element of doubt."

"You have an experienced mind. Oh, I . . ." Another flush.

"I consider that a compliment. Do please sit down."

She studied him as they sat, facing each other across the room. He has come here for what purpose? she asked herself. Men, in her experience, usually only had one purpose when visiting a woman. Did she want it to happen? Could she allow it to happen? Since her rescue by Papa she had resolutely refused to think about sex in any way. She had no desire for it, only fear. The only man with whom she felt at ease was her father. Even Alexandros she felt could not be trusted in sexual matters, although he was probably too old to do much about his desires, and she was not even sure of Johnnie.

She *was* sure that if any man ever again touched her sexually she would either scream or tear all the flesh from his face.

Yet this was what everyone, and Papa most of all, wanted to happen. In their society woman only found happiness in marriage and children. She actually thought she would love to have a child of her own, if that could be possible without the necessity of a man. As that was *not* possible, she was prepared to make do with her baby half-brother.

But this man, so apparently pleasant, well-mannered . . . She wondered if he had ever been to a brothel. More importantly, how much did he know of her background, and how much could she tell him? Telling him, of course, would be one way of ending his interest on the spot. But it might also be broadcasting it to the world.

She raised her glass. "Your health. Martina seems to imagine that you came to see me rather than Father."

"Martina . . . is she a relative?"

Anna shook her head. "Only a very dear friend. She and Uncle Alexandros are old friends of Papa's. They helped him—" She bit her lip. How easy it was to say too much.

"She seems very nice," Druce said. "And she's right. I did actually come to see you."

"Did you wish to discuss the evidence I shall give at the Karlovy trial?"

"Good heavens, no. We must not talk about it. You will be a prosecution witness and, at your father's request, we are appearing for the defence."

"Oh," she said. "Yes, I understand. Then should you be here at all?"

"I wished to see some more of you, Miss Townsend. I think you are quite the most beautiful girl I have ever seen."

"Thank you. But you know nothing of me."

She was laying a trap, and watching him most closely as she had observed his tendency to flush. And he did so now. Betraying himself?

"I would hope to correct that," he said.

"How?"

"Well . . . we could perhaps start by having dinner together."

"Where?"

He was certainly finding her directness disconcerting.

"I haven't actually decided. But I know several very good restaurants in Northampton."

"Ah," she said. "That sounds very nice. I have never been taken out to dinner, except by Papa and Lucy."

"Well, then . . ."

"You will have to ask Papa."

"I shall do that, certainly. But I felt I should first discover whether you cared for the idea."

"I think it is a very nice idea."

"Well, then . . . shall we say Friday night? I will call for you at seven."

"Thank you. But you must ask Papa."

"It is very decent of you to ask my daughter out to dinner, Druce. I assume you do know that she is only nineteen years old?"

"Soon to be twenty, I understand, sir."

"That is true, certainly."

The two men were alone in Berkeley's study, Druce having asked for a private word.

"You also are aware – it is common knowledge – that Anna was abducted as a young girl."

"Yes, sir."

"And you are then no doubt aware of just what I mean."

"The very thought makes my blood boil, sir. But if you are afraid that I shall in any way refer to the matter or cause her any embarrassment whatsoever, I beg you to believe that I shall never do so."

"Never," Berkeley said, half to himself. "It is a long time. That you are aware that there are certain lines you must not cross will suffice for the time being. However, as Anna is still only nineteen, I would be obliged if you would bring her home by ten o'clock."

"With respect, sir, could you make that eleven? I propose to take Miss Townsend to the Square Room. I doubt we will get through dinner much before half past ten."

Berkeley had been to the Square Room, which enjoyed the reputation of being Northampton's best, and most expensive, restaurant.

"Isn't that rather pushing out the boat?" he asked.

"I consider Miss Townsend worth it, sir."

"Well, in that case . . . eleven o'clock. But not a moment after."

"But what is she to wear?" Martina complained. "She has nothing to wear!"

"I have my blue dress," Anna pointed out.

"Pouf! That is for a child. You are now going out to be a woman. You are going to a famous restaurant. You must look the part." She looked at Berkeley. "You do understand this, Berkeley?"

"I think you have a point," Berkeley said. "Today is Monday. We have four days. I'll drive you into Northampton tomorrow, and the two of you can go shopping." He wagged his finger at Martina. "We are looking for something nice, but nothing daring."

She pouted. "What is daring on one woman is merely modest on another. You must trust my judgement."

Next morning, having dropped them in town, Berkeley drove out to the remand centre.

He was shown into a small, windowless room, which contained a table and two straight chairs. He waited for about five minutes, then the door opened and Helen Karlovy was shown in, a wardress at her elbow; Helen's wrists were handcuffed in front of her.

"Would you mind taking those off," Berkeley said, standing.

"This is a dangerous prisoner," the wardress said.

"She is only dangerous to me, and as I am aware of this, she is no longer dangerous. If you follow me."

The wardress obviously didn't, but she unlocked the handcuffs and Helen rubbed her wrists with her hands. Thus far she had not raised her head to look at him or at anything in the room; she looked utterly crushed, her demeanour accentuated by the severe ankle-length blue prison dress and the no less severely pulled back hair, secured on the nape of her neck.

"Thank you," Berkeley said. "Now, if you'd like to close the door behind you."

"I cannot leave the prisoner alone in here with you," the wardress protested.

"Why not?"

"It's against the rules."

"Listen," Berkeley said. "I have told you what I wish you to do. So do it, or I shall become annoyed."

"I am going to the superintendent."

"Do that. But kindly knock before again entering."

Berkeley sat opposite Helen who was shivering although the prison was well heated.

"Are they treating you badly?" he asked in Serbo-Croat.

"They are going to hang me," she muttered.

"Not here," he promised her. "I meant, are they feeding you enough? Do they beat you? Are the other prisoners all right?"

"They do not beat me," she said. "They will hang me."

"Listen," he said. "I do not believe they will hang you after the evidence I shall give. If you will cooperate, and tell me some things I need to know."

She raised her head. "I have confessed."

"You have confessed your intentions, but not the details. You told me this man Himmler arranged the documentation and finance for your visit to England. But he must have done more than that. I know you were stalking me for at least a fortnight before you attacked my house. Where were you living? The police have been looking and have advertised, but no one has come forward. And you speak very little English. Someone has been concealing you since you came here, and even now that you are awaiting trial for murder this person has not come forward. I wish to know who this is."

"Stefan speaks good English," she said. "He learned it in school. And now he is dead." Tears rolled down her cheeks.

"I still wish to know where you lived for that fortnight."

"What will happen to him?"

"Nothing."

"You will hand him to the police."

"No, I will not. I just wish to ask him one or two questions."

"About Herr Himmler?"

"Yes. Listen, Helen. You owe this man nothing. He sent you on a suicide mission. Even if you had succeeded in killing me, you would still have been caught before you could leave the country."

"You want to find him?"

"Yes."

"So you can kill him?"

"Would that be such a bad idea?"

She hesitated a moment longer, then said, "We went to the house of a man named Green, in a town called Wellingborough."

About five miles from Northampton.

"This man was an agent for Herr Himmler?"

"I think so. His name is not really Green. I think he is German."

Berkeley took out his notebook and gave it to her, together with his pen. "Write down the address."

Helen did so, and he replaced it in his pocket.

"Thank you. You are being very co-operative. As I have said, I am going to help you as much as I can."

"How can you help me?"

"By the evidence I shall give."

"What evidence?"

"I will have to reveal some secrets from my past. But if I do this, I do not believe they can condemn you to death."

"You would do this, for me?"

"I've done quite a lot to you and your family over the years."

"And we have destroyed your family."

"Not quite. Let's say I have more left than you. I would like the feud to end."

"I cannot do that. I have sworn an oath."

"That's a pity."

"Does that mean you will not help me?"

"I have said I will help you escape the gallows, if I can. You understand, however, that you will be sent to prison for the rest of your life."

She shivered.

"And prison will not be quite so easygoing as this remand centre. However, in the course of time, a parole will be considered. I imagine I will be consulted. Call off the feud and I will support your application."

"I cannot do that," she said again.

Berkeley sighed. "So be it. Then I will oppose the application, and you will spend the rest of your life behind bars."

"I am sorry," she said.

"So am I," Berkeley said.

"You and I are going to pay a visit tomorrow, Alexandros," Berkeley said.

"Ah! We have a lead?"

"I think so."

"Then why cannot I come?" Martina demanded.

"I want you to stay here with Anna."

"Of course," she said. "Anna! Come and see her. She is simply splendid."

"May I say that you look absolutely magnificent, Miss Townsend," Harry Druce said. "Or may I call you Anna?"

"Please do," Anna said.

She knew she was looking gorgeous in a black lace dinner gown which showed off her auburn hair to perfection, cut to just below her knee. The lining was black crepe de Chine, and her top flesh-coloured georgette as were her stockings. Her shoes were silver, and Berkeley had allowed her to wear some of her stepmother's jewellery, a pearl necklace and silver bracelets on her left arm. Martina had complained that her hair was most unfashionably long – not that she had ever considered cutting her own hair – but she had pinned it up in every direction.

"This is the best," she had said. "Nothing gets a man more excited than being allowed to unpin a girl's hair. Eh, Alexandros?"

Savos merely grunted. He was not looking very well, and Berkeley supposed he was feeling his age; it had been a hectic month.

But he himself was amazed, if a little disturbed, at how

grown-up his daughter looked in her new outfit, and equally at how smitten Druce was.

"Well, sir," Druce said. "If you'll excuse us."

"Have a good time," Berkeley said, and held the fox-fur cape for Anna. He shuddered to think what the entire ensemble had cost, but it had certainly been worth it.

Anna kissed all three of them; she was clearly very nervous. Then Berkeley and Martina stood in the doorway to wave them goodbye.

"I feel as if I am going to cry," Martina said. "Do you think it is going to work out?"

"Oh, come now," Berkeley said. "This is their first date."

"I so want it to work out. He seems such a nice young man."

"No matchmaking," Berkeley said. "We have just to let events take their course."

She pouted, and then they both turned sharply as there was a choking sound behind them.

"Oh, my God!" Martina ran across the hall and into the drawing room, checking to gaze at her husband. Savos had apparently poured himself another glass of champagne and was sitting in his chair, slumped, the almost full glass emptying on to the carpet beside him.

Berkeley bent over him and tried for a pulse at both wrist and neck.

Martina stood above him. "Is he . . . ?"

Berkeley nodded. "I would say he's had a heart attack. I'm afraid all the excitement has proved too much for him."

"What are we to do?"

"We need to ring for a doctor," Berkeley said. Damnation, he thought. Savos had lived a long, very full and entirely disreputable life. He could have no complaints. But Anna . . . setting out on her first date! She would believe she was cursed, that whoever she came into contact with was bound to die.

Martina was waiting. Berkeley knew she had never really been in love with Savos. She had been his secretary when he had been chief of police in Belgrade immediately after the war, and when he had summoned her to his bed she had not resisted. Equally, she had been happy to comply when he had opted, with Berkeley's assistance as a return for past favours, to flee Serbia for England.

He had no idea whether or not she had been a faithful wife; certainly Savos would have been a dangerous man on whom to cheat. But she had made advances to him, once, Berkeley recalled. Perhaps she had supposed that he was the only man in the world who could cope with her husband's trigger-happy tendencies.

But what the future might hold was less important than the present.

He called the doctor, told him what had happened. Cheam promised to be right out and said that he would bring an ambulance.

Martina sat down with a glass of champagne. "I suppose that is the best way to go," she said.

"I would say so." Berkeley sat beside her. "Now, Martina, the doctor and the ambulance will be here in half an hour, and we will have Alexandros's body removed to await a post-mortem. When that is done, we continue as normal, at least for tonight. I do not wish Anna to know what has happened."

"But . . . she must find out."

"Of course. I will tell her when the time is appropriate. If you feel you cannot cope, then it would be best for you to go to bed."

"I understand," she said. "I will do anything you wish, Berkeley." She rested her hand on his. "Anything."

They gazed at each other.

"We'll talk about it," he said. "Later."

Mr Green would have to wait.

"That was a lovely meal," Anna remarked, as Harry drove her out of Northampton and took the road to the farm.

"I thought so," he said. "And we're early. It's only ten fifteen."

"Papa will be pleased."

"That's one way of looking at it. The other is that he won't be *dis*pleased as long as we're back by eleven. From here to your home is only about fifteen minutes. That leaves half an hour."

She did not turn her head. "What will we do with half an hour?"

His heart was pounding quite painfully. He had had several glasses of wine but then, she had had two. And she had seemed to enjoy his company.

If only Walton's lecture did not keep coming back to haunt him!

"We could . . . talk," he suggested.

"It's very cold."

"I wasn't thinking of getting out of the car. We'd just park, and talk, for a few minutes."

"What would we talk about?"

She hadn't actually said no, so he eased the car to a halt and switched off the engine.

"About each other?"

"Why?"

He found, as he had done from the beginning, her habit of asking devastatingly straightforward questions completely disconcerting.

"I'd like to know all about you."

"I don't think you really would," she said.

"Well, I can't possibly know that until you've told me something."

"What?"

"Anything you like." He held her hands. "I have never been so instantly attracted to anyone as I was to you. I would like us to get to know each other as well as is possible. I would like to think we could perhaps grow to like each other, perhaps even to love each other."

"Why is that important?"

"Because I think I would like to make you my wife."

"We've only just met."

"And I said—"

"That you were instantly attracted to me. Believe me, Harry, I am very flattered. But you must also believe me when I say there is no way we can ever be married."

"You mean there is someone else."

"There is no one else. It is just not possible. I think we should go home now."

"I would like you to tell me why it is impossible."

"You will have to accept my word for it."

He got out and cranked the engine, and they drove the rest of the way in silence

"Thank you for a most enjoyable evening," she said as he stopped the car at the foot of the front steps.

Harry hurried round the car to open the door for her.

"There is no need to come up," she said. "Papa will be waiting for me."

"You're very close, you and your father," he ventured.

"Yes," she said. "We are very close."

She held out her hand, and he gave it a gentle squeeze.

"Would you like to do this again, some time?"

"Yes," she said. "I would, thank you."

He kissed her glove.

Berkeley was in the drawing room.

"How did it go?"

Anna drew off her gloves and then took off her coat. "It was very pleasant."

"Did he make advances?"

"I think he wanted to. But I put him off."

"Why?"

She shrugged. "I didn't want to give him any ideas."

"I would say he already has ideas. Didn't you like him?"

"He is very nice."

Berkeley regarded her for some seconds, and she had the impression that he wanted to say something more, but then he changed his mind.

"You go to bed," he said. "And have a pleasant dream."

Anna kissed him and went upstairs. She was in her bedroom before she wondered where the Savoses were; it was quite unlike them to go to bed before eleven. On the other hand, she reflected, Papa had probably sent them up so that he could be alone when she came in, just in case there had been some kind of crisis.

She undressed, got into bed and lay on her back to look up at the canopy. Oh, Papa, she thought. He was the only man in the world to whom she could possibly give her whole heart. She had already done so. He had fought and killed for her, like any Lancelot. She had seen him at his most grimly terrible and she had seen him at his most loving. In her heart she was almost relieved that Lucy was dead, because with Lucy she had had to share him, even if Lucy had never known the truth.

But thinking about Papa to the exclusion of all else, to live in a dream world where only the two of them existed, taking on all comers, was a dead end. Papa more than anyone wished her to marry and create for herself a normal life. Harry Druce? He had hinted that he wanted to know a great deal more about her. That was impossible, although she could not escape the suspicion that he already knew too much. But she needed to know even more about him. The problem was that what she wanted to know was not what any properly brought-up young lady should wish to know.

Have you ever shot a man, Harry? Have you ever been shot at, and hit, and gone down in a welter of pain and blood. He was probably old enough to have fought in the war, if only at the very end. But that did not mean he had seen action. Have you ridden with the Black Hand, Harry? Did you ever see the body of the woman you loved, after she had been tortured to such an extent that she hanged herself? Not only could those questions never be asked, but they were questions to which she already knew the answer. They constituted the enormous gulf between a man like Harry and a man like Papa, and thus between a man like Harry and Papa's daughter.

Anna sighed, and rolled on her side, to sleep.

When she awoke her father was in her room, standing by the bed looking down at her.

Anna sat up. "Papa?"

He sat beside her. "It seems that my family, and my friends, cannot escape misfortune," he said.

"What has happened?"

"Savos died, last night."

"But how?"

"I think he had a heart attack. We'll know today, after the autopsy."

"Oh, Papa." She threw her arms round his neck to hug him. "Do you think . . ."

"No," he said vehemently. "You had nothing to do with it."

"Is Martina very upset? What will she do? She has no friends in England."

"The answer to your first question is no. Martina's marriage was very much a convenience, and Savos was quite old. She knew it was coming. As for the second question, I agree we have a bit of a problem. She has made no friends down in Hastings, so far as I know, and her habits really do not suit her to polite society.

I would like to keep her here. She's a superb housekeeper, and well . . ."

"You would like to go to bed with her."

He raised his eyebrows.

"Oh, she would like to go to bed with you, too," Anna said. "I can tell from the way she looks at you. Have you ever had her?"

"No," Berkeley said. "I won't say I haven't been tempted and I won't claim to be virtuous, but I do not make a habit of cuckolding old friends."

"I'm glad," she said. "And I would like her to stay. She is about the only woman in the world I can talk to, because she knows all about me. And if you'd like to fuck her, Papa, now she is a widow, that is really quite all right with me."

It distressed Berkeley to hear words like that coming from such beautiful young lips, but presumably it had been an everyday word to her while she had been away.

He kissed her. "We'll see."

She caught his hand as he stood up. "Will you want to marry her?"

"I haven't thought about it. Would that bother you?"

She gave one of her utterly charming smiles. "We'll see."

There was a Serbian cemetery in London, and Alexandros Savos's body was taken there the day after the autopsy. Only Martina, Anna, Howard and Berkeley accompanied it; he did not bring the other children out of school as they had hardly known the Savoses, and only took the little boy because there was no one to leave him with. In the event, Howard enjoyed himself thoroughly, not understanding what was going on. A Serb priest conducted the brief graveside service, and the old policeman was lowered into the ground.

The four of them walked slowly back to the waiting taxi.

"I'll arrange for a headstone," Berkeley said.

"Thank you. You are very kind."

"Then we must go down to Hastings and pack up your things, and arrange for the house to be sold. But that can wait till next week."

"You are sending me back to Serbia?"

"Only if you wish to go."

She shuddered.

"Then we'd like you to come and live with us, permanently. Would you like that?"

"Oh, Berkeley!" Her eyes filled with tears. "You are so kind to me. There is nothing I would rather do."

She kissed him, and he looked above her head at Anna who waggled her eyebrows.

Whatever her true feelings, Martina had the sense to understand both that Berkeley was still in mourning for Lucy and his mother, and that she should be in mourning for Alexandros; so she returned to her job as housekeeper with as much enthusiasm as before, while continuing to share the duties of surrogate mother to Howard with Anna. As Anna had indicated, the two women – there was only ten years between them – got on very well, and there was no doubt that their shared secrets and the fact that they were both Balkan in birth and upbringing brought them together against the English world with which they were surrounded.

Berkeley had no objection although he kept a careful eye on the drug situation; but it was never in evidence. As soon as they got home, he took them into Wellingborough, to the address given him by Helen. They found the house locked and boarded up, with a FOR SALE sign in the front garden.

They went to the named estate agent, but he was no help.

"Mr and Mrs Green left over a month ago, sir. Seems Mr Green had an offer of a better job in the south."

"What did he do?" Berkeley asked.

"You know, sir, I have no idea. But there it is."

"I assume you have a forwarding address?"

"No, sir, I do not."

"But you must have somewhere to send the money, when you sell the house?"

"There is a bank account in London."

"In whose name?"

"I'm sorry, sir. I cannot tell you that. Client confidentiality, you understand."

"Well, then, let me have the name of the bank."

"No, sir, I cannot."

Berkeley kept his temper with an effort. "Very good. We'd like to look at the house if we may?"

"You wish to buy?"

"We might."

"I'll just get the keys."

He accompanied them himself, which meant it was impossible to search the place. To a casual inspection there was no evidence of any Nazi connection.

"We'll let you know," he told the agent and drove back to the farm. "A false lead," he remarked. "Just bad luck."

"He must have left the moment it came out that the murder attempt had failed," Martina said.

"So what do we do now?" Anna asked.

"We wait," Berkeley told her.

He continued to hope that something might develop between Anna and Harry Druce. Sadly, she refused Druce's next invitation to have dinner, and he did not call again.

"Can you find out," he asked Martina, "whether it is the man or the idea that puts her off?"

"I am sure it is the idea," Martina said. "This Mr Druce seems to be a very nice young man."

"Then what's to be done?"

"You are too impatient, Berkeley. Anna is not yet twenty. That would be very young to be married in any event. You must give her time."

He knew she was right and determined to take her advice, while the whole matter seemed less urgent when the other children came home for the Easter holidays. Including the two Lockwoods they made a boisterous addition to the family, but Berkeley felt it was time to have serious chats with all of them.

John was no problem, in the short term. He was due at Sandhurst in the autumn and was clearly looking forward to it. But Berkeley had a fairly good idea that his son was less interested in a military career as such than in somehow following in his father's footsteps. Explaining to him that the romantic pre-war days of cloak and dagger were history was going to be difficult, and Berkeley decided to postpone it in the hope that a year at military college might redirect his ambitions.

Alicia *was* a problem. When Berkeley asked her what she would like to do with her life, she replied, "Be like Anna."

"I think you need to tell me what you mean by that," he suggested.

"Stay at home, with you."

"Anna stays at home with me because, well, of everything that has happened. But she won't be here for ever. In the course of time she'll get married and have a home of her own. Don't you want to do that?"

"If that's what Anna wants," Alicia said. "But I don't believe she'll ever leave you, or here."

"We'll talk about it later," Berkeley said, admitting temporary defeat.

Caterina, he thought, who had created these children in her own image even if Alicia, at the least, could not possibly remember her mother, must be smiling in her grave.

The Lockwoods, although they were also half-Serbian, were easier to deal with; they were very conscious that they were the children of Berkeley's servants, even if he and his own children had always treated them as equals, and were anxious to please. Harry junior also wished to go into the army, but had no aspirations beyond being a private soldier; Berkeley undertook to use his contacts to find a good regiment. "Not," he pointed out, "that there is much prospect of your fighting in a war, except perhaps in India."

Mary was content to look to a life of domestic service, not that, since the war, there were many such posts available. But they were easier to find in counties like Northamptonshire and again Berkeley undertook to see if he could obtain her a suitable position, although he had already determined to fail in that and offer her a permanent post at the farm when she left school.

He carefully avoided all contact with Walton, and therefore Harry Druce, as Helen Karlovy's trial approached. He was visited by both Peter Watt and Douglas Jameson, who would be prosecuting, just to go through his evidence. They were not interested in the background of the feud, except in so far as it provided the Karlovys with a motive for murder; the evidence as it stood was quite sufficient to secure a conviction. To avoid the faintest hint of collusion, Berkeley pointed out that the defence knew all about the feud and would undoubtedly introduce it in cross-examination. Jameson gave a cold smile and left Berkeley in no doubt that he could take care of that.

Irritatingly, he was also subjected to periodic visits from the Horsfalls, worrying about Howard. He couldn't object to these, especially as try as they might they could not fault the care Martina and Anna were taking of the little boy. However, Joan Horsfall could not help wondering, aloud, if her grandson was being brought up in "Balkan ways", and heavy hints were dropped as to whether it might not be a good idea to remove the child to the safety, and propriety, of his grandparents' home. However, as Berkeley refused to consider that, they had to accept defeat, at least in the short term.

Then it was a matter of waiting for the assizes, which would be in May. Annoyingly, he had still had no word from Julia Hudson, who had returned to Berlin to rejoin her husband. He did hear from the Cohns, but they had no information to give him about anyone named Himmler. They suggested he write to the Berlin police commissioner, a man named Schuler, who would undoubtedly know the names of most members of the Nazi Party in Berlin. Berkeley, however, had no desire to become involved with the Berlin police.

Especially at this moment, for the English press were becoming interested in the case. At first, the reports had merely been that the home of retired British army colonel Berkeley Townsend had been attacked by a homicidal maniac who had murdered Colonel Townsend's wife and servant and caused the death of his mother, before being shot by the colonel himself. Almost everyone agreed that he had done the right, indeed the only, thing, and although he had been visited by several reporters, questions regarding whether he could think of a motive for the attack could be shrugged aside.

His brief appearance in court when answering the charge of manslaughter had changed that. Then he had been on oath, and when the magistrate had asked him if he could suggest any reason for the attack, he had been bound to relate, very briefly, the facts of the case: how, while serving with the Serb forces during the Balkan wars, he had shot and killed the boy's father, thus instigating the blood feud. This had satisfied the court and most of the journalists, even if they had found it a sinisterly romantic tale. But the London *Globe* had not been satisfied. This was partly because the editor, John Leighton, knew more about Berkeley's background than most, having allowed Berkeley to use the paper as cover on one of his previous forays into Europe, an arrangement he had come bitterly to regret. Leighton had had the intelligence to realise that as many thousand men had died in the Balkan wars, killed by other men, if death in warfare was reason for a blood feud, the entire Balkans would still be at each other's throats.

A reporter accompanied by a photographer duly arrived at the farm. They had been there before, with the rest of the pack, and been fobbed off. Now they had a whole clutch of questions.

"I'm sorry," Berkeley said, meeting them on the front porch. "You must realise that I am a witness for the prosecution, and therefore the matter is *sub judice*."

"What about the woman, Helen Karlovy? We understand that she is the sister of the assassin. What can you tell us about her?"

"Nothing at all," Berkeley said blandly.

But Leighton had also briefed his man on another aspect of the case, one which had been entirely overlooked by his rivals. "Is it not true, Colonel Townsend, that one of your children was kidnapped some years ago?"

"That is correct."

"Can you say whether this murder attempt had anything to do with that?"

"I cannot tell you anything."

"But the young lady has been returned to you?"

"Yes."

"Because you paid a ransom?"

"That is one way of putting it, yes."

"May we speak with her?"

"Certainly not," Berkeley said, well aware that Anna was standing just behind the door.

"We'd like to take a photograph of her."

"And I would like you to clear off my property," Berkeley said. "Or shall I throw you off?"

They left.

"Why won't they leave us alone?" Anna asked.

"Don't come out till they're gone," Berkeley advised. "They won't leave us alone because we might sell a few newspapers for them. A photograph of you on their front page certainly would."

"We should have shot them," Martina said

"I hope it won't be necessary to go that far," Berkeley said.

But it is very difficult to get the better of the press. The *Globe*'s headline the next day read:

> MYSTERY OF THE RETIRED COLONEL
> There seems little doubt that the recent Northampton tragedy has far more to it than the act of a madman. This newspaper has learned that Colonel Berkeley Townsend, the bereaved husband, has in fact known Stefan and Helen Karlovy for years, and that the mysterious deaths had their roots in the Balkans before the Great War. Colonel Townsend refused to discuss the matter with your reporter, leaving him to draw his own conclusions as to the origins of this so-called "blood feud". Is it possible that this murder had its origins in another murder?

"And so on and so forth," Berkeley remarked.

"The bastard," Martina said. "What will happen now?"

"Not a lot," Berkeley said. "I had intended to tell the whole truth in evidence, anyway."

"Won't that upset some people?"

"I shouldn't think so," Berkeley said. "It's all pretty ancient history."

But apparently not everyone agreed with him. Three days later, when he and Anna were in the back yard shooting at a target, Martina came hurrying out of the conservatory door, drying her hands on her apron.

"There's someone to see you," she panted. "A general. Named Shrimpton. He's from the War Office."

Part Two

The Avenger

"Into my heart an air that kills
From yon far country blows."
Alfred Edward Housman

The Trial

"This has been something of a fiasco," Josef Goebbels remarked, staring across the table at his subordinate.

"The man appears to be a devil," Heinrich Himmler remarked anxiously.

"Or the two Serbs were simply not up to the job. There is no substitute for training and determination. For belief."

"Indeed not," Himmler agreed, wondering if he dared remind the Berlin party boss that the Karlovys had been his choice. "Does the Führer know of it?"

"No, he does not. But he still wishes this man Townsend brought to book. He asked me, the last time I was in Munich, if we were making any progress in that direction. I told him we were."

"You mean you wish to try again."

"I mean it is necessary for the job to be completed," Goebbels said. He stroked his chin as he looked across the bar room to where two young women had just come in. Both were extremely attractive. Himmler sighed; Goebbels' weakness for almost anything in a skirt was well known. Himmler presumed it was a matter of compensation for the inferiority complex induced by his club foot. "Only this time," Goebbels went on, "it must be a professional job, carried out by someone who knows his business and who is prepared to die before being taken."

"Do we have such a person?" Himmler began to sweat.

"We will find one," Goebbels said. "There is no immediate hurry, as I would like the case of the Karlovy woman out of the way, with her preferably hanged, before we strike again. However, you will remain in charge of the project. Now, Heinrich, I do not wish another failure. You may not know this, but the Führer is contemplating the creation of a personal bodyguard."

"But does he not have the Brownshirts?"

"The Brownshirts are too numerous, too diffuse, and frankly, he doubts whether they are loyal to him or to Roehm."

"But as long as Roehm is loyal . . ."

"Yes," Goebbels said. "I can tell you, Heinrich, in the strictest confidence, that there are differences at the top. Chiefly between Roehm and the Führer. Roehm is a revolutionary. He would like to seize power in a gigantic bloodbath, with all those who oppose us strung up from lamp-posts."

Himmler gulped, and not only at the idea; he was being admitted into the secret conflicts at the heart of the party.

"This is entirely contrary to the Führer's approach," Goebbels said, "which is that we should remain strictly legal and gain power through the ballot box, no matter how long it takes. These differing points of view may well create a crisis, sooner than later. At that time, it will be a matter of counting heads, and when that happens, the Führer intends to be surrounded, as I have said, by a body of absolutely loyal and determined men, who will if necessary sacrifice their lives for him. Now, he has given me the privilege of selecting a shortlist of possible commanders for this new force, and I will tell you, again in confidence, that one of the names on my list is yours. This was when I was under the impression that the elimination of Townsend was being carried out with the efficiency of which I know you are capable. I will agree that the material you used was shoddy, but a reliable commander's first responsibility is to choose reliable subordinates."

Himmler opened his mouth and then closed it again, once more resisting the temptation to remind his chief that using the Karlovys had not been his idea.

"So, as I have said," Goebbels went on, "succeed this time, and it is possible that you may move into a high place within the party. When we take power, your future is incalculable. Fail me this time, my dear Heinrich, and I shall be forced to take your name from the list, and you will be doomed forever to, shall I say, serving in the ranks."

"I'll deal with it." Berkeley gave Martina his gun and hurried into the drawing room, where Major General Shrimpton was waiting before the empty grate.

The senior officer smiled and extended his hand. "Berkeley. How good to see you again."

Shrimpton was a tall, thin, alert-looking man. As General Gorman's successor at what was now being called Military Intelligence, he had first come into Berkeley's life a couple of years ago when he, or the government, had found it necessary to resurrect their tame assassin for one last job. That had turned out badly for the government's plans but excellently for Berkeley himself, because it had been on that mission that he had at last found out where Anna was being held, and had thus been able to rescue her.

He and Shrimpton had then parted, Shrimpton hinting that he might be needed again, Berkeley preferring not to consider the matter. To have the man once again standing in his drawing room, smiling that serpent's smile, was disconcerting. But he shook hands.

"I can't say the same, General," he said. "But have a seat. Drink?"

"Perhaps a little later." Shrimpton, who was in civilian clothes, sat down. "I gather from the newspapers that your past has been catching up with you."

"In a manner of speaking," Berkeley said.

"Oh, quite. You dealt with the matter in your usual manner. But it cost you your wife and mother, I understand."

"Yes," Berkeley said.

"So your poor children are orphaned again. Or is that charming young woman who opened the door for me—?"

"Martina Savos is my housekeeper," Berkeley said.

"Oh, quite. Nothing but the best for Berkeley Townsend."

Berkeley did not bother to take offence.

"Now," Shrimpton went on, "the second assassin, the one you arrested, is to be tried."

"Yes," Berkeley said.

"And will she be convicted?"

"It certainly looks likely."

"On your evidence, no doubt."

"And that of the people who were with me: Colonel and Mrs Savos – Colonel Savos, who has recently died, was Martina's husband – and my daughter Anna."

"I see. These Savos people are the ones whose entry into this country as political refugees you supported."

"Colonel Savos was of inestimable help to me while I was in the Balkans."

"Serving His Majesty's Government, in your own manner. Would I be correct in assuming that Colonel Savos was aware of the true nature of your activities?"

"I never confided in him but he was aware of most things. It was his business to be. But as I have said, he is now dead."

"But his wife is very much alive. Would he have confided any of his knowledge to her?"

"I shouldn't think he had to. She was his secretary before they left Serbia, and I imagine had access to all of his files."

"I see. Was she also around before the war?"

"Good lord, no. She was only a child then."

"However, as you say, she undoubtedly had access to her husband's files. You have of course both been subpoenaed?"

"Naturally."

"I have been reading the file on the case," Shrimpton remarked.

"Have you?" Berkeley was surprised. "I wouldn't have thought you were interested."

"My dear fellow, anything that affects one of my operatives, even one of my retired operatives, interests me. Now, it seems to me that the prosecution have a very open and shut case; a confession by the accused. What more do they need?"

"There are certain aspects of the matter which still need to be brought into the open."

"Matters which might concern you."

"You could say that."

"Berkeley, we would not like this to happen."

"By we, you mean the government."

"At this moment, I mean the War Office. But I have no doubt at all that the government will feel the same way. Dirty linen should always be kept out of sight of the public."

"I have no intention of betraying any state secrets."

"You may have no choice, if the defence counsel is up to his job. He will almost certainly attempt to instil mitigating circumstances in the minds of the jury; it is his only possible defence. To do that he needs to probe the background to this feud."

"Which was a personal matter between Karlovy and myself."

"Perhaps. But it took place while you were working undercover for us, during a very dodgy period of our history. You may well be led into giving answers which would reveal your affiliation to us, and some of the things that you were required to do on our behalf. This would be very bad, especially at a time when Europe is moving towards permanent peace."

"Do you really believe that?"

"All the evidence points that way."

"What about friend Hitler? A couple of years ago you wanted to see the back of him."

"It has been determined that he is not such a threat as we once feared. Oh, that inflammatory book of his is still being widely read, we understand, at least in Germany, but he has quite failed to make any sort of impact upon the German political scene, judging by the results of the last election, and he is not expected to do any better next year. Our fear was that his violently nationalistic ideas, if supported by big business, could create a very dangerous situation. But his poor electoral support, coming on top of the death of that fellow Grippenheimer who was one of his main backers, makes him less of a threat."

Berkeley waited, but apparently Shrimpton had no idea it was he who had killed Grippenheimer.

"So you see," the general continued, "your failure to blow up Hitler may have turned out for the best. We certainly would not like it to come out that one of our people placed that bomb. Not to mention that business with the Kaiser before the war, or your involvement in the death of the Archduke Franz Ferdinand."

"I have been subpoenaed," Berkeley reminded him.

"Yes. Thus you have two choices: one is to perjure yourself, the second is to remove yourself, and your delightful housekeeper, before the trial. As I have suggested, the prosecution don't really need you to get a conviction."

"Either way, Martina and I will have broken the law."

Shrimpton snorted. "I have never known that to bother you before."

"I may have broken the law in nearly every country in Europe, General, but I have never done so in Great Britain."

"Sometimes sacrifices of this nature are necessary. We are

prepared to finance you and Mrs Savos and your daughter, if you consider it necessary to take a long holiday out of the country. Six months, I think."

"And my other children?"

"I am sure we can sort something out."

"And when I return to England?"

"You will probably be arrested. But as the Karlovy woman will by then have been convicted and hanged, we should be able to sort something out there, too. It will only be a minor inconvenience."

"Convicted and hanged," Berkeley said. "She never actually killed anybody, you know."

"She was part of a team that came here to kill you, and did kill three people."

"Actually, they only killed two people. My mother died of natural causes," Berkeley said.

"Their presence in the house undoubtedly caused the heart attack that killed your mother," Shrimpton pointed out. "Now, we naturally do not wish to know your plans. However, I have with me a draft for one thousand pounds." He opened his briefcase and placed the piece of stiff paper on the coffee table. "Deposit that in your account and use the money to take a nice long holiday with your, ah, housekeeper, and your eldest daughter. Should you be unable to make any arrangements for your other children, ring this number," he placed another piece of paper beside the first, "and they will be taken care of until your return. I think that covers everything." He leaned back in his chair and gave an expansive smile. "We could have that drink, now."

Berkeley got up and poured two scotches, adding a splash of soda to each. "It doesn't, actually."

"Oh, don't let's have any of your haggling. You may regard the arrangement as an assignment, only instead of going away to kill somebody, you are simply going away."

"To allow somebody to be killed in my absence."

"Well, that is perfectly true. However, as it is someone who I am sure you will be very glad to see the back of, that should be very gratifying."

"Sadly, it is not my idea of justice."

"You, a professional assassin, wish to talk about justice?"

"I do not believe, except in the strictest self-defence, that I have ever killed anyone who did not deserve to die."

"It's still a pretty long list. And this woman certainly deserves to die. I would recommend you are out of the country by the end of next week. That is, before the trial commences."

"I shall remain here and give evidence," Berkeley said.

Shrimpton's eyebrows rose, and he put down his half-empty glass. "My dear fellow, I don't wish to pull rank on you but I have given you an order."

"And I do not wish to spoil your day, General, but you seem to have forgotten that I no longer work either for you or HM Government."

"You cannot defy the government."

"Try me."

The two men stared at each other, then Shrimpton stood up. "If you persist in this mad course, you will be storing up a great deal of trouble for yourself."

"And if you persist in attempting to nobble a witness in a murder trial, General, you may discover some troubles of your own. As you have suggested, I am in possession of information which could be very damaging to the government. This information is secret, and I have no intention of divulging it to anyone, unless I have to. However, I do intend to see that Helen Karlovy gets a fair trial."

Shrimpton continued to gaze at him for several seconds. Then he said, "I shall leave the draft, Colonel Townsend, as I have no doubt sober reflection will lead you to accept our proposal. You of all people, Colonel, should know that those who defy the British government invariably come to an unfortunate end. Good day to you."

Berkeley watched him leave the room and did not move until he heard the front door slam. Then he got up, picked up both the draft and the telephone number, and tore them into strips before dropping them into the wastepaper basket.

He understood that he had just received sentence of death if he disobeyed the general's instructions. If they could carry it out. If they dared try.

"Is everything all right?" Anna stood in the doorway.

"I think so."

"What did that man want? Was he really a general?"

"Oh, indeed. And an old friend of mine. Or shall I say, he was once my employer. As for what he wanted, he had a proposition which I declined."

"Oh." She looked disappointed. "Why?"

"I suppose I'm getting too old for the sort of thing he requires."

She hugged him. "You can never grow old, Papa."

"You keep telling me that," he said. "One day you'll get a nasty surprise."

But the immediate future required a good deal of serious consideration. He wondered if he should have told Shrimpton about Himmler. But, having changed his mind about the necessity of having Hitler eliminated, the general would undoubtedly have considered any differences between Berkeley and the Nazi Party to be a personal matter and would have been even more anxious that Berkeley should not be required to give evidence on oath.

So what was he going to do about it? He could not have Berkeley arrested without risking an even greater scandal. So, assassination? Berkeley knew from his own experiences that this was something the War Office would not shrink from, and although he had never been required to kill anyone British and would not have accepted such an assignment, he had no doubt there were many people who would willingly carry out the task. But they would know that he more than anyone else would be a difficult man to kill.

Once again he and his were under threat, and once again he did not wish to involve anyone else, especially Anna. For the hundredth time over the past eighteen months he regretted the absence of Lockwood, and for far more than just the loss of an old and dear friend. Lockwood had always been at his side, or more importantly, at his back, ready to protect him.

He lay on his back in bed and stared at the ceiling. He *did* possess a possible replacement. Dared he risk it? He had no doubts at all that when push came to shove, Martina was as valuable as any man. It was the long valleys between the peaks that bothered him, her ability to concentrate when there was nothing to concentrate on, when he knew, again from experience, would-be victims were at their most vulnerable. On the other hand, he had no alternative, save for Anna and possibly Johnnie, and he could not contemplate involving his own children in something that might require them to take life – or sacrifice their own. And there could be no doubt that working with Martina would be an enormous pleasure.

He got out of bed, put on a dressing gown, and opened his door. It was coming up to midnight and the house was quiet. But there was a sliver of light under the door of his parents' bedroom, which was now Martina's.

He knocked gently.

"Come."

He opened the door.

"Berkeley," she said. "I knew it was you. I knew you would come when you were ready."

He closed the door behind himself. Predictably, like himself, she slept naked and was sitting up in bed with the sheet folded just beneath her breasts while her midnight hair was spread behind her on the pillow like a shawl. He did not think she had been reading – there was no book in evidence – but what she *had* been doing was very obvious from the trace of white at her nostrils.

"Must you do that?" he asked.

She shrugged. "It is not a case of must. I enjoy it. It makes me sleep and have very pleasant dreams."

He went towards her.

"Are you going to beat me?" she asked.

"I probably would, if you weren't so obviously anxious for me to do it. We need to talk about the future."

"Oh, yes," she said. "I agree to everything you propose. Except if you wish to send me away; I will not agree to that."

"Move over."

She shifted her thighs and he sat on the side of the bed. She reached for his dressing gown but he caught her wrists.

"Later. Maybe. Now listen. That man who called this morning was a general in the British army. He used to employ me, and for him and Britain I have had to do some illegal acts."

"I know this. Alexandros has told me."

Berkeley nodded. "That also bothers him. But what bothers him most is that when we are cross-examined in court we may let something slip about my involvement with the British government; or you may. They would not like this."

"We must be careful."

"I assured him we would be. But he still thinks that a clever counsel, and Bullard is one of the best, might be able to trap us. So he offered me money to take you and Anna, and flee the country until after the trial."

"Oooh!" she said. "Where are we going to go?"

"Nowhere. I refused the offer."

"But – why?"

"For two reasons. One is that we have each received a subpoena, which means that should we not appear we will be held in contempt of court."

She blew a raspberry.

Berkeley ruffled her hair. "You would not like to spend a year in prison, now would you?"

She caught his hand and held it against her breast; he could feel the pounding of her heart. "Not if it would mean separation from you, my dearest. What is the other reason?"

"I have sworn to save Helen Karlovy from the gallows, and I can only do that by appearing in court."

"Oh!" She threw his hand away from her. "What do you have for that girl? She has been your mistress, eh? That time you kidnapped her to exchange her for Anna, you had her then, eh?"

"No, I did not. I had far too many things on my mind to have anybody then. I have never slept with Helen Karlovy. But I have destroyed her family."

"And has she not destroyed yours?"

"Not all of it, and she did not want to."

"Ha! So she says. She was still out for your blood."

"Everything she has done has been because she conceived it to be her duty to her father and sister."

"And if she gets away with this, do you not think she will continue to consider it her duty? Now she has her brother to avenge, as well."

"I am not suggesting that she get away with it. She will go to prison. But I do not want her blood on my hands. There is enough there already."

"And I am supposed to testify on her behalf, I suppose."

"You are required to do nothing except answer with absolute truthfulness any questions that may be put to you by either the prosecution or the defence."

"Then I will do that."

"There is a little more to it than that," Berkeley said. "By appearing in court at all, much less giving evidence, we shall be defying the British government."

"But we will not be breaking the law."

"No. We shall not be breaking the law."

"Then what can they do about it?"

"Defying governments is a pretty risky business. Especially this one."

"You think they may attempt to harm you?"

"I think it is very likely. I want you to understand this. I would also like to think that you will stand at my shoulder, always."

"But of course. You may rely upon me, Berkeley. I am your bodyguard, eh? And now, Berkeley, my darling Berkeley, as you are here, and I am here . . ."

And why not? he asked himself. It was more than six months since he had held a naked woman in his arms, and this woman, if by no means the equal of Caterina, was, at least in looks, about the best second he had ever known. As for loyalty, she would rank higher, because she had none of the inbuilt hatreds of the Bosnian woman.

He allowed her to untie his dressing gown and reach inside.

Martina slept in the next morning and Anna prepared breakfast. Then she rested her chin on her hand, her elbow on the table, and gazed at him. Seated in his high chair beside her, Howard looked equally intent.

"Was it good?" Anna asked.

Berkeley raised his head. "Just what do you mean by that?"

"I'm a light sleeper."

"I see. Don't tell me you listened at the door."

"Of course I did not. But I heard you go into her room and you didn't come back out, at least before I fell asleep again."

"Are you jealous?"

"I suppose I am. But I did say I was happy with the idea. I just want to know if she was worth it."

"Yes, she was."

"I'm glad. Are you going to marry her?"

"If I do, it won't be for some time yet. We actually had a lot to talk about. You do realise that in addition to the Nazi Party I now have the British government gunning for me."

"Are they in the same class?"

"Very much so. I would put the Nazi Party second."

"Well, then . . ."

Berkeley wagged his finger at her. "I don't want you involved. Martina and I will take care of any trouble."

Anna got up, came round the table, and kissed him on the forehead. "But I am involved, Daddy dear."

"All ready for the off?" Douglas Jameson said buoyantly, surveying the three people seated before him in his office. This was one occasion when Berkeley had allowed Joan Horsfall to have Howard for the morning.

"I think we are," Berkeley said.

"Excellent. There is nothing to be apprehensive about." He smiled at Anna and Martina; rather disconcertingly, neither of them was looking the least apprehensive, but this was the manner he used to all Crown witnesses. "All you have to do, in reply to my questions, is say exactly what you remember happening on that dreadful day. I know it will be an ordeal but I will be as quick as I can. I cannot, of course, answer for the defence, but I will certainly not allow Bullard to badger you, I promise."

"And the motive?" Berkeley asked.

"Well, that will have to be brought out. However, as I understand it, you found it necessary to shoot these people's father in self-defence. You had no idea that by doing so you were creating a blood feud."

"I'm afraid I did. I had lived in Serbia for several years, and was aware of their ethics."

"Well, even if you were, what were you to do, Colonel? Stand there and be shot yourself? I don't think we will have any trouble with the jury about that."

"I'm sure you know best," Berkeley murmured. "But I imagine the defence will use it."

"I am sure they will," Jameson said. "They have nothing else. And another country's ethics or mores have nothing to do with British justice. I mean to say, Colonel, if some cannibal from darkest Africa, carrying out his grisly business with the consent of his fellows, were to come to England and eat somebody, he would be guilty of murder according to our law. Anyway, this fellow Karlovy, from what I have been able to gather, was an absolute thug, a robber and a murderer."

"I have an idea that the Normans, a few hundred years ago, would so have described Robin Hood," Berkeley suggested. "But to a lot of Englishmen, then and now, he was a patriot."

Jameson regarded him for several moments, then produced one of his smiles. "No doubt, Colonel. However, English law does not recognise the right of any man to rob and murder no matter how patriotic his motives. I assure you, sir, that the defence may flog that horse for as much as they like but they will have no effect on the jury. The law is the law. I'll see you in court."

"I think you will make a lot of enemies if you speak up for that woman," Martina said as they drove home.

"I already have a lot of enemies," Berkeley said. "A few more can't make that much difference."

"What are we going to do?" Anna asked. She was sitting in the back.

"Keep a low profile," Berkeley said.

"But if those Nazi people try again—"

"I shouldn't think they will," Berkeley said. "Once bitten, twice shy, eh?"

"I wish we could go after them, and get them," Anna said. "The three of us could do it."

"Not a whole organisation," Berkeley said.

"Well then, the man Himmler. I'm sure we could find him."

"I'll think about it," Berkeley said, "when the trial is over."

He would have liked to see Helen Karlovy again but that was obviously out of the question; both Peter Watt and Jameson would throw a fit. So he would have to wait until he was called as a witness which would come early on in the trial, immediately after the police and medical evidence. Rather to his surprise, when the door of the Witness Room was opened it was Anna's name that was called first; she and Martina were the only two other witnesses for the Crown. Anna waggled her eyebrows at him and left the room.

"Why has she been called first?" Martina asked.

"I have a notion they're saving me as the *pièce de résistance*," Berkeley said. "They're using Anna to set the scene, give the jury an idea of the tragedy. You'll be next."

Martina was indeed next. Anna of course was not returned to the Witness Room, so Berkeley had no idea what she had been asked or how she had responded, or indeed, what she was presently feeling. But he knew Martina would go and sit with her as soon as she had given her evidence. Then it was just a matter of waiting. Not for very long, as it turned out.

The courtroom was crowded; this was the most sensational trial in Northampton for some years. There was no time to look over the spectators' seats but he was able to glance at the dock where Helen Karlovy stood between two wardresses. She had been given a good and well-fitting dress to wear and a little hat; without make-up and after several months in prison, her face was pale and she had lost weight, but she appeared composed. She did not look at him.

Below her were Walton and Druce, the young man looking fairly hot and bothered, and beneath them Bullard and his junior beside Jameson and *his* junior; the two KCs looked perfectly relaxed.

Berkeley climbed into the witness box and took the oath, giving a nod towards the red-robed Mr Justice Carmichael, with whom he had an acquaintance.

"You are Colonel Berkeley Townsend, of the Townsend Farm?" Jameson asked.

"That is correct."

"And you are a retired army officer?"

"That is correct."

"Would you tell the jury what you remember of the events of eight December last, Colonel Townsend?"

Berkeley recounted what had happened.

"You shot the male assassin, the man Karlovy."

"That is correct." Berkeley reflected that he had already committed perjury.

"You have testified that you had been to the railway station to pick up your friends the Savoses, and had just entered the house."

"That is correct."

"Whereupon you stumbled over the dead body of your wife. Following which this man attacked you with a knife, and you shot him."

"Yes."

"That indicates that you had a firearm on your person."

"Yes."

"Do you usually carry a loaded weapon?"

"No, I do not. However, only a few days before, I had been attacked by someone armed with a knife in Northampton. I reported the incident to the police and informed them that I intended to be armed for the next few days."

"And they gave you permission to carry a loaded firearm."

"They didn't refuse it," Berkeley said, and earned a titter from the gallery.

"But you did not find it necessary also to shoot the accused."

"No. She was arrested by my daughter."

"As the young lady has testified. A most gallant act. The accused, Miss Karlovy, was also armed with a knife."

"Yes, she was."

"You must be very proud of your daughter."

"Yes, I am."

"Now we come to the motive for this vicious and dastardly attack. In your statement to the police, Colonel Townsend, you said that in your opinion it was the outcome of what is known as a blood feud."

"That is my opinion, yes."

"A blood feud." Mr Jameson appeared to muse. "This is not something with which we in this country are familiar. Would you explain the circumstances of this, ah, feud, to the court?"

"I'm afraid, some thirteen years ago, I found it necessary to shoot and kill Georgiu Karlovy, the father of the assassin and his sister."

Jameson preferred not to pick up the deliberate separation of Stefan and Helen. "You found it necessary to kill the elder Karlovy," he said. "I assume this took place in the then Serbia?"

"Yes."

"And at the time you were an officer in the Serbian army."

"Yes."

"So, was this a military execution?"

"No, it was self-defence. Karlovy was armed, and he fired at me first."

"He attacked you. Exactly as was the case with his son. You are clearly a man who knows how to take care of himself, Colonel Townsend."

"I am a professional soldier."

"Quite so. You were no doubt aware that you might be instigating one of these blood feuds when you shot Karlovy?"

"I had then lived in Serbia for several years. I was aware of their customs, yes."

"But, being an officer in the Serb army and acting as you did in self-defence, you no doubt felt this custom would not apply to you."

"I did not really consider the matter at the time," Berkeley said.

"Quite so. Thank you, Colonel Townsend."

Jameson sat down, and Bullard stood up, a sheaf of notes in his hand. Berkeley presumed that the only persons in the court, apart from the pair of them, who knew that the notes had largely been supplied by Berkeley himself were Walton and young Druce; both were looking suitably po-faced.

"Colonel Townsend, yours has been an unusual career."

"I must object, your honour," Jameson said, standing up again. "Colonel Townsend's military career has no bearing on the case."

"Mr Bullard?"

"In my opinion, your honour, it does have a bearing on the case. Colonel Townsend has testified that he has recently retired from the British army, with the rank of colonel. This rank can only be attained by a considerable period of continuous and meritorious service. Indeed . . ." he snapped his fingers and Druce, with the air of a magician producing a rabbit from his hat, placed several bound volumes on the desk before him, "I have here a selection of Army Lists, covering the period from 1895 to 1922, which I offer in evidence to indicate that Colonel Townsend was a serving officer in the British army between those dates. The prosecution has stated that when Colonel Townsend shot and killed the man Karlovy, thus instigating this feud, he was acting both in self-defence and within his rights as an officer in the Serbian army. Now, your honour, Karlovy was shot in 1914. One of these books is the Army List for that year." He opened the book at the marked page. "And here we have the name of Colonel B. Townsend, Intelligence. I feel that Colonel Townsend should tell us if this Colonel Townsend, British Military Intelligence and Brigadier-General Townsend, Serbian cavalry, are one and the same man."

"Intriguing," remarked Mr Justice Carmichael. "I think I am going to overrule your objection, Mr Jameson, and allow the witness to answer the question. Colonel Townsend?"

"They are the same person, your honour," Berkeley said.

"Mr Bullard?"

"With your permission, your honour, I think it may be important to discover whether Colonel Townsend shot Georgiu Karlovy as a Serbian brigadier-general dealing with a mutineer, or as a British colonel dealing with someone who had perhaps penetrated his double role."

"I agree with you," Carmichael said. "Colonel?"

"I shot Karlovy in self-defence," Berkeley said. "He drew first but I was quicker. However, I was not at that moment acting as an officer in the Serbian army."

There was a rustle of comment round the court.

"You mean you were acting on behalf of British Military Intelligence," Bullard suggested.

"Indirectly."

"Would it be true to say, Colonel Townsend, that when Karlovy attacked you, it was because he had found out that although you held high rank in the Serbian army, you were actually a British agent, acting in the interests of HM Government."

"I believe he may have discovered that, yes."

"So that, in fact, he was in the process of attempting to execute a spy."

"That is one way of putting it."

"Only, as you say, you drew first and shot first. Now, Colonel Townsend, it is not the purpose of this court to enquire into what clandestine operations you may have been carrying out for the British government during this extremely critical time in the Balkans, but I am bound to ask you this: would you say that the quarrel between Mr Karlovy and yourself was a political rather than a personal matter?"

"I think that would be a fairly accurate assessment."

"Therefore it is possible to suggest that this attempt on your life was an extension of a political difference. An execution, rather than an assassination."

"Indeed."

"An execution in which the accused, Miss Karlovy, had what one might describe as a supporting role."

"I would agree with that."

"And she did not actually kill anybody, did she?"

"No, she did not."

"Now, I understand that, during your stay in Serbia or at some later date, you actually met Miss Karlovy."

"Yes, I did."

"This was after the death of her father, at your hands. Did she make any attempt to kill you then or attack you?"

"No, she did not."

"So it is reasonable to suppose that her determination to do so arose at some later date under instructions from some other party and had, perhaps, less to do with this so-called blood feud than with politics."

"That is certainly possible."

"In her statement to the police, Miss Karlovy denies having any part in the actual murders of your wife and servant. She further states that had she known what was going to happen she would have taken no further part in the execution plan. You were her target and nobody else. In the light of your knowledge of her, do you believe her when she says this?"

"Yes, I do."

"Now, Colonel Townsend, again I have no desire to probe into your duties and necessary actions while representing HM Government in the Balkans during those critical times but I need to ask you this: was Georgiu Karlovy the only person you found it necessary to kill during that period of your life?"

"No, he was not."

"You were no doubt aware that there would be reprisals for your actions?"

"I knew there was the risk of that."

"In other words, you realised that you were engaged in a war, clandestine and possibly undeclared but nevertheless a war, which is, if I remember my Clausewitz, a continuation of politics by other means."

Berkeley smiled. "Roughly."

"And therefore it is possible to regard Miss Karlovy as a soldier in an opposing army, carrying out the orders of her superiors?"

"I would agree with that."

"Thank you, Colonel Townsend."

Bullard sat down. Berkeley glanced at Jameson and, as he had expected, the prosecuting counsel was already on his feet

"Your magnanimity does you credit, Colonel Townsend. But the fact of the matter is that this 'undeclared war' to which my learned friend alludes was really a feud or series of feuds, was it not?"

"It is possible to say that a declared war is the culmination of a feud, sir," Berkeley said. "An international feud."

"As you would say, that is one way of putting it," Jameson said, clearly extremely nettled; Berkeley was supposed to be *his* witness. "I should be obliged, Colonel, if you would confine yourself to answering my questions. When your daughter so gallantly apprehended the accused, was Miss Karlovy armed with a knife? Miss Townsend has testified that she was."

Berkeley sighed. "Yes, she was."

"Thank you. And do you agree that Miss Karlovy accompanied her brother to your house for the purpose of committing murder."

"Execution."

"An unauthorised execution is murder, Colonel Townsend. Miss Karlovy accompanied her brother with the intention of assisting him in carrying out his assassination. She has admitted this and you, for all your misplaced generosity towards her, cannot deny this. Now, in the course of attempting to carry out this murder, two other people, your wife and your maidservant, were killed, and your mother died of shock. Am I right or not?"

"You are right, sir."

"Is there the slightest evidence, apart from the accused's statement, that she attempted to stop her brother from committing these murders?"

"No," Berkeley said in a low voice. He did not dare look at Helen.

"Thank you, Colonel Townsend. I have no further questions."

The Visitor

"You did everything you could," Martina said as they drove home.

Berkeley said nothing, hunched over the wheel. He had glanced at Helen as he left the witness stand and he had never seen such misery.

"Do you think she'll get off?" Anna asked from the back seat.

"There's no chance of that. It's a question of whether or not she is sentenced to death."

Neither woman made any comment on that; they both felt she deserved nothing less. And perhaps, Berkeley thought, they were right.

The phone was ringing when they entered the house. Berkeley picked it up.

"Townsend? Is that you?"

"As this is my house, that is a reasonable presumption. Who is this?"

"John Leighton."

"Ah."

"I've just had my man on the phone from the Karlovy trial."

"Yes?"

"Well, the evidence you gave . . . my God, man! I presume it's the tip of the iceberg?"

"You could say that."

"How did the defence get hold of it?"

"I have no idea."

"Well, no matter. As it's out in the open, how'd you like to do chapter and verse?"

"What exactly are you proposing?"

"That you give us the whole story of your time in the Balkans as a British agent. You'll have to name names and give dates and that sort of thing, but if you're prepared to do that, we'd pay well."

"I'd be breaking my oath of secrecy."

"You did that in court. Well, to a certain extent."

"That is because I was asked questions under oath. I could not refuse to answer without being done for contempt of court."

"We'd pay very well."

"Sorry."

"You know, if you won't play ball – we have a tame MP who will ask a question. That way it'll all come out anyway and you won't earn a brass farthing for all your trouble."

"I imagine there will be a queue of MPs wishing to ask that question, once they read the transcript of the trial."

"You're a stubborn bastard. Sure you won't change your mind?"

"Yes," Berkeley said, and hung up.

Two days later, early in the morning, Anna stood at her bedroom window and watched the car bumping down the drive. "Oh, lord," she muttered, and ran across the landing to her father's bedroom. "Papa!"

"What is it?" Berkeley made no bones about sleeping with Martina now; she was also sitting up, hair tousled with sleep.

"It's that man Druce, coming here."

"Druce?" Berkeley scrambled out of bed and grabbed his dressing gown. "He'll have the verdict. You're dressed, Anna. Go down and entertain him until I've got some clothes on."

"Me?"

"Be nice to him," Martina recommended, also getting out of bed.

Anna went down the stairs and reached the front door at the same time as Druce. She unlocked it, drawing a deep breath.

"Miss Townsend!" He raised his hat.

"Mr Druce. You're very early. Have you come to see Papa?"

"Ah, yes. But I'd rather be seeing you."

"You must explain that to Papa." She stepped back. "Please come in."

He followed her into the drawing room.

"Have you come about the trial?" she asked over her shoulder.

"Yes. The verdict came in last night."

She faced him. "And?"

"Yes," Berkeley said from the doorway, only half-dressed.

"Conspiracy to murder, sir."

"Hallelujah. Sentence?"

"Twenty-five years."

"Hell."

"There is a very faint possibility of parole after about ten years or so. Failing that, she'll be pushing fifty when she gets out. Then she's to be deported."

"Do you reckon I really did her any good?"

"Well, sir, one would suppose it is always better to be alive than dead."

"I'll remember that." Berkeley glanced from the young man to Anna; both had pink cheeks. "You'll stay for coffee?"

"That would be very kind of you, sir."

"I'll get it," Anna said.

"No, no," Berkeley said. "Martina will get it. I know she's up. You entertain Mr Druce."

He left the room.

"Do sit down," Anna invited.

Druce obeyed and Anna sat opposite.

"I'm sorry I haven't been in touch," he said. "But being on opposite sides of the case, as it were . . ."

"There is absolutely no reason for you to have been in touch, Mr Druce."

"But there is. I have spent the last months thinking of you. Seeing you in court, so beautiful, so composed . . . It made me realise how much I adore you."

"Please, Mr Druce. My father—"

"Gives every indication of looking kindly upon me. Or he would not have left us alone."

"Papa is desperate—" She bit her lip.

"To see you married? And I am desperate to marry you. Will you not at least say that I have a chance?"

"You are very kind," Anna said. "Even if I cannot believe that you have fallen in love with me at such short notice, and with, shall I say, so little encouragement."

"Love is not something that can be quantified in terms of time or encouragement or lack of it. It is there."

"You are an ardent advocate," she said, smiling, and then was serious again. "And supposing you discovered that I was not at all as you suppose me to be?"

"I already—"

Now her face was cold. "I see. May I ask how?"

He sighed. "Mr Walton told me. I don't know how he knew."

"I am sure all of Northampton knows of it."

"Anna, he told me before I first asked you out."

"Thus you thought I would be an easy conquest."

"Anna—"

"Or a very difficult one, and you relished the challenge."

"Neither of those. I fell in love with you at first sight. And I have remained in love with you. And will do so, no matter what."

"No matter what people say, you mean? Don't you realise that if we were to marry, you would be dismissed from polite society?"

"I don't give a damn for polite society."

"But your career depends upon it, does it not?"

"I can make a new career somewhere else. With you."

"And your family? Do they know about me?"

"I haven't consulted my family."

"You mean you haven't mentioned me to them?"

"Not yet."

"I think that is very wise of you. But you will have to, won't you, if . . ."

"They are my problem, Anna."

"Do you think I wish to be the cause of an estrangement between you and your family?"

"I am sure you will not be. Once they get to know you, they will love you as much as I do."

"You are very forceful. Very determined." She looked through the doorway into the hall. "It is all right, Papa. You can come in."

Berkeley entered the room, followed by Martina bearing the tray; both were now fully dressed.

Druce hastily stood up.

"How nice to see you again," Martina said, and put down the tray to squeeze his hand. "Do you take sugar?"

"Thank you."

"And you have brought news of that woman," Martina said. "She is the only thing that Berkeley and I differ about. I think she is very fortunate."

"I suspect Mr Druce agrees with you," Berkeley said. "So, what have you two been chatting about?"

"Mr Druce would like to take me out again," she said.

"With your permission, sir."

Martina clapped her hands. "I think that is a marvellous idea."

"I think you should know," Anna said, "that Mr Druce knows all about me."

Berkeley looked at Druce.

The young solicitor flushed. "Well, sir, Mr Walton knows, and when I told him I intended to ask Anna out, I suppose he felt it his duty to tell me."

"But you went ahead and asked her anyway," Berkeley said. "What exactly did you have in mind?"

Druce drew a deep breath. "I would like to ask Anna to marry me."

Again Martina clapped her hands, while Anna stared at him with her mouth open.

"Well," Berkeley said. "You are certainly very straightforward. Anna?"

Now she was flushing as well. "I have never thought of it."

"Of Mr Druce? Or of marriage?"

"Of neither."

"Well, I think you should start thinking about them both, now. As Walton appears to know so much about me, Druce, I am sure he will have told you that I am not a conventional man."

"He has indicated that to me, sir."

"Very well. Then I will tell you that I would like to see Anna married, to the right man, and up to this moment you have given every indication of perhaps being that man. I therefore give you the right to court her to your heart's content, for the next year. The marriage will not take place before then, and it will not take place at all should Anna at any time and for any reason, decide that she no longer wishes your attentions."

"I understand, sir."

"And when I say court to your heart's content, I mean you have *carte blanche.* You will be allowed every intimacy you desire. You may even take her to bed, if you wish . . . and if she also wishes. You can do her no harm, providing you always wear a contraceptive. Time enough to consider the possibility of a child after you are actually married."

Druce gulped and looked at Anna. The colour had faded from her cheeks.

"I am permitting this," Berkeley went on, "because the only hope of you achieving happiness together, and you will understand that it is Anna's happiness that concerns me, is for you to be able to have a perfectly normal sexual relationship, free of any encroachments from the past. During the course of a year together, this should be proved conclusively one way or the other."

Druce licked his lips. "I understand, sir. And thanks for giving me this opportunity to prove myself worthy of Anna's love."

Berkeley turned to Anna. "Are you content with this arrangement?"

"If it is what you think best, Papa."

He regarded her for several seconds. Then he said, "Well, will you stay the morning, Druce?"

"Believe me, sir, I would very much like to. But I am due in the office. Mr Walton only sent me out to give you the verdict."

"But you would like to stay."

"Well, of course, sir."

"Then you shall. I'll telephone Walton and tell him that I'm keeping you here to discuss the trial and the possibility of an appeal."

"I'm afraid he will tell you that there isn't any, sir."

"That is no reason why we should not discuss it. When I have made that call, Mrs Savos and I will go out for the morning. We shall be back for lunch."

"Oh . . . ah . . . yes, sir."

Berkeley nodded. "Come along, Martina."

Martina squeezed Anna's hand. "I am so happy for you. And we will take Howard, so that he will not be a nuisance."

She followed Berkeley from the room, carefully closing the door.

"Your father really is a remarkable man," Druce remarked.

"He has spent his life making things happen; he believes he can always do that," Anna replied.

Until very recently, perhaps even yesterday, she had felt that if a man ever touched her again she would scream and scratch his eyes out. But if Papa wanted this then she did too, and as quickly as possible, so that she would *know*, one way or the other.

"Does that mean that you do not, after all, really want this to happen?" Druce asked.

"I want you to make me want it to happen, Mr Druce."

"Then I am encouraged. Will you call me Harry?"

"Certainly. Have you had breakfast, Harry?"

"Yes. I breakfast very early. But you . . ."

"A glass of orange juice will suffice. When Papa and Martina have left."

"Is she now living here permanently?"

"Yes. She is Papa's mistress. They have been fond of each other for a long time but they have only been lovers since Alexandros died. Alexandros was Papa's friend."

"I understand. Will you sit beside me?"

Anna sat beside him on the settee.

He held her hands. "You understand I have never been in this position before."

"I am glad of that. Neither have I."

He looked as if he would have said something then changed his mind.

But Anna understood. "Yes," she said. "I have often sat and waited for a man to come. But the circumstances were different. It was always in a crowded salon, I was surrounded by other girls and I knew that the man would not come to me with love in his heart, only lust."

"You can talk about it so calmly?"

"It happened, Mr . . . Harry. If we are going to make any progress there can be no secrets between us."

"Absolutely. Then – may I be as frank with you?"

"I should not like it if you weren't."

"Well . . ." He licked his lips. "I would not be a human being, and I certainly would not be a man, if I did not wish to have sex with you."

She nodded. "I think it is what we should do first."

As usual, he was totally taken aback by her directness.

"Well, you see," she explained, "we can make no progress until we have established that it is at least satisfactory."

Suddenly he was nervous. "But if . . ."

She smiled. "You cannot make me climax? I would not expect you to do that, the first time. But sex is not just about orgasms. They are the least important. It is about touching, and feeling, and wanting."

"Have you . . ." Again he checked himself, about to tread on forbidden ground.

"Yes," she said. "It had to happen, sometimes. Usually with very young men, but once or twice with an older man. Perhaps they were all accidents. I think some of them just wanted to watch me in the throes of passion. But some of them were very kind."

"But not the majority."

"No," she said. "Not the majority. It is remarkable how many men just wish to hurt women."

"Oh, my dear. My dear, dear girl." Still holding her hand, he drew her against him. "I swear that no man is ever going to lay a finger on you again."

She pulled her head back, eyebrows arched. "Not even you?"

For a moment he gazed at her, uncertain of her mood, then he drew her to him again and kissed her on the mouth. It was the first time she had been so kissed in nearly three years, since Grippenheimer in fact. Although clients had not been supposed to kiss girls on the mouth, most of them had, and had wanted to tongue kiss as well. She had become so used to it that she found her mouth opened at the first touch of his.

Then for the first time she wondered what she was doing. Despite Papa's confidence, could it ever work? Did she want it to work? Yes, she thought, she did. She wanted a man, needed a man, always at her side, not for sex although she understood that would have to be a part of any deal, but because she did not think she was capable of protecting herself, at least mentally. Since her rescue, Papa had provided that essential shield but now he wanted to devote himself to Martina. She felt no real jealousy about that; she desired his happiness above even her own. So she sought a replacement. And this man was at least gentle, and had sweet breath.

Now he pulled his head back to gaze at her anxiously, and she realised that save for granting him her tongue, she had not in any way responded. She held him close to bring him back to her, and kissed him again.

Harry Druce was not quite sure whether he was in heaven. That she was utterly adorable, far more so than anyone he had ever met, was unarguable. He had hitherto found his greatest pleasure in just looking at her, watching her move, discovering her idiosyncracies, such as the sudden toss of her head which caused her magnificent hair to flutter before it settled again on her shoulders. He thought it would be the most marvellous thing in the world to watch her writhing in ecstacy and knew that her judgement had been correct: that any proper relationship between them could only come after his sexual fervour had been assuaged.

And hers? Oh, he hoped so.

And that infamous blood test? But anyone who could imagine so magnificent a creature could be diseased had to be diseased himself – in the mind.

He lay on her bed and waited for her. As instructed, he had undressed. She came into the room; and without meaning to he sat up, for she also was naked. She was far more voluptuous than any twenty-year-old girl had any right to be, with a woman's breasts but still high, and legs and thighs as strong as his own, and above them all that so beautiful face, as always, expressionless. He reckoned the most important thing he had to do with his life was bring expression into that face.

"Have you a contraceptive?" she asked.

"My God, no!"

She smiled. "You did not expect to have this event thrust at you so suddenly. I have one." She showed him the condom. "It is not mine. I took it from Papa's drawer. I do not think he means to get Martina pregnant. At least not yet." She sat on the bed beside him. "I will put it on for you. When it is time."

She got on to her knees and straddled him, then slowly came down to kiss him again. Tentatively he stroked her back, and then slipped his hands down to her buttocks.

"Relax," she whispered in his ear. "It's going to be all right. But we had better be quick, I think." She pushed herself up and affixed the condom. Her fingers were as light as a feather. "We'll have more time for real love-making after," she said. "How would you like me?"

"On your back? I want to feel every inch of you."

She smiled and lay down.

So, it's done, she thought, as she lay with her head pillowed on his arm. It had been one of the few pleasurable sexual experiences of her life. He had set out to please himself, certainly, but her also, and if he hadn't completely succeeded, that was irrelevant. He had tried; that was what mattered; he would try again, and again, and eventually he would succeed.

He caressed her breasts, still with that air of uncertain wonderment. "Happy?"

"Yes," she said. "I am happy."

"Then I also am happy."

She kissed his ear and listened to the doorbell ring.

"Damnation," he muttered. "That's not your father back already?"

Anna looked at the clock on the bedside table. "No. When he said lunch, he meant lunch. It is only half past nine. Do not worry; I will send whoever it is away."

She got up and put on her dressing gown.

"Do you wish me to come down with you?" he asked.

She smiled. "It will cause the neighbours to gossip."

"You have no neighbours."

"You just stay there," she said.

"Well, be careful."

Anna went to her bureau and took out her revolver.

Druce sat up. "Good God! Is that yours?"

"Of course."

"Do you know how to use it?"

"I practise every day. Papa says I am a crack shot. I will show you later." She put the revolver in her dressing-gown pocket and went to the door. "I will leave this open, so that you can hear."

"If you need me, I'll be there."

She blew him a kiss and went down the stairs, frowning as she looked through the glass panelling of the front door; whoever it was appeared to be in uniform but she had heard no car.

Still, someone in uniform . . . She turned the latch and allowed the door to swing in, her right hand resting on the revolver in her pocket. And gazed in surprise at the middle-aged woman in the uniform of the Salvation Army.

"Good morning," the woman said.

"Good morning," Anna replied, taking her hand from her pocket and drawing the dressing gown closer about her. "May I help you?"

"I was actually looking for Colonel Townsend."

"I'm afraid my father is out."

"Your father. Then you will be Miss Townsend? Miss Anna Townsend?"

"I am, yes."

"How nice to meet you. I have read a lot about you."

"Have you?" Anna wondered where.

"May I ask when your father will be home?"

"I expect him for lunch."

"Ah. Tell me, do you and he live alone here?"

"No, no," Anna said. "There will be five of us for lunch."

Which was technically correct, even if Howard could hardly yet be called a complete human being.

"Ah," the woman said again. "Then I will call later."

"You mean you will return at lunchtime?"

"No, I don't think I can do that. Perhaps tomorrow. Will your father be in tomorrow?"

"As far as I know. Who shall I say called?"

"My name is not important. He will not know it."

"Well, then, your business."

"I simply called to offer the colonel my condolences on the death of his wife. But she was not your mother, I believe."

"No," Anna said. "She was my friend."

"I am so sorry. Do give your father my regards. I will call again."

She looked past Anna for a moment, then turned and went down the steps, mounted the bicycle that was leaning against them, and rode away.

Anna turned, looked at Druce's feet on the stairs. "She saw you."

"I'm sorry. I wanted her to see me." He came down. "I didn't want her to get the idea that you were alone in the house."

"You're very suspicious. She was from the Salvation Army."

"You mean she was wearing a Salvation Army uniform. I don't think she was genuine."

"What makes you say that?"

"For one thing, she wasn't English."

"She looked English to me."

"Certainly she did. But she had an accent. Didn't you notice it?"

Anna frowned. "Now you mention it . . . but really, a middle-aged woman riding a bicycle . . ."

"What exactly does that prove?"

"I'll tell Papa. He'll know how to handle it. I think we should get dressed."

"All right," he said. "We'll spend the rest of the morning talking about our marriage."

Berkeley and Martina returned at twelve and Martina hurried Howard upstairs.

"He's been a ball of fire," she said. "Now he's exhausted and ready for his nap."

"I've put the lunch on," Anna said.

"I hope you've had a profitable morning?" Berkeley enquired, looking from one to the other.

"We got to know each other," Anna said. "And we had this visitor."

"Tell me."

Anna told him about the woman.

"She wasn't English," Druce said.

"So what do you reckon?"

"I think she was up to no good. I have a notion that if she hadn't seen me she might have attempted to harm Anna."

"And I would have shot her," Anna said.

"I'm still glad I was here," Druce said.

She squeezed his arm. "So am I, actually, if not entirely because of that woman."

"What are you going to do about it, sir?" Druce asked.

"Wait and see what develops. Forewarned is forearmed. It will be interesting to see what she comes up with."

"Well?" Berkeley asked, when Druce had left and he was alone with his daughter.

"I think it is going to work out, Papa."

"That sounds somewhat qualified. Did he . . . ah . . ."

"I made him. You said we should."

"So I did. And there were no problems?"

"None at all. Are you angry?"

"Not if he made you happy. Jealous, maybe."

They gazed at each other and Anna's tongue came out and circled her lips. "I would have preferred it to have been you."

"Anna! Don't ever say that again. Don't ever even think it."

"Why not? It is the truth."

"Some truths are unacceptable."

"Because it is against the law? Or because you do not find me attractive?"

"You are the most attractive woman I have ever known."

Her eyes widened. "More attractive than Mama?"

"You do not hate, the way she did. Although you have just as much reason to do so."

"But when she learned to hate, she did not have you." Another lick of the lips. "If you ever wished to come to my bed, Papa, I would welcome you."

"Anna!"

"No one would ever know. Well, Martina might, but I know she would not object."

"And Druce?"

"He would never know either."

"I was thinking of your relationship with him."

"That would not be affected."

"You mean you do not love him, and could never love him."

"I do not love him. But I like him, and I think perhaps in time I could love him."

"Do you wish to marry him?"

"If I have to marry anyone, I think he is the best."

"Marriage is not something to undertake against a background of incest as well as everything else."

"Compared with everything else, incest is a very little crime."

"You are damned difficult to argue with. Now listen, I am going to marry Martina."

"Oh, I'm so glad. She will be so happy. And she will make you happy too."

"You're not jealous?"

"Of course I am jealous, Papa. It is the other side of the same coin. If I cannot have you, then I can think of no one better suited. She is like Mama, but as you say, she does not hate. I do not think Lucy was ever a proper wife for you. You do not mind my saying this?"

"Not at all. I think you're probably right. But you see, if I am to marry Martina, you simply have to get married as well."

"Or I will be a fifth wheel to a coach," she agreed. "Then I will marry Harry. Do we still have to wait a year?"

"Well . . . perhaps a few months, at any rate."

Martina was delighted; she had not expected her own life and ambition to develop so quickly.

"Can I have a child?" she asked enthusiastically. "I so want a child. Don't suppose it will interfere with my caring for Howard."

"Of course you shall have a child," Berkeley assured her. "But I think we should wait until after we are married."

"You do not want a bastard," she said. "I am glad. Neither do I." She squeezed Anna's hand. "We shall have our first children together. I know it. When will we be married? We could have a joint wedding. That would cause a sensation."

"Everything any of us does causes a sensation," Berkeley said. "I'll have a word with Druce. That sounds like the post."

"I'll get it." Anna ran to the door and returned with several envelopes. "Bill, bill, bill, invitation? Circular. And a letter from Germany. Addressed to you, Papa."

Berkeley took the envelope. He thought he recognised the handwriting, although he could not immediately place it. But for the moment he was merely relieved; every day he expected some kind of rocket from the War Office for his evidence at the trial.

He slit the envelope, took out the single sheet of paper inside; the handwriting was in German.

> My old friend,
>
> Further to my last, I now have some positive information to give you. Heinrich Himmler has emerged as a man of some importance in the Berlin branch of the Nazi Party. He is apparently a protégé of the local party boss, a man named Goebbels, a detestable fellow. Himmler is becoming known as Goebbels' private hit man, and I have heard it rumoured that he may be destined for higher things, perhaps even as a member of Hitler's personal bodyguard.
>
> You did not tell me why you wished to know about this man and I respect your wish to keep this private, but if I may offer some advice, these people are not to be meddled with except from a position of great strength. Their methods are very brutal and they enjoy a considerable amount of political and police protection, which enables them to parade as virtuous and law-abiding citizens.
>
> Take care, my friend.
> David Cohn.

Berkeley handed the letter to Anna, who read it and then gave it to Martina; like them, the Serb woman read German.

"What are we going to do?" Anna asked.

"If we accept David's opinion, there's not a lot we can do," Berkeley said. "The Nazis may be an irrelevance in German politics but they have a considerable organisation, and Cohn suggests that it is the organisation we'd be up against rather than just Himmler. We haven't the strength or the resources to take on a political party in a shooting war."

"But they have the strength and the resources to take us on," Anna said.

"We'll just have to be careful."

"We could go away," Martina suggested.

"And become fugitives for the rest of our lives?"

"But if anything were to happen to you . . ." Anna said.

"People have been trying to kill me for twenty years," Berkeley assured her. "They haven't made it yet."

The next day Berkeley drove into Northampton to see Walton. That left Anna and Martina alone at home with Howard but he knew that of all the women in the world they were the most capable of taking care of themselves. They were aware of their situation in a way that Lucy, with her protected upbringing, could never be.

"Colonel Townsend." Walton himself ushered him into the office. "How good to see you. You must be much relieved all that terrible business is behind you."

Berkeley took the offered chair. "In my business nothing is ever quite behind me, Walton. Is young Druce around?"

"Indeed he is." Walton frowned. "He tells me you have been allowing him to court Anna. I hope he hasn't been improper?"

"To my knowledge, he has done nothing for which I have not given permission. I have every hope that they will get married, as soon as possible."

"That would be very nice. But . . . as soon as possible?"

Berkeley grinned. "You lawyers have tunnel vision. I would like the marriage to take place quickly, not because Anna is pregnant but for a reason I would like to outline to you both."

"Of course." Walton rang his bell. "Ask Mr Druce to step in here, will you, Miss Carlisle."

Druce arrived a few minutes later, looking almost as anxious as his superior. "Colonel Townsend?"

Berkeley shook hands. "Can he sit down?"

"Of course. Sit down, Harry. Colonel Townsend has something he wishes to say to us both."

"I wish to draw up a will," Berkeley said.

Both solicitors raised their eyebrows.

"You do not have a will already, Colonel?" Walton asked. His tone indicated that in his opinion for a man in Berkeley's profession that was gross negligence.

"Indeed I do. It is lodged with Howard Horsfall, as it is largely concerned with his daughter."

"Ah," Walton said. "Yes, indeed. I entirely understand."

"I can obtain it from him, of course," Berkeley said. "But I was under the impression that the most recently dated will obtains, no matter who may have possession of any previous instruments."

"That is correct, sir. But it does sometimes lead to complications and appeals and that sort of thing. I think it would be best that I inform Mr Horsfall that you have made a new will, and invite him either to destroy the original or forward it to me."

"As you think best. I agree that there may well be objections when my new will is probated."

"Always something to be avoided. But you are talking as if, well . . ."

"Yes," Berkeley said. "It could happen at any moment."

"Good heavens! An illness?" Walton looked at Druce, as if enquiring why his junior had not discovered it.

"An assassination, Mr Walton," Berkeley said. "If you recall, Mr Bullord's cross-examination elicited the fact that although the Karlovys certainly came to kill me, they did not come of their own accord."

"Well, yes, but I thought that was purely to provide a defence."

"Unfortunately, it happened to be the truth. I do not wish to involve either of you in my personal problems but in the course of my career I have managed to antagonise a powerful and ruthless organisation, and they are out for my blood. That they employed the Karlovys, who also had a reason but not the means, to kill me, is merely an example of that ruthlessness. Therefore, I must assume, the Karlovys having failed, they will try again.

"Even round-the-clock protection will not keep these people out and, as our police are not armed, we would very probably be looking at the death of at least one officer. This I do not propose to contemplate. It is a matter we will have to take care of on our own."

"We?" Druce asked.

"Anna and Martina Savos are both entirely aware of the situation and both completely capable of taking care of themselves. And me."

"But, sir . . . a twenty-year-old girl?"

"Who next year will be a twenty-one-year-old woman, Druce. Anna comes from a long line of guerilla fighters, men and women."

"Well, sir . . ."

"If you wish to withdraw your suit, you are free to do so. I will explain the situation to Anna."

"I would not dream of withdrawing my suit, sir. I would protect Anna with my life."

"Well, let's hope it won't come to that. Now, as I said, the existing will leaves the bulk of my estate to Lucy, with due provision for each of my children, and names her as my executor. When it was drawn up I had no doubt that in administering the estate she would receive all the help and support necessary from her father.

"That situation no longer obtains and my eldest child, Anna, will, as I have said, be twenty-one next June and therefore legally of age to manage her own and the family's affairs. However, she knows absolutely nothing about financial matters. I would therefore like to name you, Walton, and you, Druce as my executors, together with Mrs Martina Savos."

Both the solicitors looked somewhat anxious at this.

"Mrs Savos and I intend to get married in the very near future," Berkeley explained. "At which time she will, as Mrs Townsend, be fully entitled to that position. This will is merely to tide us over until then. My pension will of course cease with my life, but my investments should be sufficient to keep things going, certainly in the short term."

"Do the children know of this arrangement?" Walton asked, still doubtful.

"I intend to acquaint Anna with it immediately. I know she will be content, as she and Martina are the best of friends. I will tell the other children when they are home for their holidays, which will be in a couple of weeks. Now, Druce, when you marry Anna – if you have not changed your mind – you will share the responsibility of handling the family's affairs with Martina. Should Martina wish to marry again, she will forfeit her position and share in the estate and you will be sole administrator; I hope this will not happen and it is unlikely that it would, or could, happen before Anna's twenty-first birthday. I wish all of this incorporated in the will."

"I shall have it drawn up immediately," Walton said. "Druce will bring it out tomorrow for you to study. It would be better, however, if you came into the office to sign it. Obviously any witnesses you may obtain at the farm will be interested parties. Including Druce."

Berkeley nodded. "That makes sense. I'll look forward to seeing you tomorrow, Druce."

"Come back in, Harry," Walton said, when the young man had shown his prospective father-in-law out of the office. "And close the door."

Druce did so.

"Sit," Walton said. "What do you think?"

"He's a remarkable man. In every possible way."

"He's also something of a fool."

"Sir?"

"This business of the Savos woman. For God's sake, she's little more than a tart."

"She appears devoted to Colonel Townsend."

"Appears is the operative word. She knows which side her bread is buttered all right. But if something *were* to happen to him . . ."

"It would be up to me, acting on Anna's behalf, to make sure the estate was administered properly."

"Yes," Walton said thoughtfully. "You've had no second thoughts?"

"None. I think I love her more and more with every day."

Walton did not comment on that in words, although his expression did. "What do your parents think of her?"

"They have never met her."

Walton raised his eyebrows. "But if you are to marry, and soon . . ."

"I had not realised it was going to be that soon," Druce said. "When I first proposed, Colonel Townsend spoke of waiting a year. I have not actually mentioned anything to my parents yet."

"Bless my soul," Walton commented. He knew the older Druces quite well; they were not the most liberal couple he had ever met. "Well, my boy, I think you need to do so, very urgently."

Druce nodded. "I realise that now. Would you give me your support?"

Walton scratched his nose. "I assume you have asked that because you suspect they may not approve."

"Yes."

"Well, I really do not feel I can, or should, interfere between a son and his parents, Harry. I can, if asked, give an opinion on the Townsends, in which case I will say that the Colonel is a valued client and an honourable man, and his daughter is both beautiful and charming, and I would say intelligent. That she has recovered so well from her horrifying ordeal is entirely to her credit, and I personally would be very happy to have her as the wife of one of my partners."

"I do not think I could ask for anything more, sir," Druce said.

Berkeley drove home in a more relaxed frame of mind than for a long time. He felt he had put his affairs in order and taken care of the immediate future. He felt quite sure of Martina's loyalty, not because of any love she might feel for him – which was purely physical – but because she had nowhere to go, nor could she possibly improve her position, save by marrying again, and he had taken care of that. And Anna and Druce would hopefully find the happiness he so desperately wanted for the girl.

He even found himself whistling as he turned down the lane, the house clearly visible in the valley beneath him, bathed in autumnal colours. Now he could go ahead wth plans for both weddings. They would be held next summer, while Johnnie and Alicia were home. Why, it could be that joint wedding Martina had suggested.

He braked as someone waved at him from the hedge beside the road; it was a middle-aged woman wearing the uniform and bonnet of the Salvation Army.

"Lost?" he asked, stopping beside her and rolling down his window.

"I've been waiting," she said. "You are Colonel Berkeley Townsend?"

"Yes, I am. And you're the woman who came to the house a few days ago."

"That's right."

Berkeley considered her. He had been as suspicious as Anna

and Martina when he had first heard of her, but quite apart from the uniform and the large prayer book lying in the basket on her handlebars, he had never seen such an ineffective-looking woman.

"Well, follow me down and have a cup of coffee."

"I don't think I need to do that," the woman said, pulling his door open and in virtually the same movement flipping open the prayer book to reveal, in its cut-out interior, an automatic pistol, which she now aimed and fired.

The Wound

Anna stood at the front window and watched her father's car come over the top of the low hill.

"Papa's home," she called down to Martina.

"Just in time for lunch," Martina called back.

Anna turned away from the window and then checked, looking back at the lane. The car had stopped. Because of the trees and bushes which lined the lane, she couldn't tell why, but it had definitely stopped, and hadn't started moving again.

She ran down the stairs.

"I think Papa has had a puncture," she told Martina, who emerged from the kitchen, drying her hands on a towel.

"That'll annoy him."

"I'll go up and see if he needs a hand."

"We're not supposed to leave the house," Martina reminded her.

"I'm only going a quarter of a mile. And it's almost all on our property."

"That doesn't make it any safer. If you must go, take your gun."

Anna ran upstairs again and took her revolver from the drawer. She was wearing a dress but it had a pocket, and she put the gun in there.

"I'll be watching you," Martina said. She kept her gun handy in the kitchen, and now stood at the window with it in her hand.

"Just don't shoot me by mistake." Anna giggled. She hurried out of the yard and up the gentle slope. For a few minutes she was out of sight of the car but then it came into view, stopped in the middle of the road, the engine still running but the handbrake obviously on . . . and one of her father's legs hanging half out of the driver's door.

"Papa!" she screamed, running up the last of the hill. Berkeley was still behind the wheel, but turned away from it and the open door as if he had realised what was about to happen and had tried to avoid the bullet. There was blood everywhere – on his back and down his legs, inside the car and on the ground beneath it. Instinctively she looked left and right, but there was no one to be seen.

She leaned over her father, realised he was breathing. But still bleeding. He had been shot at least once, but there was so much blood it was difficult to tell where.

"Martina!" she screamed, and then realised that inside the house Martina would probably not hear her. She stood up, drew her revolver, and fired six shots into the air.

Then she knelt beside Berkeley again. "Oh, Papa," she said. "Don't die. Please, Papa, don't die."

"God," he muttered. "How stupid can you get."

"You're alive!" Tears were rolling down her face. "Oh, Papa . . ." With an enormous effort she turned him over and got him upright.

Feet pounded on the lane; Martina had heard the shots. "Oh, Jesus," she said. "Berkeley . . ."

"He's alive," Anna panted. "But all this blood . . ."

"We must stop it. Was it a bullet?"

"Yes," Berkeley groaned. "At point blank range. Fired by that Salvationist."

"All right. I will find it. Anna, go down and telephone Dr Cheam. Tell him it is very urgent. Then telephone Inspector Watt."

Anna straightened; the front of her dress was a mass of blood. "Is he . . ."

"Get on with it," Martina commanded.

Anna ran down the hill.

Martina gently pulled Berkeley forward so that he lay half across her knees. She lifted his jacket, pulled his shirt out of his trousers and gasped.

"Am I done?" Berkeley asked.

"You should be. But the bullet hit your wallet. It is a good thing you keep a lot of cash on you." Tongue between her teeth, she extracted the leather from his hip pocket; the bullet had gone right through it and was somewhere in his pelvic region.

"She fired twice," Berkeley said.

Martina tore strips from her dress to place over the wound.

"I can't move you. You must lie as still as you can. Dr Cheam is on his way and he will have an ambulance."

Berkeley nodded, teeth gritted.

"Is it very painful?"

"Yes."

"Try to keep still. I am not going to let you die, my darling."

"I'm glad of that. That woman . . ."

"I will deal with her," Martina said. "Now let us find this other wound."

"Good heavens," said Peter Watt. "Shot, you say? I'll be right out. Have you called the doctor?"

"Yes," Anna said. "Please hurry, Mr Watt."

"I'm on my way," Watt assured her.

Anna replaced the receiver. Her mind was spinning. Papa shot! Of course he had been wounded before, at least three times. That man Karlovy had shot him in the chest, and he had survived. But he had been younger then. Oh, Papa! Tears flooded down her cheeks.

She picked up the receiver again, and gave the number of Walton's chambers. A tremendous desire to kill the Salvationist and whoever had sent her was mingled with an equally overwhelming desire to be held in her lover's arms and comforted.

"Walton, Harrison and Druce."

"Please let me speak to Mr Druce," Anna said.

"I'm afraid Mr Druce is in a meeting. If you'd leave your name and telephone number—"

"I must speak to him, now. Tell him it's Anna."

"Oh, Miss Townsend. Why didn't you say? I'll get him right away."

Druce was on the phone a few moments later. "Anna? What's the matter?"

"Papa! He's been shot."

"Good God! Is he . . ."

"I don't know. God, I don't know. The doctor's coming, and the police. Harry . . ."

"I'm on my way. Hold on, my dearest girl. I'll be there in half an hour."

Anna replaced the phone, remained sitting on the floor for several minutes. I'm the head of the family, she thought. If Papa is dead. But he couldn't be dead, surely. You'll never grow old, she had said, so often and so confidently. There was so much to be done. But nothing could be done until she knew whether Papa was going to live or die.

She pushed herself up again and went outside. It was a beautiful day, blue skies and warm sunshine . . . but Papa could be dying.

She climbed the hill. Martina heard her coming. "Anna!" she shouted. "Berkeley is in so much pain. Fetch a sedative."

"What?"

"God, I don't know. At least some aspirin."

Anna looked past her at her father. His face was pale, and she thought he was still bleeding; Martina had torn her entire skirt into strips and bandaged up his chest as best she could, as well as one leg which was folded at a very awkward angle. He had been hit twice!

Anna stumbled back down the hill into the house, tore open cupboards and boxes, found various boxes of pills . . . and then thought of Martina's habit. Cocaine might ease the pain or at least make him less aware of it. She ran into Martina's room, again tore open drawers, and found a packet of the white powder. She dropped it into her pocket beside the gun, and ran out of the house and back up the hill. But now she heard the reassuring roar of car engines, and by the time she reached the top both Dr Cheam and the ambulance were there.

"He's fainted. He was in such pain," Martina was saying. "And he's lost so much blood."

Cheam, a heavy-set man who normally had a most reassuring bedside manner and who had been the Townsends' GP for more than twenty years, was looking distinctly agitated. "We'll get him to hospital and a transfusion," he said.

"You must stop the bleeding," Martina said. "I tried, but I don't think I have."

Cheam nodded. "Put him inside," he told the ambulance men, who were hovering with their stretcher. "Carefully now."

"Is he going to live?" Anna asked.

Cheam seemed to realise who she was for the first time.

"My dear child! You're covered in blood."

"Daddy's blood. Doctor . . ."

He looked from woman to woman as Berkeley was laid on the stretcher and carefully conveyed into the ambulance. "Are you all right? Would you like a sedative?"

It wasn't clear which of them he was addressing.

"We have everything we need," Martina said.

"Very good." He was remembering her as well. "You are the widow of the old gentleman who died a few months ago."

"I am Colonel Townsend's fiancée," Martina said, proudly.

Cheam looked at Anna.

"Martina is my dearest friend," Anna said.

"I will telephone this evening. I really should go."

The ambulance, after some shunting to and fro across the narrow lane, had already moved off. Dr Cheam hadn't quite completed turning his car to follow the ambulance when there was a blast on a horn and a police car came down the lane. The two cars stopped beside each other and the occupants exchanged words, then the doctor drove away, and the police car stopped behind Berkeley's vehicle. Chief Inspector Watt got out, followed by two constables; the third remained behind the wheel.

"Oh, Miss Anna, I am so very sorry."

"Thank you," Anna said. She had regained her composure, her fear and distress covered, as had been necessary so often in the past, by ice-cold anger.

"Did you see what happened?"

"I saw Papa's car stop and thought he'd had a puncture."

"That woman must have waved him down," Martina said.

"Woman?"

"She was dressed as a member of the Salvation Army," Anna explained.

"You saw her."

"No. Papa said before he passed out. But I have seen her. She once came to the house, looking for Papa, only he wasn't in."

"Can you describe her?"

"She was, well . . . a little taller than me," Anna said.

"Age?"

"I thought about forty."

"Colouring?"

"Her hair was mostly tucked up beneath the bonnet. But I would say she was fair."

"Can you describe her features?"

"Well, not really. They were just . . . ordinary."

"No distinguishing marks?"

"She wore glasses."

Watt reflected that glasses could easily be discarded.

"That's not a lot to go on, but we'll see what we can do."

"Wait a moment," Anna said. "She was foreign."

"How do you know?"

"Her voice. I didn't notice it myself. But Harry was sure she had an accent."

"Harry being?"

"Mr Druce. My fiancé."

Watt was taken aback by the news. "Would that be Mr Druce the lawyer?"

"Yes."

"And he's your fiancé?"

A spicy bit of gossip to tell the wife.

"We're to be married, yes."

"How very nice for you. Do you mind if I have a word with him? If he actually spoke to this woman."

"He didn't actually speak to her. He heard me speaking to her."

"But he saw her."

Anna frowned. "I'm not sure. But he's coming here now. You can ask him yourself."

"Ah," Watt said. "Then I'll wait for him. May I use your phone?"

"Of course. Can one of your people move Papa's car? It's blocking the road."

"I can see that, miss. But I don't want to move it right now. I'm going to telephone our forensic department and have them come down to photograph the vehicle and dust it for fingerprints. Don't worry. We're in charge now. Everything will be sorted out."

"We should bathe and get changed," Martina said. "I think I'm soaked right through to my undies."

Chief Inspector Watt gave a discreet cough.

* * *

Anna left the bloodstained dress and vest and knickers lying on the floor. She supposed the blood could be washed out but she still intended to burn them; she would never be able to wear them again.

In the privacy of the bathroom she let herself go and began to cry all over again. Papa would be on the operating table now, while Cheam searched for the bullets and determined just how badly he was hurt. How she wanted the phone to ring, to reassure her. But at the same time she didn't want it to ring, just in case it was bad news. It couldn't ring, in any event, because Chief Inspector Watt was monopolising it, giving instructions here and there.

Johnnie and Alicia, she thought. They would have to be told; they would have to be brought home from school. But she didn't want to tell them what had happened until she *knew* what had happened. To tell them that Papa had been shot but not killed and have them come home to find he had died would be unbearable. But equally, to tell them he was dead and have them then discover he had survived would be hardly less traumatic.

Head of the family. She had to keep telling herself that over and over again, to make herself believe it. If Papa died. She had no idea of their financial position, but Harry would know.

Martina opened the door. She had also undressed but was wearing a dressing gown. "You've been in there long enough," she said.

Anna climbed out of the bath and towelled vigorously; she had washed her hair as well. "I was daydreaming. Do I need to dress?"

Martina smiled at her. "You should. But you can wear a dressing gown and slippers. Give them a thrill. Harry is here."

"Harry!" She hadn't heard the car. But of course, he would have had to leave it up the hill and walk down. She dashed into her bedroom, pulled on a dressing gown, thrust her feet into slippers, ignored her still wet hair and ran down the stairs. "Harry!"

Her appearance in extreme *déshabillé*, white legs emerging from the dressing gown, had them all startled. Harry had been talking with Watt. He was the first to recover and got up to put his arms around her, while Watt looked at the ceiling and the two constables stared out of the window.

"Oh, my darling," Druce said, holding her close. "We thought this business was over."

"He knew it wasn't."

"I know. He was in the office this morning, making a new will. My God!"

Anna raised her head. "What?"

"If he . . . your father . . ."

"You mean if he dies."

"Well, without signing the will, then the original one will stand. It virtually names Howard Horsfall as executor."

"But you can fight that, Harry. We can."

"You bet. But hopefully the colonel won't die."

"Ahem," Watt remarked.

Druce's hand was sliding up and down Anna's back as he caressed her, and with every upward movement the dressing gown got higher; it was already up to her knees.

"Oh, Chief Inspector," Anna said, disengaging herself. "I am sorry. We're engaged."

"So you mentioned, miss. I wonder if you would sit down and give a statement to the constable over there."

"Of course." Anna sat on the settee and patted the space beside her for the embarrassed constable.

"I assume Mrs Savos is coming down?" Watt asked.

"I am here." Martina, another conversation stopper in dressing gown with wet hair, appeared in the doorway.

It took over an hour for the police to take statements and obtain all the information they needed. By then the car had been examined, photographed and dusted, and one of the policemen had driven it down into the yard.

"It'll need a proper going-over," Watt remarked.

"I'll see to it," Druce volunteered.

"Yes. Well, we'll put out a bulletin on this mysterious woman and see what we can find. If we do pick her up, we'll need you for an identification parade, Miss Anna."

Anna nodded. "Chief Inspector, do you think I should phone the hospital?"

"I know it's a terrible time for you, miss, but I'd recommend that you don't. I imagine the colonel is still on the table, or just off it. I'm sure Dr Cheam will telephone the moment he has some news. And we'll certainly be in touch, hopefully sooner than later." He nodded to Druce and got into the waiting car.

Martina emerged from the kitchen. "Lunch is quite spoiled, but I can do something with eggs. You'll stay, Harry?"

"I'd like to."

"I want you to," Anna said. "But I couldn't eat a thing."

"I think you should," Martina said.

"Perhaps later."

"Well, I'll get something for Harry and me, anyway."

"What you need is a drink," Harry decided. He mixed three whisky and sodas.

Anna drank, and shuddered.

"Haven't you tried Scotch before?"

She shook her head. "Papa didn't want me to. Oh, Harry . . ."

He sat beside her and held her hand. "Think of it as medicine. We have a lot of decisions to make."

She nodded. "Like avenging Papa."

"Don't talk like that."

"I must. And Johnnie and Alicia will feel like that too."

"Listen, you're not Helen Karlovy."

"I'm Serbian. Just like her."

"You're not. You're only half, and the half is Bosnian, not Serbian."

"We have the same traditions."

"What you need to remember is that your other half is English, and English young ladies do not go around carrying out acts of vengeance. Even if you knew who to go after."

"But I do know who to go after. A man named Himmler, a German. He's behind all this."

"You mean you know this man?"

"I don't, personally. But Papa knows of him."

"Have you told Chief Inspector Watt?"

"Why should I do that?"

"Because he's obviously a chief suspect. Watt can at least have him investigated."

"Watt can't do anything about it. Himmler doesn't live in England. He lives in Germany."

Druce stared at her with his mouth open. "And you mean to go to Germany?"

"I know Germany well. I speak the language fluently."

Druce turned his head to look at Martina, standing in the doorway.

"Lunch is ready," she announced.

"Martina," Druce said, "Anna is talking about going to Germany to look for a man called Himmler. She thinks he is responsible for this."

"That is what Berkeley thinks, yes," Martina said.

"Well, do please tell her that anything like that would be absolute madness."

"I think it is what we must do," Martina said seriously. "I shall go with her."

Sitting down to lunch, Druce decided that his best course was to be as matter-of-fact as possible.

"The first thing we need to do," he said, "is get married."

"Don't you think that should wait until after I return from Germany?"

"No. It is your father's wish. He told Mr Walton and I this morning that he wanted the marriage to take place as soon as possible. Anyway, you can't possibly think of leaving England while the colonel is seriously ill."

Anna looked at Martina.

"That is true," Martina agreed.

"Neither can I think of getting married," Anna said.

"Even if it was, I mean is, his wish?"

Anna sighed. "We can do nothing, think of nothing, until we hear from Dr Cheam."

Walton willingly gave Druce permission to remain at the farm for the rest of the day, and to spend the night, if he thought it necessary.

"There is really no need to put yourself out," Anna said. "That woman and her employer were after Papa, not me and Martina. She will not come back."

"Don't you want me to stay?"

"Of course I want you to stay. But I do not wish sex."

"I did not expect you to," he said.

He was aware that there had been a subtle change in their relationship. In the few hours since Berkeley had been shot, Anna had moved away from him and towards Martina. He knew that she and Martina had always been close, but now they had become melded in their desire for revenge. He did not think they had actually discussed the matter – he had been with them all day – but it was a meeting of minds from which he was excluded. Because of their shared background or because he had rejected the the idea of vendetta? Or was it because they doubted he was man enough to help them? That thought hurt. They needed another Berkeley, and he was not that. If he had fired a rifle during the war, it had only been during the last few months, and he had no idea if he had ever hit anyone; since returning to civilian life he had not touched a firearm, much less owned one. On the other hand, he did not remember being afraid when under fire; he had been nineteen and quite sure he would not be hit.

Now he was faced with what he supposed was the biggest decision of his life. Go along with them in a madcap adventure which could result in all of their deaths and which went entirely against his personality, his upbringing and his profession? Or refuse, try to stop them and end his relationship with Anna. Because he knew that would happen. Part of her attraction was her total commitment to whatever she was doing, or whatever she regarded as important. And the most important thing in her life was her father.

The afternoon was very tense, and to Druce, increasingly alarming, as Martina and Anna went into the back yard with their revolvers and engaged in target practice. When he was invited to join in, his aim was so very poor that he reckoned he had gone even further down in their estimation.

It was a relief when, just after dinner, Dr Cheam's car came bumping into the yard.

Anna ran down the front steps to greet him.

Cheam embraced her. "Your father is going to live."

"Oh, Doctor."

"Really and truly?" Martina joined them.

"Really and truly," Cheam said. "We managed to get both bullets out, and he has received a transfusion. There will be another one tonight."

"Oh, thank God," Martina said. "Harry! Harry! Did you hear that?"

"That is the most splendid news, Doctor," Druce said.

"He is certainly lucky to be alive," Cheam agreed. "However . . . may we go inside?"

Anna escorted him into the house, still holding his arm. "However what?"

"Shall we all sit down?"

Anna and Martina sat to either side of him on the settee. Druce stood in front of them.

"What is the matter?" Martina said. "*Isn't* he going to be all right?"

"The colonel is going to live and, with fortune, will be able to enjoy most aspects of life," Cheam said carefully. "But there is something else, yes. That is why I thought it best to come out and see you in person rather than telephone. One of the bullets shattered his left leg. The breaking of the bones was accentuated by his effort to avoid the second shot. We have set the bones, but I'm afraid the damage is very severe and I cannot promise that he will ever be able to walk without the aid of a stick."

"But he's alive," Anna said, determined to be optimistic.

"That is, should he ever be able to walk again," Cheam said.

"What do you mean?" Martina asked, her voice a snap of concern.

Cheam sighed. "The second bullet entered just above his right thigh. It struck his wallet and went through it – it was fired at very close range."

"I saw that," Martina said. "Didn't the wallet save him from more serious injury?"

"Unfortunately, no. Had it gone straight on, it might well have penetrated the stomach. That would have been very serious, but we should have been able to cope. Sadly, it was diverted by the wallet and moved to the left, still travelling at considerable speed. It therefore lodged at the base of the spine."

"What does that mean?" Martina asked.

"It damaged the nerves. We have, as I say, taken it out. But the damage has been done. Your father is paralysed from the waist down."

The Avenger

"Oh, my God!" Anna clasped both hands to her neck and looked at Martina.

Who licked her lips. "You mean . . ."

"What I have said," Cheam said. "Colonel Townsend is paralysed from the waist down."

"He has no functions at all?"

"At the moment, no, apart from involuntary movements of the bowels. He may recover some usage of his extremities in the course of time, but for the moment he will need the care of a baby." He looked from one woman to the other. "I know he is fortunate in having two ladies such as yourselves to look after him."

"Yes," Anna said. "We will look after him. When will he come home?"

"I'm afraid not for some time."

"But we can go to the hospital to see him?"

"Of course. However, he is not yet aware of his condition. The moment I consider that he is psychologically strong enough to know, I shall tell him. You should therefore be guardedly optimistic in what you say."

"I understand," Anna said.

Martina was staring into space.

"Is he capable of doing any business?" Druce asked. "I have a most important document for him to read and sign. I'm sorry, Anna, but it is most necessary he sign the will."

"Of course. How soon can we see him, Doctor?"

"Tomorrow. You will find him weak, but there is nothing the matter with his brain, save a certain amount of depression. You may cheer him up. Now, I must be off. I'm sorry the news is so bad. On the other hand, it could have been so much worse."

"Doctor," Martina said, appearing to wake up. "When you say he will gradually recover his faculties, can you put any sort of timescale on that?"

"I'm sorry Mrs Savos, but the word I used was may, not will. A great deal will depend on his strength, both mental and physical. As for a timescale, that is quite impossible at this moment."

"Will there be a big splash about this?" Anna asked.

"I'm afraid there will be, Anna. It is a police matter, and I suppose it has to be linked to that Karlovy business. Well, if there is anything I can do to help, any tranquillisers . . ."

"We'll manage," Anna said.

"Very good." Cheam looked at Martina. He had a strong suspicion that she had a drug habit. "Don't forget, I'm at the end of a telephone if you need me. Druce."

Druce accompanied him to the front door.

"Do you think they can cope?" Cheam asked.

"Oh, they can cope. But . . . you realise that the family has a stormy past."

"I know all about their stormy past. Twenty-one years ago I extracted a bullet from Berkeley Townsend's ribs, fired by the man Karlovy. So you think the family reaction may be . . . unusual?"

"That is putting it mildly."

"May I ask what your interest is in this? As the family laywer, or a family friend?"

"Anna and I are engaged to be married."

"Then I shall congratulate you. When is this wedding to take place?"

"It was to have been as soon as possible."

"Berkeley's idea?"

"Yes, it was, actually."

"I should think he would be even more anxious to have it happen now. Don't delay. Then you should be able to assume a position as head of the family, subject to Berkeley's agreement, of course, and thus keep Anna, and her siblings, under control."

"Yes," Druce said, somewhat hesitantly.

"I know," Cheam said. "That is quite a responsibility to take on at your age. But it does have to be done. Now tell me about this Savos woman. I only met her for the first time the night her husband died. She didn't seem too overcome. I'm surprised to find her still here."

"She is, or was, Berkeley's mistress."

Cheam blew through his teeth. "I'm afraid that is now definitely was."

"I happen to know it was Berkeley's plan to marry her."

"Presumably she knew of this?"

"She's all for it. Or she was."

"Well, try to persuade her not leave right this minute. That will only increase his depression."

"I don't think she will leave," Druce said, remembering Walton's thoughts on the matter. "She has nowhere to go."

"Well, as I say, I can only commiserate with you on having landed yourself in such a situation."

"Please don't. I love Anna, very much."

"I can see she would be very easy to love. I met her mother during the very brief period she lived here. I would have classed her as even more beautiful than Anna, but she was a tormented soul. It was to do with her background, the execution of her father and the murder of her mother. I suppose you know that Caterina committed suicide after being tortured by the Austrians?"

Druce stared at him in consternation.

"And now her father has all but been murdered. And she herself suffered that horrendous experience . . ." He peered at the young man. "You do know about that?"

"Yes," Druce said. "I do know about that."

"So you'll see, she is a young woman whose emotions are certainly just as disturbed as were her mother's, and she is going to need a great deal of tender loving care for the foreseeable future."

"I'm just realising that. Thanks for everything, Doctor."

Druce watched Cheam get into his car and drive away, remaining on the steps for several minutes longer. What had he got himself into? Whatever he thought he had learned about the girl he was going to marry, there always seemed something else he didn't know. Could any girl have grown up with such a past and be entirely normal?

He returned into the drawing room. Anna and Martina were

sitting together on the settee, arms round each other, heads together, whispering.

"My darlings!" Berkeley's voice was weak, and a nurse hovered, anxious that he should not become overtired.

"Papa!" Anna kissed him.

"Dearest." Martina followed her example, and then held up Howard for a kiss.

"Papa in bed," the little boy commented.

"I am a lazy fellow, aren't I?" Berkeley looked past them at Druce. "All under control?"

"For the moment, sir."

"How are you?" Anna asked.

"Better than I have any right to expect, after such crass stupidity. I was daydreaming, there was the trouble. I saw this woman waving at me and stopped without thinking. Me, of all people. Have they got her yet?"

"Not as far as we know," Martina said.

"I doubt they will, now. Peter Watt is coming in to see me today, I believe, looking for a better description. But she'll have changed beyond recognition within minutes of shooting me. Take away the uniform, the glasses . . . The hair could have been a wig. Get rid of the bicycle . . . It makes the blood boil."

"I meant, how do you feel in yourself?" Anna asked.

"Oh . . ." Berkeley attempted a shrug, and winced. "I have some kind of multiple fracture of my leg. Would you believe it? I have been speared in one thigh and shot in the other. Now my shin has been shot to hell. Cheam says I may have difficulty walking for a while."

"And the other bullet?" Martina, like Anna and Druce, was holding her breath.

"No one seems quite sure about that. It obviously missed anywhere vital, and they've taken it out. No doubt they'll tell me about it in due course."

"But are you in pain?"

He grinned. "I'm drugged to the eyeballs. But amazingly, I don't feel any pain at all. Even in my leg."

"And your back? I mean," she hastily added, "wherever the other bullet went?"

"I don't feel a thing from that one, either. I suppose it clipped a nerve or something, but I can't even feel myself when that pretty girl over there gets going with the bedpan."

"Well, that's good news," Druce said. "I have that new will here, if you'd care to look at it and sign it some time. Two of the nurses can act as witnesses."

"Yes," Berkeley said. "Leave it and I'll look at it. Now tell me, have Johnnie and Alicia been informed?"

"Not yet," Anna said. "I wanted to be sure you were all right before I involved them."

"That was responsible thinking. Now you can tell them that I'm as fit as a fiddle. And you can go ahead with plans for our weddings. Both our weddings, just as soon as I get out of here."

"I feel so desperately unhappy for him," Martina said as Druce drove them back to the farm.

"What about yourself?" Druce asked.

"There is nothing the matter with me."

"I mean, with Colonel Townsend still wishing to get married . . ."

"Of course we shall get married. I love him. But he will have to be married in bed."

Druce had nothing more to say on that subject. He was only relieved that Walton and himself had been, apparently, so wrong about her. "If we are going to be married soon," he said to Anna, "I would like you to meet my parents."

"Of course," she said. "I am looking forward to that."

"May I go ahead and make a date?"

"You need to make a date to call on your parents?"

"Well, I don't live at home, you see. Talking about that, I have only a bachelor flat in town, so . . ."

"That is not a problem," Anna said. "When we are married you will move to the farm."

"To the . . . Yes, I suppose I could."

"I will have to be here to help Martina look after Papa. And Howard." She ruffled the little boy's hair.

"Of course." He parked at the foot of the steps. "Well, look, I'm afraid I have been playing truant for too long. I simply must get into the office. Would you like me to come out this evening?"

"I would love to see you. We both would." Anna glanced at Martina.

"Oh, yes," Martina said. "We'd like that. Come along Howard." She got out, followed by the boy and Anna.

Once again Druce felt an outsider. "By then I'll hopefully have set a date with my parents," he said.

"That would be nice," Anna said, and leaned into the car to kiss him before following Martina and Howard up the steps.

"You go into the garden and play," Martina told Howard, "while Anna and I get lunch."

Anna followed her into the kitchen. "I wish to thank you."

"For what?"

"For keeping Papa happy, at least for the time being."

"I intend to keep him happy for the rest of his life."

Anna started peeling potatoes. "You do understand that you will not be able to have sex with him?"

"For the time being. Yes, I understand that."

"You mean you do still intend to marry him?"

"Certainly. I am betrothed. Where I come from, to be betrothed is the same as being married. Don't you intend to marry Harry Druce?"

Anna sighed. "I suppose I must."

Martina frowned at her. "Don't you want to? Don't you love him?"

"No, on both counts."

"But you allowed him to have you."

"That was because Papa wanted me to. Oh, I wanted to, too. I wanted to see if I could still do it."

"And you found out that you could but he couldn't do anything for you."

"No, no. He was very good. Very sweet and gentle."

"What more do you want?"

"You can't love a man just because you have had good sex with him. The trouble is, I could love him. I am sure he will make a very good and loving husband,"

"He certainly loves you," Martina agreed. "So what is the problem?"

"He's not one of *us*."

"You mean because he doesn't shoot straight? He can learn. We can teach him."

"Martina, he doesn't shoot straight because he has no desire to shoot straight. He doesn't approve of our attitude to life. The concept of vengeance, of taking care of one's own, is totally foreign to him. Do you realise that in the last hundred-odd years Britain and the Scandinavian countries are the only countries in Europe that have not seen violent revolution or been invaded by enemy troops? There is no longer a culture of self-protection."

Martina nodded. "I have observed this. Well, at least it makes life easier."

"It hasn't for Papa. It didn't for my stepmother and grandmother. It didn't for me, either."

Martina abandoned the stove to sit beside her and put her arm round her shoulders. "Be thankful for small mercies. Berkeley is at least alive, and he will recover. I know this. I think we owe it to him to do as he wishes."

"And when these people try again?"

Martina's frown was back. "You think they will?"

"They've tried twice and failed both times. They aren't going to give up now."

Martina released her and returned to the stove, absently stirring her gravy. "When, do you think?"

"Just as soon as they realise that he isn't dead. That woman must have thought she'd killed him, or she would have shot him again."

"I would like to get my hands on her."

"We're not likely to have that pleasure," Anna said.

"Then we must ask Berkeley what we must do."

"No," Anna said. "It would only agitate him."

"Then who? Druce?"

"Definitely not. He would insist we leave it to the police. Whatever we are going to do, it has to be you and I. And maybe Johnnie and Alicia when they know about it."

"But what are we going to do? Are you serious about trying to track down this man in Germany? What about our weddings?"

"I am serious," Anna said. "But we must humour Papa by going through with our marriages. We need to buy some time."

"How can we do that? As you say, the moment this Himmler

man learns that Berkeley has only been wounded, he will try again."

"We must make him think otherwise. Have you any money?"

"Some. I was going to ask Berkeley to write me a cheque for cash the next time we visit him."

"Just give me enough for the return fare to London and something to eat while I'm there."

"London? You're going to London? Why?"

"There is a man there I believe will be able to help us. Maybe two."

"Should I not come with you?"

"You have to stay here with Howard."

"When will you be back?"

"I am only going for the day. I will take the early train tomorrow morning and be back in the evening."

"Are you going to tell Druce?"

"No. And neither are you. He would only fuss. Now I must write to Johnnie and Alicia."

"I wish to see Howard," Joan Horsfall announced.

She stood on the porch, her husband at her shoulder, looking somewhat embarrassed.

Martina had watched the car come down the drive from the kitchen window and had carefully placed her revolver beside the sink, just in case. But when she recognised the Horsfalls, she decided to leave it where it was, even if she would cheerfully have used it on them.

"Then you had better come in," she said. "He is in the garden."

"Is he all right?"

"Why should he not be all right?" She led them down the hall to the back door.

"Well, with all this shooting . . ."

"Are you asking after Berkeley?"

"How is he?" Howard Horsfall asked, before his wife could reply.

"He is very badly hurt." Martina opened the door. "Mr and Mrs Horsfall are here," she announced.

Howard was scrabbling about in his sandpit, watched by Anna, who now turned.

"Hello," she said. "It is good of you to call."

"That child is filthy," Joan Horsfall remarked.

"So he is," Anna agreed. "That's what sandpits are for."

"Well, he'll have to have a bath before he can come home," Joan said.

"He'll have his bath this evening, as usual," Anna said.

"We cannot possibly wait until then. Kindly do it now."

"I said, he'll have it this evening," Anna repeated.

"Now, you listen to me, my girl, I do not wish him to remain here for a moment longer than is absolutely necessary."

"I'm sorry, I'm not with you," Anna said. "He lives here. This is his home."

"Not any more," Joan declared. "Do you suppose I am going to leave my grandson in this place, to be shot at?"

"No one has shot at your grandson, who also happens to be my brother, Mrs Horsfall. He is staying here."

"And who is going to look after him? You? A chit of a girl?"

"I have Martina to help me."

Joan swung round to look at Martina, standing in the doorway. Martina smiled.

"Martina is about to become my stepmother," Anna said. "Then she will be Howard's stepmother as well."

"You . . ." Joan turned to her husband. "Howard! Do something. Say something."

"Ah . . ."

"Who dat woman shouting?" little Howard enquired.

"I think we had better leave, my dear," his grandfather suggested.

"We are going to take this matter to court!" Joan shouted.

"You're welcome," Anna said.

Joan glared at her a last time, then marched through the house to the waiting car. Her husband followed, apologetically.

"Can she?" Martina asked. "Go to court?"

"She can do whatever she likes," Anna said. "She must think Papa is going to die. So she's not going to get anywhere. You and I have more important things to worry about."

* * *

"Miss Townsend?" John Leighton peered at his visitor. "Not *the* Miss Townsend?"

"I don't know who *the* Miss Townsend is, Mr Leighton." Anna drew off her gloves. She had borrowed a broad-brimmed black straw hat from Martina to wear with a modest blue dress and knew she was looking her best.

"But of course you are," Leighton said. "Berkeley Townsend's daughter. May I say that the descriptions I have had of you hardly do you justice."

"Thank you."

"Do please sit down. My dear girl, I am so terribly sorry. Your father does appear to attract trouble."

"It is the nature of his business."

"Ah . . . yes, I suppose it would be. I must say, you are taking this latest attempt on his life very calmly. But then—"

"Yes, Mr Leighton, I have had a lot of experience at taking quite unacceptable events calmly."

Leighton was lost for words, not a very usual occurrence.

"I bought a copy of your newspaper at the station," Anna said. "Is what was reported everything you know?"

"That your father was shot and seriously wounded by an unknown woman, yes. I have sent a reporter up to Northampon to get some more facts."

"I can give you all the facts you need," Anna said. "In return for a small favour."

"What favour could I possibly do for you." Obviously, from the way his eyes caressed her, he could think of several, but he preferred the invitation to come from her.

"Your reporter will learn from the hospital in Northampton that my father's wounds, though serious, are not life-threatening."

"That must be a great relief to you."

"Yes. However, when you print the back-up story tomorrow, I would like you to contradict the hospital version and say that you have learned, from a source very close to Colonel Townsend's family, that he is actually very badly hurt indeed and is not expected to survive, although he may hang on to life for a week or two yet."

Leighton gazed at her for several seconds. Then he asked, "And which version is true?"

"You may accept mine as the truth."

Another long stare. "I do not believe you. You are asking my newspaper to print a false story. You will have to tell me why."

"I will tell you why when you agree to print that story."

Leighton stroked his chin. "May I ask how old you are, Miss Townsend?"

"I am twenty years old, Mr Leighton."

"And you seriously think you can come in here and give instructions to a grizzled old editor like myself?"

"If I have offended you, I apologise." Anna stood and picked up her gloves and handbag. "I will have to go elsewhere. I am sure I will find some editor willing to help me."

"Oh, sit down," he said. "Don't be so touchy. I would very much like to help you. But you must understand that it is a serious matter for a newspaper knowingly to print a falsehood."

"Then do not do it knowingly. I have given you this version of what has happened. Anyone would have to agree that I should know better than anyone else. Nor is there any conceivable reason for me to lie about it. When, or if, it is discovered that I have lied, then you may correct the story and claim, correctly, that you were misled."

He smiled at her. "By a pretty face."

"If that is how you wish to put it, I have no objection."

"However, may I remind you that you have not yet given me your, inside, story of what happened, nor the reason why you wish your father to appear to the world as dying."

"Will you print the story?"

"If you will have lunch with me."

He took her to a very good restaurant and they studied each other as they ate. She told him all the facts she could remember about Berkeley's shooting; he made notes, but she knew it was the studying that mattered. She wondered how much he knew about her. He would know that she had been kidnapped as a girl; everyone knew that. But did he know about the brothels? It seemed quite a few people did, certainly in Northampton. But in London?

"Now tell me why you wish your father to be presumed dying," he said, when she had finished her meal.

"Very simply, as long as this man Himmler and his friends think he is dying they will assume that their task has been completed and thus will not return."

"You are accusing a German political party, these Nazi people, of attempting to kill your father?"

"There can be no doubt about it. But I would not like that to be printed, at least at this time."

Leighton nodded. "I can appreciate that. But what good do you suppose a fortnight will do? They must eventually find out that he is alive."

"It gives me a chance to take certain steps."

"You?" His smile was condescending. "What steps?"

"I prefer to keep that private, if you don't mind. Now I have a train to catch. Thank you for a lovely lunch, Mr Leighton. Can I expect to see that story in tomorrow's paper?"

"You're not finished yet, young lady."

"I assure you I am."

"And I assure you that you're not. You have not told me the most important fact of all: why is the Nazi Party so eager to kill your father?"

"You will have to ask *him* that, when he is stronger. I have no idea."

"I think you do. I think it is to do with undercover work he carried out for the government. We know, from his evidence in court, that he infiltrated the Serbian army before the war. I know, because I provided the cover, that he went to Germany in 1921 and there met the Nazi leaders, including Herr Hitler, although they were hardly yet a party. There is also a rumour that the bomb which so nearly did for Hitler a couple of years ago was his work."

"If you know so much about my father's activities, what more do you want from me?"

"I want you to tell me if he did actually infiltrate the Nazi Party, perhaps became a member of it."

"And, as I have said, you will have to ask him."

They gazed at each other for several seconds. Then Leighton said. "Perhaps I will."

"Then I'll say goodbye, and again, thanks for the lunch."

"Do you know what it means when a man takes a woman out to lunch?"

"It can mean a great many things, Mr Leighton, depending on the man and the circumstances. As you are a prominent newspaper editor, I am assuming that you are interested in my story. If you were a handsome young man, I would asume that you also wished to form a relationship, and I might be interested. If you were an ugly old man, I would assume that you wished to get me into bed, and I should not be in the least interested. And if, in the role of an ugly old man seeking sex, you were to make any indecent advances to me, I should up-end this carafe of water over your head, and take my story to another editor. Good day to you, Mr Leighton."

"Miss Townsend?" The secretary was a very stiff young man, smart in his khaki uniform with its brass-buttoned tunic and Sam Browne. "General Shrimpton will see you now."

He seemed rather surprised.

"Thank you." Anna allowed him a dazzling smile, then went past the door he was holding open.

Shrimpton was seated behind his desk but stood up as she entered. "Miss Townsend? Good heavens."

Anna was by now used to this reaction. "General Shrimpton. My father has often spoken of you."

"He has never spoken of you at all. Do sit down."

"Thank you." Anna sat down and crossed her legs.

Shrimpton sat opposite her. "Forgive me, but are you the young lady who—"

"Yes, General. I was kidnapped when I was twelve years old and held in various houses for five years until my father rescued me. I am sure you have a file on it."

"Indeed. Your father acted with our blessing. It had to be unofficial, of course, but we were very pleased that he was successful. It is a shame that since then his relationship with the army has turned sour."

"My father did, as he has always done, what he thought to be right."

"It is a point of view which sadly cannot always obtain in

matters which are at once important and secret. Has he sent you here to offer an apology?"

"My father does not know I am here, General. He is at present in hospital, very seriously ill."

Shrimpton's eyes flickered, and she realised he knew what had happened. "That must be very worrying for you. May I ask the nature of this illness?"

"Three days ago, my father was shot, twice, at close range."

"Good heavens. And he survived?"

"Yes, General. He has survived, so far. He is a difficult man to kill."

"So his record indicates," Shrimpton commented. "Are you telling me that the Karlovy woman somehow escaped from prison?"

"It was not the Karlovy woman. This was an entirely different woman. But we suppose she came from the same source. The attempts on my father's life were set up and paid for by a political party in Germany. The Nazis."

"Oh, come now."

"That is fact, General. The Karlovy woman confessed it to my father before she was tried."

"And he never told anyone?"

"He told me. He did not consider coming to you because you had fallen out."

"But now you have come to me. With what in mind?"

"I wish to protect my father from a further attempt on his life. Each of the last two could easily have succeeded."

"And you wish the War Office to give him protection? I'm afraid that is not possible, Miss Townsend. Your father did not quarrel with me, he quarrelled with our superiors; they regard what he said in court as a betrayal of his oath of secrecy, and very nearly treason. There is no possibility of them agreeing to help him."

"Even if they know that he is in this position because of the work he did for them? And that he has spilt a lot of blood, his blood, on their behalf?"

"I'm afraid these are occupational hazards for a man like Berkeley Townsend."

"I see. Then I have wasted my time in coming to you."

Shrimpton stroked his chin as he looked at her. Here we go again, she thought.

"I wouldn't necessarily call it a waste of time," he said. "I have explained that there is no point in looking to the War Office for help. But it may be possible to do something privately."

"How privately?"

"I have certain officers who work undercover and who might be persuaded to help your father."

"I must tell you, General, that I have no money to pay them with. Nor does my father."

"I am sure that you have other assets you can realise."

Anna met his gaze. "My father always told me that British officers were usually gentlemen. Sadly, as I grow older, I am beginning to understand that he was wrong about several things."

Shrimpton's smile was cold. "Both your father and I, and yourself, Miss Townsend, have been forced to live in the real world. So please, none of your pseudo-morality. How many men would you estimate you have serviced since the age of twelve?"

"I would say perhaps half a dozen."

"Oh, come now."

"You asked me how many *men*. If your question had been how many filthy perverts, I would have said several hundred. Are you seeking to make it several hundred and one?"

His head came up and he stared at her, his eyes glittering. "A chip off the old block," he remarked. "But not a chip which is going to cause me the slightest concern, Miss Townsend. You are a most desirable young woman. You are also a whore and the daughter of the man I most dislike in this entire country. You have come to ask me for help in preserving his miserable life. As far as I am concerned, it is a simple business transaction in which, for all your beauty, I cannot be sure I will be getting a good bargain. However, I will take the risk, while you are certain to make a profit. In exchange for the use of your body for one night, tonight, I will provide, free of charge, a bodyguard for your father. I would say you will be making far more of a profit than I."

Anna stared at him. "I would not have believed it possible. You are a general in the British army."

"Generals are also men. Kindly make up your mind. I am a busy man."

Anna continued to stare at him while her brain raced. He had been her very last resort; for all her determined talk she knew that there was no hope of Martina and herself going to Germany and discovering the man Himmler, or taking on his party. Who would look after Papa and Howard while they were away?

Equally she knew that the pair of them had little hope of defending the farmhouse against a determined assassin. She and Papa, backed up by Savos and Martina, had been unable to do that.

"How do I know you will carry out your side of the bargain?"

Another cold smile. "You have the word of an officer and a gentleman. As I take it that you are agreeing to my proposal, I will tell you what you must do. I have a flat in Mayfair." He pulled a block of paper towards him, wrote rapidly, tore off the sheet and slid it across the desk. "There is the address. Go there at six o'clock. Ring the bell and give the woman who answers that piece of paper. She will admit you and make you comfortable; I will join you shortly afterwards."

Anna folded the paper into her handbag; as she did so, her fingers touched the cold steel of her revolver. He deserved nothing better. But he might be Papa's salvation. She stood up.

"Six o'clock," he said. "And please, I am anticipating something better than a sack of potatoes."

"You shall have it," she promised.

It was four o'clock; she had only two hours to wait. Presumably it would be a long night but at least she would be in bed; she did not have sufficient money for an hotel room. And tomorrow she would be back in the farmhouse.

There would be questions, of course. Harry had got into the habit of driving out to the farm every evening. He would be angry and alarmed when she did not turn up, and he was already in a state of nerves over her meeting with his parents, which was to take place tomorrow evening. How nice it would be to tell him the truth. But as she had said to Martina, he lived in a different world to them. His concepts of honour and ethics, those of the average well-bred Englishman, centred on words like chastity and notions like obedience to the law. He would not understand and she didn't think he ever would.

She spent the time window-shopping, attracting glances of envy and admiration from women and men. This was not the first time she had been to London but it was the first time she had been in the city entirely on her own, and she found it fascinating, so much so that she lost track of time and recalled herself only at half past five when it was time to hurry towards the address in Mayfair. She was panting by the time she got there, and as it was still only five to the hour she gave herself five minutes to catch her breath before ringing the bell against the name Shrimpton. Fortunately, the street was deserted and she did not have to endure any more stares.

"I am opening the door," a woman's voice said.

Anna frowned. There was something . . . but the door was open. She stepped into a hall. The flat was up two flights of stairs. She climbed these slowly, keeping her breathing under control. It had to be coincidence, of course. Or her imagination running away with her. But Shrimpton's housekeeper or tame assassin would not know who his latest acquisition was – she would certainly not have given her employer any details of her visit to Northampton. Anna recalled what her father had told her: the general never wanted to know exactly how his orders were carried out, only that they had been. He had assumed Berkeley was dead and had been surprised at learning that he wasn't.

What have I done? she asked herself. Not only had she told Shrimpton that her father was alive, she had actually invited him to place one of his men in the farmhouse so that he could complete the job! She almost turned and ran down the stairs and all the way to the railway station, and thence home to warn Martina.

What good would that do? If she had already realised that she and Martina had very little hope of taking on the Nazis, what hope did they have of resisting the Nazis *and* the War Office? But this one threat could be ended now, and she owed it to Papa's poor, bullet-ridden, paralysed body. She had no doubt she could do it, no feeling of uncertainty as to right or wrong. These people were killers. They needed to be taught that there were others in the world more deadly even than they.

She rang the flat bell, and the door was opened. "You have something for me?" the woman asked.

"A piece of paper," Anna told her.

The woman raised her head in surprised alarm, recognising her immediately. "You!" she gasped, and tried to close the door.

Anna did not recognise her at all without the uniform and the glasses and with her mousy hair loose and straggly. But the voice was unmistakable.

"Me," she said, placing her left hand on the woman's chest and pushing her back across a small hallway and against an inner door. Anna kicked the outer door closed behind her and unclipped her handbag. "In there," she said.

The woman opened the door and backed into a small lounge. "I did what I was told to do," she said, her voice high.

"And I do what I have to do," Anna said, and shot her in the chest, firing through the handbag so that the noise would be muffled.

"I have Miss Townsend on the line, Mr Druce," Miss Carlisle said.

"Oh, thank God for that. Do forgive me, Mr Harman," Druce said to the client on the far side of his desk. "A domestic crisis. Anna?" he said into the phone. "Where in the name of God are you?"

"I am in Roade."

This was a village on the railway line a few miles south of Northampton.

Druce looked at his watch; it was just after eleven in the morning. "What on earth are you doing there? Where were you last night?"

"I'll explain when I see you. Would you come down and pick me up?"

"Now?"

"That would be very nice. I am in a hurry to get home."

"Why couldn't you take the train into Northampton?"

"I said, I'll explain when I see you. Please hurry. I'll be waiting for you in the station yard."

She hung up.

Druce regarded the phone for several seconds before replacing the receiver. Then he gave his client a winning smile. "I do apologise," he said, "but it seems my fiancée has had some kind of accident."

"Then you must go to her at once," the farmer said. "My business can wait."

"That's very kind of you. Perhaps tomorrow?"

"I'll make another appointment with your secretary."

"Thank you." Druce grabbed his hat and hurried from the office. "Will you tell Mr Walton I have been called out on urgent business," he told Miss Carlisle.

She goggled after him, reflecting that since he had got involved with these Townsend people Mr Druce had been behaving very oddly.

Druce got into his car and took the road south. His head was spinning, but then it had been spinning for the last twelve hours.

When he had driven out to the farm last evening, he had been dismayed to find Anna not there and alarmed when Martina had told him she had gone to London. On business of which he, as her lawyer, her advisor, her fiancé and virtually her guardian until Berkeley was back on his feet, had known nothing.

"She will be here on the last train," Martina had explained.

"But how did she get into Northampton?"

"She took Hannibal and the trap."

His concern had grown when the time for the last train had come and gone, and she had not returned. Martina had offered him a bed for the night but he had declined and returned to Northampton. At the station he had found the horse, which Anna had left in the care of the stationmaster and which had spent a pleasant day grazing in that worthy's paddock.

"Weren't you expecting her back this evening?" he had asked.

"The young lady did say she might be delayed," the stationmaster had said.

Druce had spent a sleepless night. At first he had been inclined to call the police but after all that had happened he had no doubt that Anna could take care of herself. He had also forgotten to ask Martina if Anna had taken her gun and could only pray that she had not.

Roade was a sleepy little town, and in the middle of the morning the station yard was empty. Save for a woman, waiting by the steps to the platform. Druce braked and peered at her uncertainly. She wore a dress he had never seen before with a hat he had never seen before either and her hair was a brilliant yellow; she carried a large paper shopping bag together with her handbag.

"You made good time," she said, sitting beside him and tossing her bags into the back seat.

"Anna?"

"Who were you expecting? Please take me home."

Druce engaged gear and drove out of the yard. Once they were clear of the houses, Anna took off her hat and the wig beneath and threw these into the back seat as well; then she fluffed out her hair.

"Where in the name of God have you been? Martina said something about London. And why are you wearing that peculiar disguise?"

"I didn't wish to be recognised."

"Why? What were you doing in London?"

"I was tracking Papa's assassin."

"You . . . my God!"

"Do keep your eyes on the road, Harry. We don't want to have an accident. Especially now."

Druce attempted to concentrate, but it was very difficult.

"Your father's would-be assassin was a German agent."

"No, she wasn't. We were meant to think she was. She was actually English, even if she did have an accent. Actually, I think the accent was assumed, as part of her disguise, again to make us think she was foreign."

"And you say you tracked her down? Just like that?"

"I had a lead and I followed it, and it turned out to be right."

"And you handed her over to the police?"

"No. That wouldn't have done any good. She was working for the British government."

"The government? I can't believe that."

"They regarded Papa as a traitor, because of the evidence he gave in court for the Karlovy woman. They didn't dare do anything about it publicly so they sent along an executioner, setting it up for the whole world to think it was another German paid assassin."

"So you say you tracked her down. What did you do then, if you didn't go to the police?"

Anna drew a very deep breath. "How much do you love me?"

"I love you more than life itself."

"Is that the absolute truth?"

"Of course it is."

"Then you'd better stop the car."

Druce obligingly pulled into the side of the deserted road. "Tell me."

Another deep breath. "I shot her."

Druce stared at her with his mouth open.

"And when her boss came home," Anna said, "he had designs on taking me to bed and I shot him too."

Part Three

The Pursuit

"Conscience and grace, to the profoundest pit!
I dare damnation."

William Shakespeare

The Police

"Well," Josef Goebbels said, "I suppose you are to be congratulated."

Heinrich Himmler blinked at him from behind his glasses; he had no idea what his boss was talking about.

"It is not entirely satisfactory, of course," Goebbels went on. "But according to this . . ." he tapped the German edition of the *Globe* which lay on his desk, "he is very badly hurt and perhaps crippled for life."

Himmler attempted to look at the paper, upside down, without letting on that he didn't know what it had to say.

"Still, that is a step in the right direction," Goebbels said. "And perhaps a Townsend, lying in bed, crippled and in pain, waiting helplessly for us to strike again, is even better than a Townsend dead. What I particularly admire, Heinrich, is the way you have handled this, so close to your chest, so cunningly. I take it this woman is absolutely trustworthy?"

"Oh, yes. Absolutely."

"But still, I think, when she returns from England, it might be best for her to be eliminated. Is she handsome?"

"Ah . . . yes, she is handsome, Josef."

"Well, then perhaps I will interview her myself when she returns. Before I hand her back to you for a final solution. But as I say, I like the way you have handled this. I can tell you that I am putting your name forward as my recommendation for commander of the new Blackshirts."

"Thank you, Josef. Thank you."

"You will understand that people like Hess and Goering and Roehm will have their own recommendations. But I doubt they will have anyone with credentials to equal yours."

"Thank you," Himmler said again, and stood up. "May I

borrow that paper? I would like to see how they treated the incident."

Druce felt physically sick. "You have shot and killed two people?" he asked, not at all sure it was actually him speaking.

"I executed the two people responsible for Papa's shooting," Anna said.

"My God! Oh, my God! And one was a general?"

"That's right. He is, was, Papa's enemy."

"But . . . my darling girl, you will be arrested and charged. My God, you'll be hanged!"

He just couldn't contemplate such a prospect.

"I will only be arrested and charged, and then hanged, if you betray me."

He stared at her. "You cannot get away with murder."

"I keep telling you that it was not murder; it was an execution."

"That's not how the police will think of it. What are we going to do? You can't possibly hope to get away with it. Everyone knows you went to London yesterday."

"But no one knows when I left."

"What do you mean?"

"I went to London yesterday morning and had an interview with the editor of the *Globe*. I wanted him to do something for me. Whether he will or not, I don't know. Have you seen a copy of the paper this morning?"

"I have been far too distraught to look at newspapers."

"Well, we'll have to get hold of a copy. Anyway, after lunch I went to see this General Shrimpton. He used to employ Papa and I thought he might help. He said he would, but only if I spent the night with him."

"My God!"

"I agreed to." She stared at him. "I didn't think I had a choice. He sent me to a flat and the door was opened by the pretend Salvationist woman. So I shot her."

Druce groaned and held his head in his hands.

"Then I waited for this Shrimpton to turn up and shot him as well."

Druce tried to visualise this girl, to whom he had given

his heart, calmly pointing a revolver at someone and pulling the trigger. "And you don't suppose all London knows of it by now?"

"By now, very probably. But they don't know of my part in it. Listen. Shrimpton gave me the address of the flat. What he was doing was nothing he could be proud of so it is almost certain that he did not tell anyone about it. He did not even telephone the woman, because she was as surprised to see me as I was to see her. So, no one save Shrimpton knows I went to that flat."

"You'd have been seen on the street. No one is going to see you and not remember you."

"There was no one in the street when I got to the address. No one saw me go in."

"But the noise of the shot . . ."

"I closed the door before I fired, and I fired through my handbag. The hole is there. Both holes. I shot Shrimpton through the bag as well. There was no indication that anyone else in the building heard either shot. Certainly no one came to investigate."

"All right." Druce was intrigued, despite his distress. "Where did you spend the night?"

"Right there."

"You spent the night in a flat with two dead bodies?"

"There was food and a bed, and I had nowhere else to go."

He was speechless for a moment. "But when you finally left, surely someone saw you then? Or at the railway station?"

"Yes. But as soon as I had shot Shrimpton, I went out. He had money in his wallet. Some of the shops were still open, and I was able to buy this dress and the wig and a new hat."

"And the saleswoman won't remember you?"

"I don't see why she should. Before leaving the flat I put on one of the woman's bandannas and used one of her hats as well. Besides, who's going to ask? That would require not only working out what I did but which shop I went to."

Druce scratched his head. "So you left the flat this morning, in disguise, and caught the train to Roade."

"Well, I couldn't go into Northampton wearing a disguise."

He nodded. "What are you going to pretend to have done between leaving Shrimpton's office and this morning?"

"I returned here and spent the night with you." She gazed at him.

"That is what you would wish me to say in court."

"If we both make up our minds that that is what happened, it will never come to court."

"My darling . . ." he held her hands, "it just will not work. You would claim to have caught the train at what time?"

She shrugged. "I left Shrimpton just after four. I would then have gone straight to King's Cross and caught the next train. We can look up the times."

"But you can't prove you caught that train."

"No one can prove I didn't."

"Your ticket?"

"I handed it in just now. The collector never looked at me twice."

"So you're going to pretend you returned last night. But you didn't pick up the trap."

"Because I was in a hurry to get back to you. And make love. We can go along and collect Hannibal and the trap this morning"

"Unfortunately, when you didn't come back last night, I went to the station to find out what had happened. I spoke to the stationmaster. He'll remember that."

"Oh. That was sweet of you. What time did you go?"

"After the last train. Must have been about ten. So there is no way you could have come back last night. Jennings would have remembered you, not only because he knows you but because you would have collected the trap."

"Then the best thing we can do is not attempt to offer an explanation. As I said, we'll just collect it today."

"He'll wonder what was going on."

"Of course. He'll assume we're having an affair, which we are, and that my appearance or non-appearance was an aspect of that."

"And when the police ask him about it?"

"Why should they?"

"For God's sake, Anna, when they find the bodies . . ." He looked at his watch. "They'll have done that by now, and when they start checking they'll discover that you were one of the last people to see Shrimpton alive. Whether or not they suspect you had anything to do with his death at this stage, they'll certainly want to interview you."

"So? I saw Shrimpton, he refused to help me, I caught a train and came home. There is absolutely no reason for them to connect me with his death."

"Save that you have a motive."

"The only people in the world still alive who can possibly know I had a motive are Papa, Martina and you. That woman was Shrimpton's tame assassin, and no one save she and him knew she tried to kill Papa."

They gazed at each other while Druce attempted to think straight. Of course she was right. There was no way anyone in the world could look into those angelic features and associate them with death. Save that he would always know. So which was she really? A beautiful, tragic girl whose life had been forced into the most vicious paths by the accidents of her birth and parentage? Or a devil from hell masquerading as the most lovely woman he had ever seen?

"So all you require from me is that I perjure myself," he said slowly.

"And that you love me."

He knew it was a time for bargaining, for laying down certain lines of conduct in exchange for his support. But he was afraid of losing her. Besides, he now knew her well enough to understand that those she did not regard as friends she considered enemies.

"I presume you still have your gun," he said.

"Of course."

"You don't think it might be a good idea to get rid of it? Ballistics and all that."

"If the police ever get as far as comparing the bullets they take out of Shrimpton with my gun," she said, "I'm done, anyway."

"You mean, we're done. I would like you to get rid of the gun, Anna. Everything you have said is plausible but that gun is a certain link between you and those dead bodies."

She kissed him. "I hoped you'd say we and not me. All right, I'll get rid of the gun. Let's go home."

* * *

Martina, predictably, was delighted with what Anna had to tell her. "Oh, I wish I could have been with you."

"It was a job for one person."

"Yes. I can see that. What do we do now?"

"We sit absolutely tight," Anna said, "and take care of Papa."

Druce clapped his hands to his forehead. "My God!"

"What's the matter?"

"I'd forgotten. You were supposed to be coming with me to meet my parents this evening."

"Oh, splendid. I *am* looking forward to that."

"You mean you want to go through with it? Now?"

"Why not?"

He wiped his brow with his handkerchief. "Then I'll pick you up. Now I really must get back to the office."

"Of course. Will you give me five minutes to change my clothes, then perhaps you could drop Martina, Howard and me in town."

"To do what?"

"Firstly to get the trap. Then we can go to the hospital and see Papa."

Druce swallowed. "Are you going to tell him what happened?"

Anna shook her head. "Not till he's safely home."

"Why, Miss Townsend," the stationmaster said. "That Mr Druce was here last night, looking for you."

"I know," Anna said. "It was so stupid of me. I had so much on my mind that when I got back I forgot all about the trap and took a taxi home."

He scratched his head. "You came back through here last night?"

"Of course I did," Anna said. "How else was I to get home?"

"It's just that I don't remember you."

Anna took a fairly safe shot in the dark. "I was on the six o'clock. There was such a crowd. I remember *you*."

"There was a crowd. You'll find Hannibal in good nick."

"Thank you, Mr Jennings," she said.

"Do you think that'll work?" Martina asked, as they drove out of the yard.

"I would say so. Jennings is a simple soul."

"What about Druce? Do you trust him?"

"Yes," Anna said. "For two reasons. One, he loves me. Two, by simply doing what I asked he's committing himself to us. He'd go to prison as an accessory if he ever changed his mind."

"He's a lawyer," Martina said darkly. "Lawyers are devious."

Before going to the hospital, they bought a copy of the *Globe*. As the bodies of Shrimpton and his housekeeper would not have been found until this morning, there was no report of the double assassination in the paper as yet. And as Anna had suspected would be the case, the follow-up story on the shooting of Berkeley contained no suggestion that he might be more seriously hurt than was suspected; it simply concentrated on the possible link between this attempt on his life and the Karlovys.

"The bastard," she muttered. "I should've shot him as well."

"But if that woman had nothing to do with the Nazis," Martina said, "does that mean they have given up?"

"No," Anna said.

They found Peter Watt with Berkeley, who was already looking much stronger although he still could only move his head and arms. They had encountered Cheam in the corridor, and he had warned them that Berkeley did not know the truth of his situation. So they were as bright and cheerful as before.

Watt was less so. "I'm sorry to say, Miss Anna, that the woman has just disappeared. She must have changed her clothing and appearance within minutes of shooting the colonel. We haven't even found the bicycle. She must have had an accomplice close by, because we would certainly have had a sighting of a woman bicycling by herself. She must have been picked up in a motor car and driven away."

"But you'll keep looking," Anna suggested.

"Of course. And we've put a watch on all the seaports, although our people don't really have a worthwhile description to go on. But I have a feeling she's already out of the country. The only positive evidence we have is the two bullets. Our experts say they came from a German-made automatic pistol, called a Luger." He paused, hopefully.

"Which increases the possibility that she is somehow connected with the Karlovys."

"That's the point, Miss Anna."

"I think it might be a good idea to have a talk with Helen Karlovy."

Watt nodded. "I shall do that right away."

Anna realised that Watt's conclusions had added another dimension to the situation: if the woman *had* had an accomplice waiting to pick her up, then there was a third person who would know the Townsends had a motive for revenge; it was hardly likely to have been Shrimpton himself.

On the other hand, that third person, as an accomplice to an attempted murder, would not dare come forward however much he might try to settle things on his own. In which case, she thought with grim satisfaction, even if she had buried her revolver in the garden, she still had the guns belonging to both Martina and Alexandros, not to mention Papa's heavy Browning. She was quite willing for number three to try.

Cheam was waiting for them in the lobby.

"I've been giving the matter some thought," he said. "And I have concluded that it would be best dealt with at the farm and in your presence. Do you agree?"

"Yes," Anna said. "When?"

"I think we will be able to move him next week."

"Will he not begin to suspect after a week?" Martina asked.

"I think we should be able to keep him happy until then. You do understand that this is going to be a considerable shock? For a man who has lived such an active life where survival has so often depended on his strength, his speed, suddenly to have to face the fact that he has none of those assets left, well . . . I am sure you know him better than I."

"We understand," Anna said. "But I think he will cope."

"I hope to God you're right."

"What makes you so sure he will be able to cope?" Martina asked, as they drove the trap back out to the farm. "I am scared stiff."

"He will cope," Anna said, "because I intend to tell him exactly what has happened; what I have done."

"Are you sure that is wise?"

"Yes," Anna said. "It will reassure him that there is someone at hand who will take care of his future."

Martina swallowed. She also was realising that she was in the presence of someone she did not really know.

Druce called for Anna at six. He was in a highly nervous state, as he had been all day.

"How do you feel?" he asked Anna.

"I feel fine," she said. She had dressed demurely in a short but very plain frock, and tucked her hair virtually out of sight beneath a cloche, while to add to the general suggestion of somewhat dowdy chic she wore white stockings and low-heeled button-strap shoes. "Do I look all right?"

"You look superb." He cast an anxious glance at her handbag. "Do you, I mean, have you . . ."

"My revolver has been discarded," she said. "I am leaving it up to you to protect me." She gave a wicked smile. "Even from your parents."

"Well . . ." He kissed Martina and they drove out of the yard. "I have had to put them in the picture."

"How big a picture?"

"Well, I told them that you are Colonel Townsend's daughter."

"Does that mean they know I was kidnapped as a girl?"

"I'm afraid it does."

"And everything that entailed?"

"*I* haven't told them about that."

"But it's fairly common gossip."

"I'm afraid it is. Does that bother you?"

"Of course it does; I'm a human being." She glanced at him. "Or don't you believe that any more?"

He swallowed. "I love you and I wish you to be my wife." Did he mean that? he wondered. Or was he just playing the gentleman with a damsel in distress?

Anna squeezed his hand. "I am so grateful. And so lucky to have you."

"Mother, Father, I'd like you to meet Anna Townsend. Anna, my mother and father."

He almost thought Anna was going to offer them her hand to kiss, but she merely shook hands, while the elder Druces took her in.

"You are very lovely, my dear," Mrs Druce said.

"Thank you," Anna said.

"Terrible thing about your father," Mr Druce remarked.

"He is alive, Mr Druce. That is what matters," Anna said.

"Of course," Mrs Druce said. "But come in and sit down, my dear. You'll take tea?"

"That would be very nice, thank you."

Anna sat on the settee, leaving room beside herself. After a momentary hesitation, Druce sat beside her.

His father sat opposite. "Shooting people here in England. They're saying it was a member of the Salvation Army."

"And a woman," his wife added. She had rung the bell, and the maid was bringing in the tea tray.

"She was certainly a woman," Anna agreed.

"But we think her uniform was a disguise," Druce added.

"Don't know what the country is coming to," his father said.

"But your father will recover?" Mrs Druce asked.

"My father is not going to die of his wounds. As to whether he will ever recover from them, no one can say."

"Oh, you poor child," Mrs Druce said. "All this, after . . ." She checked herself. "You may pour, Louise."

The maid obliged.

"After everything else," Druce said. "Anna has had a very difficult life."

"Oh, indeed," Mrs Druce said. "We are so sorry for you, my dear."

"Please don't be," Anna requested, and looked at Druce.

Who licked his lips. "The fact is, Mother, Father, I have been privileged to be able to take Anna out on several occasions, and, well, I have asked her to be my wife."

The Druces stared at the young couple, and Anna smiled at them and drank some tea.

"I am happy to say that Anna has consented to our union," Druce went on. "Her father's approval was given shortly before he was shot. I had intended to speak to you of it before, but at that time we had been contemplating a long engagement. Now things have changed, and . . ."

He paused, as his parents' gazes had remained hostile.

"Marriage?" his mother asked. "Are you not both somewhat young?"

"Mother," Druce said, "I am twenty-nine years old. And Anna will be twenty-one in a few months."

Mrs Druce looked at her husband.

"I do think you need to consider the matter a while longer," Druce senior said.

"I have considered the matter in all its aspects, Father. I love Anna, and she loves me. There is nothing more to be considered."

"Unfortunately, there is," Mrs Druce said. "My dear Miss Townsend, do forgive us, but I am sure you appreciate that this is a very important matter. Harry is our only son, and, well . . ." She flushed. "Do you think you could possibly wait in another room while we discuss this?"

Anna looked at Druce.

Who was now becoming angry. "Whatever you have to say, Mother, whatever we have to discuss, needs to be said and discussed in Anna's presence, as it concerns her and as she is going to become a member of our family."

His father cleared his throat while his mother looked as if she had been slapped in the face. But she too was now becoming angry. "Very well, if you will have it so. Miss Townsend, were you not abducted as a little girl?"

"I was twelve when I was kidnapped, Mrs Druce."

"And were you not in the hands of the kidnappers for several years?"

"I was separated from my family for five years," Anna said, carefully.

Mrs Druce again looked at her husband. But he clearly intended to leave the interrogation to her, so she returned to the charge.

"I assume these kidnappers were mainly men?"

"They were mainly women. But I was rented to men on a regular basis."

"Rented . . ." Mrs Druce looked as if she were about to faint.

"Through no fault of her own," Druce said, "Anna was forced to spend those five years in various brothels."

Mrs Druce opened her mouth and then closed it again; that was not a word used in polite society.

"But she was eventually rescued by her father," Druce said.

"After five years," Mrs Druce said, faintly.

Mr Druce finally accepted that he had to offer his wife some help. "Are you . . . I mean, have you ever been . . ."

"If you mean, have I ever been a mother," Anna said, "the answer is no. My madames always took every precaution. But I hope to become a mother now, for Harry."

Mr Druce retired hurt. Mrs Druce took up the challenge. "This fact, that you were kidnapped as a child, is fairly widely known."

"I suppose it is," Anna said. "It was mentioned during the trial of Helen Karlovy."

"Oh, yes." Mrs Druce's tone indicated that being involved in criminal trials was just another count against her prospective daughter-in-law. "And all the . . . er . . . ramifications?"

"I have no idea," Anna said. "I imagine the ramifications, as you put it, must be fairly obvious to anyone who thinks about it." She stood up. "And now, Mrs Druce, I have had all of this that I am prepared to stand. Will you take me home, please, Harry?"

Druce also stood up. He was looking most unhappy.

"I have no desire to hurt your feelings, Miss Townsend," Mrs Druce said. "I understand and appreciate that yours has been a singularly tragic life. However, surely you can appreciate that a marriage between you and my son is entirely out of the question. Harry has an important and hopefully successful career in front of him. This could be irrevocably damaged were he to marry a . . ."

"The word is whore, Mrs Druce."

"Well . . ."

"Thank you for tea," Anna said. "I won't say it has been a pleasure meeting you." She went through the doorway.

"Will you be returning for supper, after you have dropped Miss Townsend home?" Mrs Druce asked.

"I don't think so, Mother," Harry said. "I may call tomorrow."

They drove in silence until they were in the country. "I am most terribly sorry," Druce said.

"But you thought this might happen."

"I was afraid it might."

"So what happens now?"

"I will see what can be done. But there's a chance they will not be at the wedding."

"Oh, Harry! You mean there is still going to be a wedding?"

"Of course there is. I have asked you to marry me and you have accepted."

"I do not wish you to go through with it simply from a sense of duty or honour."

"I am marrying you because I love you."

"I am so glad. Will it really affect your career?"

"Perhaps. But only in a small degree. Walton knows we are going to be married and he has raised no objection."

"Perhaps he thought your parents would object so strongly that you would call it off without the necessity of his interfering."

"That's not so. He has offered to stand up for both you and your father if necessary."

"A character witness," she said softly.

"If you like." He gazed at the road unfolding in front of them. "But you do understand that I am, well, going out on a limb for you."

"Are you not happy to do that?"

"Of course I am. It's just that . . . am I entitled to ask for anything in return?"

"Certainly you are. And you will have my love, my faithfulness and my support for the rest of our lives."

"May I ask for something more?"

"Certainly."

"I would like to ask you to renounce your past."

"I don't think anyone can do that, Harry."

"I was thinking of this blood feud, and your determination to be avenged on the man Himmler."

"Those are duties to my father and my family."

"They are duties that are beyond your ability or strength to carry out, Anna. Attempting to do so will only bring additional misfortune on your family. I am asking you to devote your life, to your father's health, certainly, but also to me and hopefully our children."

"I will willingly do those things, in so far as I can."

"But you will not renounce vengeance."

"No," she said.

Druce stayed for dinner but declined Anna's bed for the night. Conversation had been stilted and commonplace, and it was not until after he had left that Martina was able to sit down beside Anna and release her suppressed curiosity.

"How did it go?"

"It was a total and unmitigated disaster."

"Oh, my dear! Do you mean the wedding is off?"

"That is up to Harry. He wants to marry me; he swears he loves me. But he wants me to renounce any thoughts of hitting back at Himmler."

"Did you agree to that?"

"No, I did not. So we'll just have to wait and see."

"You don't think—"

"He's not going to betray me, Martina. I am sure of that. Has anything happened while I was out?"

"Johnnie rang. He just got your letter."

"Is he very upset?"

"Yes. He wanted to come home. But I talked him out of it, at least until Berkeley is installed and that other matter has been cleared up. Do you think . . ."

"I am sure of it," Anna said. "But we have nothing to fear."

Yet she was apprehensive. The next day's paper had the murder of General Shrimpton as front-page news, with several theories being put forward, but the fact that he had been murdered in his *pied-à-terre*, the address of which was apparently known to very few people, was inclining speculation in the direction of murder and suicide involving himself and his housekeeper. But Anna had no doubt that the police would leave no stone unturned and, sure enough, on Monday morning, the day before Berkeley was due home, Chief Inspector Watt arrived at the farm, accompanied by another man with detective written all over him.

"This is Detective Inspector Harriman from Scotland Yard, Miss Anna," Watt explained.

"Oooh," Martina commented.

Howard clapped his hands.

"You've caught the woman who shot Papa!" Anna said.

Detective Inspector Harriman looked somewhat taken aback by the domesticity with which he was confronted and the beauty of the two women.

"Sadly, no," Watt said. "Mr Harriman is here on another matter."

"Well, do come in and sit down," Anna invited.

"Will you take coffee, or tea?" Martina asked.

Harriman glanced at Watt and received a quick nod.

"Tea, thank you very much, Miss . . ."

"Mrs Savos. I am Colonel Townsend's fiancée."

This seemed to make Harriman more bemused yet. He followed Anna into the drawing room where she sat down, taking Howard on her knee.

"This is my half-brother," she explained. "His mother was murdered last year."

Bemusement was joined by embarrassment. Both policemen sat down.

"So, tell me what I have done," Anna invited.

Harriman coughed, and left it to his superior.

"We are merely hoping that you may be able to give us some information," Watt explained.

"Well, I do not think I can add anything to what I have already told you," Anna said. "The woman—"

"As I said, unfortunately we are not here about the woman who shot your father," Watt said. "At least not directly. Did you read about the murder of a General Shrimpton in the newspapers?"

"Oh, yes," Anna said. "He used to be Papa's boss in the army. We were very shocked."

"What did your father say?" Harriman asked.

"Papa doesn't know yet. He really has been very weak since he was shot, and he hasn't been reading the papers. I felt I shouldn't tell him until he was stronger, in case it upset him."

"Absolutely," Watt agreed.

"Especially as I must have been one of the last people to see the general alive," Anna added. "Papa is actually coming home tomorrow. I'll probably tell him then."

"It is the fact that you were one of the last people to see General Shrimpton alive that we would like to discuss," Harriman said.

"Of course. It gives me goose pimples every time I think about it."

Harriman opened his notebook. "You visited General Shrimpton at approximately half past three last Wednesday afternoon."

Anna nodded. Martina brought in the tea and started pouring.

"May I ask what you saw General Shrimpton about?" Harriman asked.

"It was about that woman; the attempt on Daddy's life."

"You went to London, two days after your father had been shot, specifically to see the general?"

"Not entirely," Anna said, well aware of possible traps. "I was very upset, as I am sure you'll understand."

"Of course you were," Watt agreed.

"I could think only that once the assassin, or whoever was employing her, learned that Papa was not dead, they would try again. I therefore went to see Mr Leighton, at the *Globe*. I knew he was an old friend of Papa's. My idea was that if he would print in his paper that Papa was actually even more badly hurt than had been reported and was in fact likely to die, the assassins would leave us alone, at least for a while, which would give Papa time to recover his strength." She gave a little sob. "I now know, of course, that he is not ever going to recover his strength."

"You poor girl." Watt leaned across to squeeze her hand.

Harriman was looking a little impatient. "But this second story has not been printed."

"No," Anna said. "Mr Leighton refused to do it."

"You cannot blame him. For a reputable newspaper deliberately to print a false story is a serious business."

"I thought he would help," Anna said.

"And when you left the *Globe* offices, you went to the War Office. What did you do in between?"

"Mr Leighton took me out to lunch. When I left the restaurant I went directly to see General Shrimpton."

"What did you wish to see the General about? I'm afraid he left no record of your conversation."

"I wanted to ask him if he could offer Papa some protection. I mean, there is just Martina and me, and Baby Howard. If any more people like the Karlovys, or even that woman, were to come here determined to kill my father, we would be absolutely helpless."

She looked from one policeman to the other, fluttering her eyelashes.

"Absolutely," Watt agreed.

"I am terrified," Martina confessed, doing some fluttering of her own.

"Quite so." Harriman felt called upon to agree. "And did General Shrimpton agree to furnish such protection?"

Anna shook her head. "He explained that he could not."

"How unfortunate. Then what did you do?"

"There was nothing more I could do. I left the War Office, went to King's Cross Station and caught the next train to Northampton."

"That would have been at what time?"

"I don't really know. I suppose I left the War Office before four. I know I was back in Northampton just after six."

"You were home here by seven," Martina said.

"I see," Harriman said. "I wonder if you could tell me, Miss Townsend, what General Shrimpton's demeanour was like when you were with him? I mean, was it quite normal?"

"I really cannot say," Anna said. "It was the first time I had ever met him."

Harriman raised his eyebrows. "You said he was a friend of your father's."

"I never said that," Anna protested. "I said he was my father's immediate superior in the army, and Papa often spoke of him. But he never came here."

"He did," Martina contradicted. "Once. I remember. But you were in the garden."

Once again Harriman was showing signs of impatience. "When you met the general, Miss Townsend, did he give any suggestion of being agitated or preoccupied?"

"No," Anna said.

"Did he wish to arrange a further meeting with you?"

"No," Anna said. "Once he told me that he could not help Papa, there was nothing more to be discussed."

"Well, I think that is all I can ask you. Thank you very much for your cooperation." He stood up. "Oh, by the way, Chief Inspector Watt tells me your father keeps firearms on the premises."

"I think he does," Anna said. "Would you like to see them?"

"If I may."

"Come up to his room." Anna led the way. She opened the top drawer of Berkeley's bureau. "There they are."

Harriman peered at them. "A Browning nine-millimetre automatic and a Smith and Wesson point three eight revolver." He looked at Watt.

"He also holds a licence for a Smith and Wesson point three two," Watt said.

"We don't have that one any more."

"What has happened to it?"

"Well, you see, he actually bought that gun for me. But after the attack by the Karlovys, well, I didn't want it any more. I think I became afraid of the whole idea of guns. I had never seen anyone shot before." Another flutter of the eyelashes.

"I should think so too," Watt agreed. "What did the colonel do with the gun?"

"I don't know. I think he sold it."

Watt looked at Harriman.

"Can you remember when this was, Miss Townsend?"

"Oh, ages ago."

"Yet he still has the licence."

"Does he?" Anna asked.

"But the gun is not here," Harriman pointed out. "Would you know who he sold it to?"

"No."

Harriman regarded her for a few seconds. Then he said, "A gun is the personal responsibility of the person to whom it is licensed. For it to be sold or go missing and that fact not be reported to the police, could be a serious matter."

"Well," Anna said, "you will have to ask Papa. When," she added hastily, "he is well enough to speak with you."

"Of course. May I leave that with you, Chief Inspector?"

Watt nodded. "I'm quite sure there is an adequate explanation. You see, Miss Anna, we are interested simply because General Shrimpton and—"

Harriman gave a warning cough.

"General Shrimpton was shot with a point three two revolver, and we are fairly sure it was a Smith and Wesson."

"But the papers said he was shot by his mistress, or committed suicide after shooting her."

"I'm afraid there is no possibility of that," Harriman said. "Quite apart from the forensic indication that neither of the deaths could have been suicide, there is also the matter of the murder weapon. It isn't there."

"So it seems certain there was a a third person present," Watt said. "The murderer."

"And you think it was Papa?" Anna cried. "Papa is in hospital unable to move. Anyway, why should he do such a thing?"

"Of course we do not suppose the colonel did it," Watt said, very embarrassed. "It's just that there is the possibility that the general's murder was connected with the attempts on your father's life, and if Colonel Townsend did sell that gun, or it was stolen and he did not report it, well, it could provide a link."

"I understand," Anna said.

"I will have a word with the colonel today," Watt said. "Just to clear the matter up."

"Oh, please don't," Anna begged. Both policemen looked at her.

"He doesn't know about the general. He doesn't even know he's crippled yet. He's very weak. Well, you know that, Mr Watt."

Watt nodded vigorously. "I do indeed."

"He's coming home tomorrow. Dr Cheam is coming with him and the three of us are going to tell him what's happened to him. Depending on how he takes that, we will tell him about General Shrimpton. If all goes well, I will telephone you, Mr Watt, and you can come out and talk to him about the missing gun on Sunday. I really don't want him to become agitated in his state."

"It would be terrible," Martina said.

"I quite understand," Watt said. "I'll wait for your call. We must leave now. And thank you again for being so frank with us."

The two policemen went down the front steps and got into their car.

"Such brave women," Watt commented as they drove away. "Particularly that lovely girl. When you think what she has gone through, and is going to go through, with a permanently crippled father . . ."

"Yes," Harriman said drily. "May I ask, Mr Watt, are you married?"

"Oh, yes," Watt said.

"Children?"

"Two sons."

"But no daughters."

"Sadly, no. We would have liked one but it was not to be."

"Pity. Having daughters, especially when they are teenagers growing into women, can give you a marvellous insight into the wiles of the female sex."

"I suppose they can." Watt frowned. "I'm not sure I take your meaning."

"That beautiful young lady," Harriman said, "whose eyes would melt a stone idol and in whose mouth butter would not melt, knows a great deal more than she was willing to admit."

"A great deal more about what?"

"General Shrimpton's death."

"My dear fellow, you're not suggesting—"

"I am not suggesting anything, Mr Watt; I am making one or two observations. Such as, it is well known that the general was a womaniser; he has been named in two divorce suits and has been attacked by at least one angry husband."

"Then isn't that where your investigations should take you?"

"They are doing so. However, I would say there is as much chance of the general coming into contact with a girl like Anna Townsend and not wishing to pursue the matter than there is of Australia regaining the Ashes. Miss Townsend is an intelligent young woman. She would have noticed his interest."

"She is also a very modest young woman," Watt argued, "who would have been embarrassed to suggest it."

Harriman gave him an old-fashioned look. "There is a file on Colonel Townsend, which I have read. It covers the kidnapping of his daughter and his eventual rescuing of her. After five years in various European brothels."

"That does not mean she cannot be modest," Watt snapped. Anna was one of his favourite women.

"Possibly not. But it is unlikely. And, as I have said, I also consider it just about impossible that Shrimpton, being the man he was, would have said, hello Miss Townsend, sorry I can't help you, goodbye Miss Townsend. He would almost certainly have suggested another meeting."

"Again . . ."

"She might have been too modest to mention it? But I specifically asked her, Mr Watt, and she said he had not done that. I would have said that Shrimpton, again being the man he was, may well have invited her to that *pied-à-terre* where he conducted most of his affairs."

"Then you *are* suggesting—"

"I am observing, Mr Watt. And when you consider the coincidence of the general being shot with a revolver of the same calibre as that owned by her father, which has now so conveniently disappeared . . ."

"Are you accusing that unfortunate girl of shooting Shrimpton and his housekeeper?"

"No, I am not, at this time. I am accusing her of lying about her visit to London. I would be much obliged if you would keep an eye on the young lady, Mr Watt."

The Adventure

Anna and Martina had the house spick and span, and suitably rearranged, for Berkeley's homecoming, with Baby Howard neatly dressed and highly excited.

Druce arrived an hour before the ambulance and hurried Anna into the drawing room. He hadn't been out the previous day, although he had telephoned; he had been back to see his parents but had not sounded very optimistic on the phone. Anna could guess that he had been endeavouring to come to terms with the possibility of a permanent estrangement, which was not something she either wanted or had set out to create.

She supposed she was being very selfish. She liked Druce enormously, had found him a stimulating companion and a reassuring lover; she admired many things about him but did not love him in the sense that she could devote her entire life to him. That might be possible in the future, after she had carried out the several tasks that were her duty. But she could not be certain even of that. Yet she wanted to be married to him, to have the security of his presence. Did that entitle her to disrupt and possibly destroy his life? Of course it did not, in civilised terms. Her problem was that she could not afford to consider life in civilised terms until this business was finished.

This morning he was definitely agitated.

"I saw Peter Watt yesterday," he said as soon as they were alone.

"Don't tell me he's been questioning you as well."

"This was another matter. But he did mention that he had been out to see you with a Scotland Yard fellow."

"That's right."

"But my God, Anna, that means they're on to you."

"Of course they are not. They're merely interviewing everyone who saw General Shrimpton on the day he died. As it happens, apart from his staff, I was the last person to see him alive." She gave one of her roguish smiles. "Apart from the person who killed him, of course."

"Anna," he held her hands, "I am terrified."

"Well, don't be. Nothing is going to happen. How are your parents?"

He sighed. "They're going to take a lot of work."

"Well, we can't wait. I want us to be married just as soon as it can be arranged. I know Papa will want that too."

"Yes," he agreed. "I've been thinking about that. If we were to have a child, that might bring them round. Continuing the family name and all that."

"After we've talked with Papa," she said. "I hear the ambulance."

She left him standing in the doorway to run outside and be with Martina as the ambulance drove into the yard, followed by Dr Cheam's car.

"Are you nervous?"

"I am scared stiff," Martina confessed.

"Well, leave it to me," Anna said.

Martina glanced at her; she was still trying to come to terms with the realisation that this girl had taken over all of their lives and was now planning to take over the life of even her own father.

The vehicles stopped, and white-clad men got out to fuss. Berkeley had apparently made the journey in a wheelchair, and this was now carefully wheeled down a ramp at the rear of the ambulance.

The two women hurried forward. "Papa!" Anna cried, embracing him.

He hugged her. "They insisted I travel in this contraption. Martina." He turned up his face to be kissed. And then Anna lifted Howard for a hug.

"Home, Papa, home," Howard said.

"And it's good to be here," Berkeley said.

Cheam joined them. "You'd better help us get him up the steps," he told the ambulance men, and they obligingly lifted the chair and deposited it on the porch. "What we will have to do," Cheam said to Anna, "is fix up some kind of a ramp at the side of the steps, so that you can get him up and down."

"You're making it sound as if I'm going to be immobile for some time to come," Berkeley remarked. "We won't be having that. Druce. Good to see you." He shook Druce's hand.

Cheam dismissed the ambulance men, and Anna wheeled Berkeley into the drawing room.

"You'll see we've arranged a bed for you down here," Martina said enthusiastically.

"In the drawing room?"

"Well, we're not going to be entertaining for a while," Anna said. "And you don't want to be coping with the stairs, do you?"

Berkeley grunted, and Anna knew he was becoming suspicious. "I think we should all have a drink," she said brightly. "To celebrate your homecoming."

"I'll do it," Druce said. He was perhaps the most nervous of them all.

"Do sit down, Doctor," Anna invited, and did so herself, next to where the wheelchair had been placed. Druce produced a tray of whisky and sodas.

"Am I permitted?" Berkeley asked.

"I don't see any reason why not," Cheam said. "It's not as if you were taking drugs."

Berkeley drank deeply. "That tastes good. But there's the point, Doctor: why am I not taking drugs? Or at least painkillers. You said you'd explain when I got home."

"Yes, I did," Cheam agreed. "Well . . ."

"I should do this," Anna said, and held her father's hand. "Papa, I know you have been through some pretty narrow scrapes in your time. You could have been killed a dozen times."

"But they've always missed," Berkeley pointed out. "What are you trying to tell me?"

"A miss is not always quite as much of a miss as one would like," Anna said.

"So I'm going to have a gammy leg for the rest of my life. I'll get used to it."

"I am sure you will, Papa. It's not the leg that is worrying us."

He gazed at her for several seconds, then looked at Cheam, and lastly at Martina.

"Oh, Berkeley," Martina said, bursting into tears.

"How long?" Berkeley asked.

"Nerves do grow back," Cheam said. "And join up, as it were. But it can take a while."

"How long?" Berkeley asked again.

"Age is an important factor, too," Cheam went on. "Perhaps not so much with regard to the speed at which the healing process will work but simply in terms of, well, if you were twenty years old . . ."

"I see," Berkeley said. "I am crippled for the rest of my life."

"Oh, no, no," Cheam protested. "We shall work on it. I am laying on a team of physiotherapists to work with you as soon as you are strong enough, and there are other things we can do."

"Cheam," Berkeley said. "Am I crippled or not?"

"Well, at the moment . . ."

"Therefore the bedpan situation continues."

"I'm afraid so. For the time being. Anna and Mrs Savos are quite prepared to cope."

"And sexual matters? You'll excuse me, Druce, but this is important."

"Of course, sir," Druce said, flushing.

"Again, we must put our trust in time," Cheam said.

"Which, in that respect, is running out anyway, even if I was as fit as a horse."

"It will make no difference," Martina said.

He squeezed her hand. "I need to have a private chat with Martina and Anna," he said. "Thanks for everything, Cheam."

"I'll be out again in a day or so to see how you're getting on."

"You mean to make sure I haven't committed suicide?" Berkeley grinned. "I'm not going to do that, Cheam."

"I'll see you out, Doctor."

Anna accompanied him out to the porch. "I would say he's taking it very well."

"Too well," Cheam commented. "It either hasn't sunk in yet—"

"Or it is what he has suspected for the past week and he has already decided how to deal with it."

"Yes," Cheam said. "Which bothers me."

"I believe him when he says he is not contemplating suicide. I'll keep you informed of his mental state."

"Anna . . . I don't know how to say this. Yours has been such a tragic life. And now it seems set to continue. If there is anything I can do, anything I can give you . . ."

"Thanks all the same, Doctor. But we'll manage."

"Now then," Berkeley said. "First things first." He had known, subconsciously, that something was very wrong from the moment he had regained full consciousness. Known, but refused to accept. Now the unacceptable had to be accepted. He had only lowered his guard on a few occasions in his life, and it had nearly always brought him close to catastrophe. Now the catastrophe was here. He, Berkeley Townsend, once considered the most dangerous man in Europe – a title he had not sought but of which he had been proud – was now one of the most helpless men in Europe, a sitting duck. His only reassuring thought was that, as he still had the use of his arms, when it happened he should be able to take at least one of the bastards with him.

But there were others to be considered. "I release you, Martina, from any obligations you may feel you owe to me, and certainly the obligation of marriage."

"That is nonsense," Martina declared. "I told you once that I would obey anything you asked me to do except leave you."

"My dear girl, any marriage between us can only be in name."

"I do not accept that either. Have we not already consummated our love? Marriage is merely a formality. But we will be married."

Berkeley looked at Druce.

"I intend to marry Anna, sir, unless you have withdrawn your permission."

"You understand that there may be other attempts on my life?"

"I understand that is possible, sir. It is Anna's wish that I move in here after our marriage."

"Which puts you in the firing line. What do your parents think of this?"

"I'm afraid they do not approve of the marriage, sir. This has nothing to do with any knowledge they may have of the Karlovys, or the German connection, or . . ." He glanced at Anna, who had just returned.

Berkeley caught the glance. "All right," he said. "Something has happened while I was in hospital. Out with it."

Anna sat beside him and told him everything she could remember of the events of the past week. He listened in silence. When she was finished, he looked at Druce. "What do you say to this?"

"I was deeply shocked, sir. I still am."

"But you still wish to marry her."

"I will support her in every way I can, sir."

"Understanding that if this ever comes out, you will go to prison?"

"Yes, sir."

"You haven't told me if you think I did the right thing, Papa," Anna said.

"You did the wrong thing."

"Papa!"

"Not in killing that woman; she deserved to die. Probably not even in killing Shrimpton; he was just as guilty. But in killing on impulse. Execution should only be undertaken as part of a deliberate and carefully thought-out exercise."

"I'm sorry Papa. But when I recognised her—"

"I understand that – but our business now is to make sure the police don't track us down. You say Watt is coming here tomorrow to ask about that gun?"

Anna nodded.

"I'll handle it."

"Wih respect, sir," Druce said.

"Yes?" Berkeley asked, slightly impatient.

Druce's flush was back. "Anna and I differ on this matter, as I am sure you will appreciate. While I understand and admire her loyalty to her family and to what she considers her duty, I am sure you will agree with me that what she has done certainly cannot bear the possibility of a repetition in the future."

"That depends on the future," Berkeley pointed out. "I am not quite sure what you're driving at."

"Harry would like you to forbid me ever to do anything like that again," Anna said.

"I would appreciate that, sir," Druce agreed.

"Have you asked her not to?"

"She will not promise."

"Then neither can I. If you marry into this family, Druce, it has got to be warts and all. I thought you understood that."

"I did, sir. But I thought—"

"That it was simply a matter of accepting what happened to Anna. Perhaps the fault is ours for not making it clear. You see, Druce, what happened to Anna was merely a concomitant of everything else that has happened in this family over the past twenty years. Anna was kidnapped because I killed Karlovy. I killed Karlovy in a vain attempt to prevent the murder of the Archduke Franz Ferdinand. That I was involved at all was because of my love for Anna's mother who was, to all intents and purposes, murdered by the Austrian secret police, as had been her father; while her mother, Anna's grandmother and the woman after whom she is named, was killed by the Austrian army. This family is steeped in blood and battle, Druce. I had hoped it might be over, but now I know it can never be over. It had been my intention that Johnnie, in the fullness of time, would take over the protection of his sisters, and I still hope that will happen. But we have been rather overtaken by events and my own carelessness. So for the moment it is only Anna, and of course Martina, who can protect us."

"If I may say so, sir, that is a very sombre, uncivilised, and certainly un-Christian attitude."

"Sadly, we are dealing with uncivilised and un-Christian enemies."

"Into which category you would place the British War Office."

"Certainly. There is nothing the least civilised or Christian about the British War Office. To believe otherwise is pure hypocrisy. I am sorry to have to accuse you of that, but I am sure it is is simply because you have never considered the matter deeply enough."

"So you believe that if anyone attempts to kill you, their lives are immediately forfeit? Without due and proper recourse to the law?"

"I might go for due process of law if I believed that it would be the least effective. Sadly we are not dealing with a man who poisons his wife, or even an habitual criminal who commits murder in the course of a robbery; we are dealing with organised forces with immense resources at their disposal. When one of these forces determines that I am to be disposed of, I reserve the right to riposte with every force at my disposal."

"Including your own daughter."

"Had I been up and about I would not have allowed Anna to do what she did. As I was not up and about, she took the law into her own hands. In doing this, she acted entirely as her mother and her grandmother would have done."

"And as you have reminded us, they are both dead," Druce said bitterly.

"Sadly, yes. But looking over one's shoulder is nearly always a waste of time. I think you need to think very clearly about this, Druce. I understand and sympathise with your point of view. You were brought up in a totally different world to that of Anna and her siblings. The decision as to whether you . . ." he chose his words with care, "wish, or can afford, to abandon your world for ours, has got to be yours alone. If you decide that you cannot do so then I shall not hold it against you. And neither, I am sure, will Anna."

He glanced at Anna, who had been following the conversation, as had Martina, with interest.

"But the commitment," Berkeley went on, "if you join forces with us, will have to be total and irrevocable."

"I am to stand at Anna's shoulder and load her gun while she shoots at someone else," Druce said bitterly.

"It could come to that," Berkeley said, urbanely.

"And of course, if I were to break the engagement I would immediately have to be executed myself, as knowing too much."

"I hope it would not come to that," Berkeley said. "I understand that you have already pledged yourself to support Anna, in this matter at least. Besides, as it is nearly a week since Shrimpton was killed and in that time you have helped Anna in every way possible, that makes you an accessory after the fact. Were you to attempt to turn her in now you would find yourself in serious trouble. You may be able to do a deal with the police for turning

King's evidence, but your career as a solicitor would be ended. Moreover, so that you are in no doubt, should you, to use the hackneyed term, shop my daughter, then you had better hire yourself a bodyguard immediately, not that I think it would do you much good."

Druce stared at him for a moment, then got up and went into the hall.

Anna followed him. "I am sorry you quarrelled with Papa. But I suppose your conflicting attitudes did need bringing into the open."

"Conflicting attitudes! Your father is—"

"A remarkable man," she quickly interjected. "You were very happy about that, once."

He sighed, and held her hands. "Anna, do you suppose Martina can take care of him?"

"I should think so."

"Well, then, can you not marry me, come and live in Northampton, and turn your back on all this?"

"You know that is impossible, Harry. The family must stick together, more than ever now. It is us against the whole world."

"And you glory in that."

She smiled. "It is a challenge."

"And you are asking me to abandon everything to join you in facing that challenge."

"I suppose I am."

He sighed, and drew her forward for a kiss on the forehead. "You know it will end in your death."

"Maybe, but I will not abandon Papa, Harry."

"And I cannot abandon my beliefs – in right and wrong, in the rule of law, in the sanctity of human life – any more than you can abandon yours."

"Then it is goodbye. At least your parents will be pleased."

"Anna . . ."

She freed her hands. "I think you should go now; I must go back to Papa."

Anna closed the door behind Druce and leaned against it. She supposed she should feel like weeping, but she did not. She had always known it was not going to work.

Nor was she even very concerned at the realisation that she

would probably never marry and have children of her own. The world, or at least the English world, was full of Harry Druces but there was only one Berkeley Townsend.

She found herself thinking of what Druce had said, all so reasoned, sensible, Christian . . . and civilised Papa had called it, almost contemptuously. Papa had been right, of course; the ability to be so civilised existed only in a few relatively small parts of the world. There had been no such civilisation in the Balkans of her mother and grandmother; she doubted it had arrived yet.

But that did not mean it was not an ideal to be sought. Could someone who had spent five years of her life being raped and maltreated and who had now killed two people ever become civilised? Why not? What of the millions of men who had spent four years killing other millions of men and who were now living civilised Christian lives? They had fought and killed, and then, when the war was over and they had been called upon to lay down their arms, they had done so and resumed their normal lives as law-abiding citizens. She would do the same . . . when the war was over.

Her war!

She went into the drawing room, and Martina got up to embrace her. "My darling," she said. "I am most terribly sorry."

"It was never possible," Anna said, and sat beside her father. "Are you all right?"

"I'm in the company of my two favourite women. What more can I ask."

"We need to plan."

"We do indeed. But as I said, I can handle Peter Watt. I don't think they'll be able to take that any further, at least in our direction."

"You think you can trust Druce?" Martina asked.

"I think we can. Anna?"

"I believe so. At least for the time being. I am thinking of this Himmler business."

"I'm afraid that is too hot for us to handle," Berkeley said.

"And when he sends another assassin?"

"We'll have to cope with that as best we can."

"Of course. But it will be difficult, as we won't know where or when or how."

"The where and the how are simple enough," Berkeley pointed out. "As I can no longer move about, the where has got to be right here at the farmhouse and the how will have to be either a gun or a knife. It is the when that we do not know."

"And that is his trump card," Anna said. "He must know that we cannot keep up a state of readiness for an indefinite period. There must come a time when we lower our guard."

"I'm afraid that's true."

"We cannot permit that to happen, Papa."

"I don't see how we can prevent it."

"I have been thinking about it. This Nazi Party is just a fringe organisation, isn't it? I mean, it doesn't have any real political power?"

"No, it doesn't. Which doesn't mean it doesn't have power, though. It seems to have its tentacles everywhere."

"That is one point. The other is that it is surely as subject to the law as any other group or individual."

"Yes," Berkeley agreed. "But if you're thinking of taking it, or Himmler, to court in Germany on a charge of attempted murder, you won't get very far."

"Is there not a saying, in chess, that the threat is greater than the execution?"

"I'm not with you."

"As you have just said, Papa, the chance of getting a conviction against Himmler in Germany for attempting to kill you, and for killing Lucy and Grandma and Maria, is remote, especially as he has used people who cannot easily be connected to him. But according to our Cohn friends, as the Nazis are presently committed to seeking power in an entirely legitimate manner, can they afford to let such a case come to court?"

Berkeley stroked his chin.

"Now," Anna went on. "Himmler will know by now that you have been shot and badly hurt by some other organisation. He may wish to let the dust settle before coming after you again, and he may suppose that he has all the time in the world. But if he learns that we are taking counter steps, he will realise that he does not have so much time after all."

"You are thinking that we should advertise that we know who he is?" Martina asked.

"The next best thing," Anna said. "David Cohn recommended we talk to the Berlin Chief of Police, this man Schuler. I know you didn't want to do that, Papa; you wanted to deal with it on your own. But circumstances have changed. If I were to go to Berlin and see this man Schuler, tell him what we know, tell him that Helen Karlovy told us it was Himmler, tell him also that the story about your being badly hurt isn't true but was put out by us to put the Nazis off the track . . ." She smiled. "I wanted Leighton to go the other way. Thank God he didn't."

"This police chief would have you deported," Martina said.

"That would depend on whether or not he is in the pay of the Nazis," Berkeley said.

"It doesn't matter whether he is in their pay or not," Anna said. "Or whether he has me deported or not. I am quite sure there are people in his department who *are* Nazis, so the news will get back to Himmler pretty quickly. I believe that he will then feel obliged to do something about it, and we will be waiting for him."

Berkeley shook his head. "Too dangerous. Oh, I am quite sure you're right as to his reaction, but he may well decide to do something about you first."

"What would be the point? I am only a messenger girl from you to him. Anyway, he will never catch me. I will go to Berlin and make an appointment to see this Schuler. One hour after the time of that appointment, I will take the train for Poland. I will be out of Germany in an hour. From Warsaw, I will take the train for Vienna, then Paris and home: the exact route we took when escaping from Berlin after Grippenheimer's death."

"Brilliant!" Martina clapped her hands. "I will come with you. Oh!"

She gazed at Berkeley.

"The idea was that you both should stay here and look after me," Berkeley said.

"I will only be gone a couple of days," Anna said. "I could leave tomorrow and be back by the end of next week."

Berkeley didn't doubt she could do it, but the thought of allowing her to go back to Germany, or indeed anywhere on her own, was terrifying. On the other hand, he knew he couldn't keep her at his side for ever.

"You'll wait until I have had a chance to write to David Cohn," he said. "To arrange your meeting with Schuler."

"We are to leave Berlin," Heinrich Himmler told his secretary.

The young woman frowned. "To go where?"

"I am to go to Munich, to join the Führer's personal entourage." He dared not say more than that at this moment, however much he wanted to. "You will like Munich. Do you ski?"

The secretary hesitated. She found working for Heinrich Himmler incredibly boring. He was an incredibly boring man. And apparently totally asexual; he had never made the slightest pass at her, and she considered herself a handsome woman with all the right curves in all the right places. When she thought of the tales her friend Eva told her of Herr Schuler's advances . . .

"I don't ski," she said. "And the fact is, Herr Himmler, I would not like to leave Berlin. All my family and friends are here."

She paused, but her boss did not appear to be concerned. In fact he was distracted. But then, he had been distracted for the past couple of days; probably it was to do with this move, not that *he* would be leaving any friends behind; he didn't have any friends.

"The decision must be yours," he said. "Now fetch Herr Bruckner."

The secretary left the office, and Himmler could study the newspaper once again. Who on earth could this strange woman assassin be? He had as yet sent no one to replace the Karlovys. Gerber was certainly capable of carrying out an assassination, but he was also very firmly planted in England, as a result of years of fitting into the community, and to waste all that subtle work the goal would have to be very worthwhile . . . and as Goebbels apparently thought that he had organised Townsend's shooting, the temptation to do nothing was enormous. But if he did nothing, and Goebbels found out the truth . . . There were many things of which Heinrich Himmler was afraid but, when it came to people, Josef Goebbels headed the list.

"You sent for me, sir?" Bruckner, a large, heavy-set man, stood before his desk.

"Yes. What is the latest word from Gerber?"

"I have heard nothing from him for some time."

"Have you seen this?" Himmler pushed the newspaper across the desk.

Bruckner studied it. "This was one of ours?"

"No. But everyone thinks it was, and it might be to our advantage to let them suppose so, for the time being. However, you will see that the woman, whoever she was, botched the job. They say Townsend may be crippled for life but our business is still not completed. Is Hassler standing by?"

Bruckner nodded.

"Then send him over. The job must be completed this time. For God's sake, if the man is a cripple, it should not be difficult."

"I will despatch him immediately."

"I wish it clearly understood that should anything go wrong, he must not be traced back to us."

"I understand," Bruckner said. "Hassler does too. He speaks perfect English and will have all the necessary documents. You wish me to advise Gerber?"

"Gerber," Himmler sneered. "That man is a waste of time. What is he doing now?"

"I imagine he is still keeping the house under observation," Bruckner said. "But of course since the Karlovy fiasco he has had to move from the area."

"The man is a failure," Himmler said. "No, do not advise him of this plan. But give Hassler his new address just in case contact is necessary. This time, Bruckner . . ."

"This time, Herr Himmler," Bruckner said.

"Believe me, Colonel, this is very embarrassing for me," Peter Watt explained.

"You are doing your duty, Peter," Berkeley pointed out.

"And with you lying there . . ."

The two women had put Berkeley to bed in the drawing room. It was filled with vases of flowers as well as Howard, while both Martina and Anna hovered protectively.

"I'm very comfortable," Berkeley pointed out. "Now, you wanted to ask me about one of my guns."

"Yes," Watt said. "That thirty-two you had. Anna says you got rid of it."

"Why, yes, so I did."

"May I ask why?"

"Well . . . how many guns does a man need? You remember that thirty-eight I absent-mindedly picked up? The one with which I shot the Karlovy boy, and which I had forgotten to license?"

"You have licensed it since?" Watt asked anxiously.

"Of course. But then I had three guns, so I got rid of the thirty-two."

"You mean you returned it to the gunsmith? Or sold it?"

"Neither. I threw it into the canal."

"May I ask where?"

"By Weedon Beck. Did you need the gun for something, Chief Inspector?"

"Well, not really. You see, General Shrimpton was shot with a Smith and Wesson thirty-two."

"And you thought I had done it? My dear fellow, I was in hospital."

"Absolutely. But you see, well . . ." Red in the face, Watt glanced at Anna.

"The police know that I was in town that day, Papa."

"And you think that Anna—"

"No, no, sir," Watt protested. "I would never dream of such a thing. But you know what Scotland Yard is like. They're trying to round up every Smith and Wesson thirty-two that could possibly have been connected, and hope to match up the bullets. But you say your gun had been thrown into the canal. How long ago?"

"At least six months."

"Well, that's it, then. We could look for it, I suppose, but after six months, well, there's not much chance of finding it. Still, I doubt it matters."

"And my own business?" Berkeley asked.

"Ah, well, sir, I'm sorry to say I have nothing to report there. Very slick, it seems to have been. Do you think they'll try again?"

"I wouldn't be at all surprised."

"I could mount a patrol out here. It would be expensive, and there might be questions asked. But for you, sir . . ."

"Fortunately, Chief Inspector, that woman left me the use of my arms and I still have two guns, for which I have licences."

"Yes, sir." Watt's face had assumed its usual disapproving expression when Berkeley talked about protecting himself. "I was thinking of Anna. And Mrs Savos, of course."

"Their constant company and support are my chief assets."

Watt now looked dubious as well as disapproving. "Well, sir, you know I'm just at the end of a telephone."

"I do indeed," Berkeley said.

Anna left three days later; they were anxious for her to be back before the start of the school holidays. Neither Johnnie nor Alicia knew anything of what was going on, and it was Berkeley's intention that they should not. He telephoned his bank manager in Northampton arranging for Anna to call and receive suficient Deutschmarks for her journey. On the same visit she bought her train and boat tickets: Northampton–Dover, Dover–Boulogne, Boulogne–Berlin. The Cohns had been requested both to meet her and to arrange her exit from Berlin, and although there had been no time for them to reply to Berkeley's letter, he had no doubt that they would help in every way possible; he gave Anna their address, just in case they failed to meet the train. Cohn was also to arrange a meeting with Schuler, giving as reason that she had information regarding the death of Hans von Grippenheimer four years previously.

The risks were high, but Berkeley knew that she was right: they could not just sit at the farm waiting to be hit, and if they could force Himmler into the open they might be able to end the threat. Besides, Anna clearly felt she needed to repay him for his five-year search and eventual rescue of her. He also understood that she had other reasons, not all of them admirable. Perhaps the most sinister was that she had tasted blood, and from here on could never be anything other than what she was – Berkeley Townsend's daughter. He had a suspicion that her admiration for him and for what he had been called – the most dangerous man in Europe – had created an ambition to become the most dangerous woman. A twenty-year-old girl!

"May I take your gun, Papa?" she asked.

"No. Listen to me. You are going to Berlin to put the wind

up Himmler. You will have your meeting with Herr Schuler; you will then immediately leave Berlin and come home."

"And if I am stopped, or arrested for any reason?"

"There is no reason for you to be stopped, save by Himmler's people, and if you are in and out of Germany as rapidly as you should be they will never have the chance. If you do happen to be stopped, you are young, you are pretty, you are innocent, and you have a British passport. Those assets should be sufficient to make sure you are all right."

"As you wish, Papa."

"I wish I was coming with you," Martina said, giving her a hug.

"I wish you were coming too. But it is more important that you stay here and look after Papa."

Anna was exhilarated as she caught the train south. The launching of her career as Papa's closest associate had been accidental; she had not gone to London with the intention of killing anyone. If she had carried a revolver that was because it had become second nature to do so. And indeed, today she felt almost naked without its reassuring weight in her handbag. But of course Papa was right; her youth and beauty and obvious innocence were far more useful weapons.

And she was adventuring. This was necessary. She had to get Harry Druce right out of her system. He had never really been there, but she had wanted him to be. Now she was just grateful to him for having freed her mind from so many traumas and felt that she was at last truly a woman rather than a frightened girl.

She lunched on the train; then it was necessary to take a taxi across London to Victoria and the boat train to Folkestone. She joined the queue outside King's Cross, kicking her bag along the ground as the line slowly advanced, and suddenly realised she was being watched.

She turned her head left and right, and then looked over her shoulder. There were several people, of both sexes, looking at her. She was used to this, as most people gave her a second look – certainly most men – and nobody appeared the least bit sinister. Yet the peculiar prickling at the nape of her neck persisted until she actually got into the taxi. Half an hour later she was on the train to Folkestone. Martina, no doubt instructed by Papa, had booked her a First-Class seat but for this leg she preferred to join the crowd in Third; she felt safer. Yet the prickling feeling was back as she boarded the ferry.

She spent the hour-long voyage in the main saloon, again surrounded by people and bustling stewards.

Arriving at Boulogne, customs formalities were brief, especially as she was passing through, and she boarded the waiting train with a sigh of relief. It was now late in the afternoon, but she had a sleeper. She stowed her bag, opened a novel she had brought with her but found herself unable to concentrate; instead she stared out of the window at the darkening countryside as the train headed south. It stopped in Paris, a city she only vaguely remembered, discharged some passengers and acquired others. Dinner was served as soon as they left the French capital. She had a glass of wine with her meal and smiled graciously at her fellow diners, none of whom she had ever seen before. But that was how it should be.

It was ten o'clock when she regained her compartment, carefully locking the door. The steward had been in and made up her bed, using only the lower bunk. She undressed, cleaned her teeth, and was just getting into the bunk when there was a tap on the door.

"Who is it?" she asked.

"It is your steward, mademoiselle."

"Do you require something?" Anna asked.

"Your passport, mademoiselle."

Ann rolled out of the bunk, pulled on her dressing gown, and opened the door. The steward was a personable young man. "Why do you wish my passport?"

"Well mademoiselle, we do not cross the German border for another two hours. By that time I assume you will be asleep. But the Germans require to inspect the passports of everyone on the train. So I collect all the passports," he indicated the pile of little books he already had on his tray, "give them to the Germans for stamping, and tomorrow morning I return them to their owners, who have not had to be woken up in the middle of the night."

"I see." She gave him her passport.

"Thank you mademoiselle. Sleep well."

Anna locked the door again, got back into bed and switched off the light. It was an extremely pleasant feeling, racing through the night. The noise was fairly loud, but rhythmic and almost hypnotic, broken only occasionally by the distant wail of the whistle.

She was adventuring, she thought. Doing Papa's business and thus, however remotely, Mama's business, and even Grandmama's business as well. And afterwards? Afterwards meant taking care of Papa and Howard until they became capable of taking care of themselves. She had to believe that was going to happen, in both instances. And men? She did not suppose she would miss them physically. She had had all the men any woman was entitled to expect . . . or suffer. And for support – there was always Martina, she supposed.

She slept, and awoke when the train stopped and there was much shouting on the platform beyond her window. They must be in Germany, she thought. The noise died, and she went back to asleep, to waken again, suddenly, as her compartment door opened.

The Prisoner

There were two men in the doorway, for a second silhouetted against the light in the corridor before the door was closed. Anna sat up, pushing herself against the wall, trying desperately to think.

"What do you want?" she snapped. "Who are you?"

"We want you, little girl," one of the men said in accented English, and switched on the overhead light.

Anna blinked at them. They both wore top coats and slouch hats, they both had heavy moustaches and they both had big chins. She opened her mouth to call for help and one of the men grasped her throat, his other hand grabbing at her nightdress and the flesh beneath.

The whistle howled.

"Five minutes," the other man said, and Anna realised he was carrying a suitcase. This he now laid on the floor, opened, and took out several lengths of tape as well as a hooded cloak.

She got free of the sheet and blanket and kicked savagely, but to very little avail; the man with the suitcase merely gathered her legs together and passed some tape round her ankles to secure them. Then he taped her mouth, and both men turned her over to tape her wrists together behind her back. While doing this they availed themselves of the opportunity to manhandle her, squeezing her breasts and belly and buttocks; at least the nightdress stopped them getting between her legs – thus far.

"This is a lot of woman," one said in German, perhaps unaware that she understood the language.

"Maybe they will let you have her for a while, when they are finished with her," the other said.

Now utterly helpless, Anna was dragged to her feet and

wrapped in the cloak, the hood was pulled over her head, and this too was taped, across her nose.

She was being kidnapped! For the second time in her life. The first time she had gone willingly because she had believed she was being taken to the mother she had supposed dead. She had been only eleven years old, desperately innocent. Now she was a grown woman, in a way these men could not possibly suspect. She was Berkeley Townsend's daughter. Certainly they would know that, or their employers would. But they could not possibly know how much of his daughter she was. All she had to do was be patient, until they gave her the opportunity.

The train slowed. One of the men slung Anna over his shoulder as if she were a bolt of cloth. She was carried helpless into the deserted corridor, past the doors of the other sleeping compartments, to the external door; the other man followed, carrying both suitcases, his and hers. As they reached the door, the train came to a halt. The door opened, the two men stepped on to the platform, the door banged shut behind them, and the train moved off again, into the night.

Harry Druce sat at his desk and doodled on his blotting pad. He had just completed a meeting. His next client was not for another hour. He looked at the clock. A quarter to ten. He wondered if he could go out.

To do what? There were so many things that needed doing. He certainly should visit his parents to inform them that his engagement was broken. But he didn't want to do that. This was partly because it would seem like climbdown on his part, another mistake. There had been so many.

But it was also because . . . *was* his engagement over? Could it not be resurrected? That would mean another climbdown, but this one would be worth it. And anyway, he was at least an accessory after the fact. She would surely change once she was a mother. Besides, her life for the immediate future would be bound up in caring for that old devil of a father. He needed to marry her, and get her pregnant, long before Berkeley Townsend showed the slightest sign of recovery.

His door opened. "All well, Harry?"

"Ah . . ." But Geoffrey Walton was a very observant man.
"Just a lovers' tiff, sir," Druce said.

"They do happen. May I ask how the meeting with your parents went?"

Druce hesitated; he had no idea whether or not his father had been in touch with the senior partner. "I don't think they altogether approve," he said. "But they will, eventually. I wonder, sir, if I might nip out for an hour."

"I don't see why not. I'll wish you luck."

Truly had he entered a world of lies and concealments, Druce thought, as he drove out to the farm. It was only as he swung down the drive that he realised she might refuse to see him. But they had not actually parted on bad terms, merely in mutual regret.

He braked before the steps, and Hannibal whinnied from the stables. He stepped down, and the front door opened. But it was Martina rather than Anna.

Druce raised his hat. "Forgive this intrusion, Martina. Is Anna around?"

"Why do you wish to know?"

She was definitely hostile.

"I would like to see her."

"What about?"

"Oh, for God's sake. I have come to apologise. To make it up."

Martina considered. Then she said, "You'd better come in."

Frowning, Druce climbed the steps and followed her into the drawing room. As he did so he heard sounds behind him, and turned to see Harry and Mary Lockwood cycling down the drive. He had actually passed them on the road without registering who they were. He went into the drawing room where Berkeley was sitting up in bed, reading.

"He wants to see Anna," Martina explained.

Druce began to feel uneasy. "She's not ill, is she?"

"No, she's not ill," Berkeley said. "What did you wish to see her about?"

Druce sighed. "I have come to make it up, sir. I have realised that I love her over and above any ordinary consideration of morals or ethics. Or law."

"I see," Berkeley said. "Well, I will be honest and tell you that I am very happy to have you on board. And I am sure Anna will be also."

"Then can I see her?"

"Not right this minute. She isn't here."

"May I ask where she is?"

"We are expecting her back the day after tomorrow. She is doing something for the family," Martina explained.

"For the . . . Where is she? I am entitled to know."

Berkeley looked at his watch. "They are a couple of hours ahead of us. Let's see; she arrived in Berlin early this morning, she had a meeting during the day, and she was catching a train to Warsaw as soon as the meeting was completed. I would say she is probably in Warsaw by now."

"Berlin? Warsaw? My God! What have you sent her to do?"

"Simmer down. She has gone to Berlin to have a meeting with someone, following which she will return here."

"You have sent her to the man Himmler?"

"Of course not."

"But it is to do with him."

"Yes, it is. Indirectly." Berkeley turned his head. "What is that noise? Another visitor?"

"That is a motor bike," Druce said.

"I had better go see what it is." Martina left the room.

"I still feel it was incredibly dangerous of Anna to go to Germany by herself," Druce said.

"Well, you weren't here to go with her, were you?"

"It is a telegram," Martina announced, returning. "Addressed to you, Berkeley."

Berkeley slit the envelope and frowned as he read. "Damned odd," he remarked. He gave the sheet of paper to Martina.

"Oh, Lord," she said.

"May I see?" Druce asked.

Berkeley nodded, and Martina gave the lawyer the paper.

PLEASE ADVISE CHANGE OF PLANS STOP HAVE MET PARIS TRAIN AND LATER BUT ANNA NOT ARRIVED STOP HAVE POSTPONED MEETING

WITH SCHULER STOP HAS SOMETHING HAPPENED QUESTION COHN

Druce raised his head. "What does this mean?"

"I wish to God I knew. Anna left here yesterday morning. She was catching the afternoon ferry from Folkestone. In Boulogne she was catching the overnight train to Berlin, to arrive this morning. As I told you, she was to have a meeting with Schuler and then leave immediately for Poland."

"Who is Schuler?"

"The Berlin chief of police."

"Only she never got there." The words fell from Druce's lips like drops of vitriol.

Berkeley looked at Martina. "Can she have missed her train? Missed the boat, perhaps?"

"Yes," Martina said. "That is what must have happened."

"That is not what happened," Druce said. "Someone didn't want her to have that appointment with Schuler."

"Who? No one knew she was going, save Martina and myself."

"And presumably Schuler."

"Cohn wasn't to make the appointment until yesterday afternoon. By then Anna was already on her way, and no one knew how or when she was travelling."

"This man Cohn certainly did."

"Cohn would never betray us. I saved his life, and that of his wife."

"And he helped us escape from Grippenheimer's," Martina put in.

"Four years ago," Druce pointed out.

"I cannot believe Cohn would let us down," Berkeley said. "In any event, if he did, he would hardly wire us to tell us what he had done. But, my God, if she's been kidnapped again . . ."

He looked at Martina.

"We must find her," Martina said. "But how can I leave you?"

"I will find her," Druce said.

"You?" Berkeley and Martina spoke together.

"She is my fiancée," Druce said.

"But you know nothing of this game," Berkeley said. "If Anna *has* been kidnapped . . ." Eight years ago he had not hesitated, had charged into the Balkans with guns blazing, and even then it had taken him five years to reclaim his daughter. Now he could only lie on his back, could only leave his bed with Martina's assistance.

Martina!

She could read his expression. "How can I leave you and Howard?" she asked.

"Would you go, all else being equal?"

Martina smiled; sometimes she could look very like a tigress watching her next meal approaching. "Of course I will go."

"Right. Mary will look after me and Howard. She is about due to leave school in any event. And Johnnie and Alicia will be home in a fortnight. You will be back before they return to school."

"And suppose these Nazis come after you while I am away?"

"Just give me my Browning. I'm safer here than anywhere else in the world, don't you see? There is only one way they can get at me, through that door. Anyway," . . . he grinned, "I am relying on you to keep them busy until you return."

"With respect, sir," Druce said, "are you suggesting that Martina and I should go to Germany together?"

"Martina is going, certainly," Berkeley said. "If you wish to accompany her . . ."

"I regard it as my duty to find out what has happened to Anna," Druce said. "And to bring her home, if that is possible. But it would be more seemly if I went alone."

"Druce," Berkeley said. "Unless it is your intention to commit suicide, you have simply got to forget these quaint ideas. Are you worried about what people may say if you take off with a woman?"

Druce flushed.

"You are going to be partners in a venture which will put you under considerable stress, and which may require you to kill. What you do to sustain each other is your business, and will mean nothing to me, or to Anna, should we ever learn of it. However, I must make it perfectly clear that Martina is in command of this expedition. Martina knows the score, knows the country in which you will be operating, and has forgotten more about skullduggery than you will ever learn. So tell me, are you on board?"

Druce swallowed and looked at Martina, who gave him one of her encouraging smiles.

"Yes, sir," he said.

"Right. How soon can you be ready?"

"I will have to square it with Mr Walton."

Berkeley nodded. "If there is a problem, ask him to give me a ring. But you must be on the lunchtime train to London. That way you will still catch the last sailing to Boulogne, and be in Berlin tomorrow morning. Your parents?"

"Well . . ."

"You cannot under any circumstances tell them what you are doing, but I think you will have to tell them that you are going away for a few days."

"Yes, sir."

He was allowing his entire life to be taken over by the grim old man, but he could not deny that it was exhilarating.

"Then you had better get moving. You'll meet Martina at the station in two hours' time."

Druce swallowed. "Our passages . . ."

"We will look after that. There is one more thing: do you own a gun?"

"I'm afraid not."

"There's a problem."

"No," Martina said. "I will take my gun, and I will take Anna's as well. If there is any shooting to be done, I will do it. He is not very good with a gun, anyway."

"I'm afraid that is true, sir," Druce admitted.

"Very well. Now go and make your arrangements."

"Yes, sir." Druce hesitated, looked at Martina again, then hurried from the room.

"What do you reckon?" Berkeley asked.

Martina shrugged. "It will be amusing."

"I imagine it could be. I meant, do you think he will be any use at all, or will he let you down at the first critical moment?"

"I do not think he will let me down. He would be too ashamed."

"You have *carte blanche*," Berkeley said.

"I am not that desperate. Yet."

"I meant, as regards dealing with him if he does not measure up."

"I understand. Now tell me what is it you wish me to do?"

"I wish you to get Anna back."

"You think these Nazi people have her?"

"Not necessarily. My understanding is that the Nazis are striving for respectability. Kidnapping foreign nationals is not the way to accomplish that. There is also the matter of who found out where she was going, and how. That can only have been done by constant surveillance. We know that the last attempt on my life was not Himmler-inspired but that he is unlikely to abandon his attempts on my life simply because the Karlovys failed. I suspect that he has had his agents watching us but has always refused to use anyone who could be traced back to him. Therefore I believe that whoever snatched Anna made the decision without reference to Himmler, or the party. This person or persons will have been watching us and will have followed Anna as a matter of course. When they discovered she was on the train for Berlin, they decided to act on their own initiative; there just wasn't enough time between tracking Anna to France, ascertaining that she was headed for Berlin, contacting Himmler and getting her off the train – which must have been done somewhere between Boulogne and Berlin. Again, my bet would be it happened in Germany; taking someone off a train who doesn't want to go is a difficult matter. Those overnight sleepers are expresses; they stop only in big cities, which means bright lights and crowded platforms. I think it may well be possible to trace what happened. I am going to wire Cohn to expect you, and to set up another meeting with Schuler. I can't tell you what to say as I don't know how cooperative this man will be, or how much he knows. You will have to use your judgement. Can you handle it?"

"I will handle it," Martina said.

He smiled and ruffled her hair. "And no shooting, except as a last resort."

Martina kissed him, and held him close. "And you," she said. "You must not worry."

He raised his head.

"Oh, I know that was a stupid thing to say," she admitted.

"Let's get married. We can get a special licence first thing tomorrow and be married before you leave."

"We will be married when I return with Anna."

"You mean you don't want to start our married life by committing adultery."

"I mean I don't want to start our married life by making you a widower."

"Martina . . ." He held her hand.

"I do not expect that to happen," she said. "But just in case, I shall sleep with you tonight."

"A week's holiday? Now?" Geoffrey Walton stroked his chin. "I think I'm entitled to ask for a reason."

Druce had already made up his mind to confide in his employer. He felt he needed to confide in someone, if only to offset Berkeley Townsend's overwhelming personality, and his relations with Walton were far closer than with his own father.

Walton listened to what he had to say, his expression growing more grave by the moment. When Druce had finished, he said. "The only sensible advice I can give you is to abandon this lunacy forthwith. But I don't suppose you will take that advice."

"Sir . . ."

"I know. I know. You will never meet another young woman like Anna Townsend. I have a notion we should all say, thank God for that. All right, so she has gone to Germany to see off this fellow Himmler. How come his name never came up at the Karlovy trial?"

"Colonel Townsend wanted to settle that matter personally."

"And got himself a bullet in the spine for his trouble."

Druce had not told his senior the truth about that.

"So we have here some people who believe in playing very rough," Walton said. "You realise that your fiancée may have been murdered by now?"

"But sir, I am sure you'll agree I can hardly sit here drawing up conveyances while there is a chance she is still alive."

"Of course not. What about this Savos woman? I have a feeling that she is somewhat trigger-happy. Can you keep her under control?"

"I shall endeavour to do so, sir."

Something else he had not confided was that Martina was to be in command.

"Hm. Well . . . would you have any objection if I offered some help?"

"What kind of help?" Druce asked, suspiciously.

"Well, you may remember that my brother is in the FO. Quite senior. He gave me all that background information about Townsend."

"I do remember, sir. But I do not think Colonel Townsend would wish to involve the Foreign Office in this."

"Then there is no need to tell him. There is no harm in having a back-up. I will acquaint Claude with the situation and request him to get in touch with our Berlin embassy. Not only may they be able to help in locating Miss Townsend, or at least discovering what has happened to her, but they may be very helpful in the event of any trouble. As a matter of fact, I happen to know that one of the under-secretaries in the embassy, a man called Hudson, is married to Julia Gracey that was."

"Not the woman from the Gracey Farm?"

"That's right. But she is also a childhood friend of Townsend. I'm quite sure they'd be willing to help in every possible way."

"I cannot possibly approach them."

"I am not suggesting that you do, if all goes well. But they will be there in case, for instance, you wind up in a German police cell. I want you to come back, Harry, preferably in one piece. And of course, bringing your bride with you. But first, go and say goodbye to your parents."

"Going away?" Annette Druce demanded. "Isn't this rather sudden? Is it to do with a case?"

"It is to do with Anna Townsend," Druce said.

His mother raised her eyebrows.

"I'm afraid she was seriously upset by your attitude, Mother," Druce said. "And she has left the country. Mr Walton has given me permission to go after her and make it up."

"And then?"

"We shall be married."

"Harry, I will not receive that girl."

"That is entirely up to you, Mother. Father. I shall say goodbye."

"Where are you going?" his father asked.

"I am not at liberty to divulge that."

"This whole business is very strange. When will you be back?"

"I have no idea," Druce said. "Goodbye."

His mother and father watched the door close.

"That girl seems to have bewitched him," Mrs Druce remarked.

"Something has," her husband agreed. "I think I should have a word with Walton."

There was a car waiting in the station yard. Anna was laid on the back seat, and one of the men sat beside her; she could see no point in attempting to fight them and in any event she was unable to move either her arms or her legs. The other got into the front beside the driver.

"Any trouble?" the driver asked.

"None."

"I am to take you to Berlin headquarters."

"That is best."

The car drove out of the yard. It was very difficult to see through the folded and taped hood but Anna guessed that it was a small town, for a few minutes later they were away from houses and increasing speed.

It was a long drive. The man seated beside Anna prodded her from time to time, but it seemed this was for his own amusement for he never actually spoke to her. His companions kept up a flow of conversation, which Anna found interesting if not entirely reassuring.

"They are not pleased," the driver pointed out.

"I did what I thought necessary."

"It is not just the girl," the driver said. "I think they are unhappy that you may have blown your cover. The Mr Green masquerade."

"I had to blow my cover when that Karlovy woman was arrested," Green said. "That whole business was a shambles. My business was to keep watching the Townsend house and the Townsend family, and to hide the executioners and give them all assistance in my power. I was surely entitled to expect the executioners to be competent. Berlin knows all of this, but I am still commanded to keep the Townsends under surveillance pending the arrival of a new executioner. Then they send someone without informing me at all. Another shambles."

"I think there is some confusion about that one," the driver said. "I do not blame you for being agitated. But to kidnap the girl . . . That is an overreaction."

"I did what I thought best," Green said again.

Slowly the darkness began to fade, although as it was a cloudy morning there was no immediate sign of the sun. But now they were amidst houses again. Anna knew Berlin very well and soon enough she was picking out familiar landmarks. It was broad daylight before they turned through an archway into an enclosed yard. She had expected to be freed sufficiently to walk but her captor preferred to carry her, and once again she was slung across his shoulder, as he lifted her out into the crisp morning air, and then through a doorway. Now there were other people around, and several comments in German. She was carried along a corridor and then through another doorway into a room, on the floor of which she was laid, not at all gently.

"I need to use a toilet," she said in English. She was not going to give away any of her advantages.

"Awake, eh?" Green said, standing above her.

"It is urgent," Anna said.

He snorted, but untaped the hood and rolled her out of the cloak. Then he freed her wrists and ankles, and she experienced the painful pleasure of returning circulation.

"Through there," he said.

She scrambled to her feet, straightened her nightdress and moved uncertainly towards the doorway he had indicated. There were still people in the corridor, if less than before, but they were definitely interested in the girl and she was actually relieved to have Green at her elbow, even if it was apparent that he intended to accompany her to the toilet, which was across the hall.

"What is going to happen to me?" she asked, keeping her composure.

"I do not know, Fräulein. Tell me why you were coming to Berlin."

"That is my business," Anna said.

"You may find that other people consider it to be theirs," Green said, and followed her back into the first room, which she now realised was an office with a desk and some chairs but no windows; light was provided by a single naked bulb hanging from the ceiling.

"Sit," Green said.

Anna sat in one of the straight chairs before the desk. "I am very thirsty."

Green considered this, then opened the door and called for someone to bring a carafe of water.

"Thank you," Anna said, and drank. "I would like to get dressed."

He grinned at her and sat down himself. "That can wait. Perhaps it will not be necessary, eh?"

Anna stared at him, and he looked away.

Again she had to practise patience. She looked at her wristwatch; it was just after eight. The train would be arriving about now, and David Cohn would be on the platform to greet her. What would he do when she did not arrive? Wait for another train, perhaps, reckoning she might have missed the first one. Then he would send a telegram to Papa. For the first time she felt a real pang of alarm. Papa, paralysed and helpless! He had only Martina to turn to, and he needed Martina there, both to nurse and protect him.

What would he do? What *could* he do?

The door opened; Green stood up and came to attention. Anna turned her head. Would this be Himmler?

She didn't think so. The man was short and walked with a limp; his right shoe had been artificially enlarged. He wore a trench coat and carried a cane. His face was peculiarly ugly, the features heavy and oddly misshaped, but his eyes were magnetic.

"This is the girl?" he asked in German.

"This is she, Herr Goebbels," Green said.

"You acted on your own initiative?"

"Well, Herr—"

"I have spoken with Herr Himmler, and he says he gave no instructions that anyone was to be kidnapped. He tells me he knows nothing of this."

"Well, Herr Goebbels, I felt something was wrong, in that she was coming to Berlin. What reason can she have had for coming here?"

"As she is here, I am sure we can persuade her to tell us." Goebbels limped across the room to stand in front of Anna, seeming to take her in for the first time.

Anna clenched her fists in her lap. She had seen men look at her like that before.

"You have caught a treasure," Goebbels remarked. "Does she speak German?"

"I do not believe so, sir."

"But you say she is Townsend's daughter?"

"Yes, sir."

"Then would she not be the girl he rescued from Grippenheimer, killing him in the process?"

"I think she is, sir."

"Then of course she speaks German. Is that not true, Anna?"

Anna gazed at him.

Goebbels smiled. "Oh, yes. I have heard a lot about you. I was not then sufficiently important in the party to be invited to Grippenheimer's house, to sample some of his delights. But now, what do I see? You have come to me. Is it not true that everything comes to he who waits?"

Still Anna gazed at him, while her brain raced. She knew what he wanted, what he intended to have. But men, she had observed, were at their most helpless when in the throes of sexual endeavour.

Perhaps he could read her mind. "Bundle her up," he said, "and take her to Amhasser, number three. Tell Hannah to see to her until I get there. But I do not wish her harmed in any way." He chucked her under the chin. "If you *are* to be harmed, I would prefer to do it myself."

Keep calm, Anna told herself, as Green summoned his accomplice to tape her up again, watched by Goebbels. This is no different to Shrimpton's behaviour. The difference was that now she did not have a gun . . . Ankles and wrists again secured, she was wrapped up in the cloak, carried out of the building and replaced in the back seat of the car It was broad daylight now and the city was bustling, so she was made to lie on her side on the seat, her head on Green's lap, in order that no one might see her. But it also meant that she couldn't see out, and she had no idea where she was being taken. Amhasser. It was not an address she knew.

At least, Goebbels having staked his claim, Green did not attempt to interfere with her. "So you do speak German, Fräulein? Who's a smart-ass then?"

"It is not difficult, dealing with a halfwit like you," Anna said.

His hand, resting on her shoulder, gripped her flesh hard for a moment, then relaxed. "When Herr Goebbels is finished with you, I will ask him to give you to me for execution," he said. "Then we will hear you squeal."

The car turned into another yard from which rose a high building. Someone must have telephoned ahead because a woman was waiting for them, opening doors. The woman took Anna's suitcase, Green carried Anna into the lift, and they moved upwards. There was no evidence of anyone else in the building.

"Where did he find this one?" the woman asked.

"I found her," Green said. "I didn't know it was for him."

"They are always for him," the woman remarked.

The lift stopped, the gate opened, and the woman unlocked a door on the other side of the lobby. Green carried Anna through, and through another lobby into a light and airy if somewhat overfurnished lounge.

"Where do you want her?"

"The floor will do. Then you can unwrap her."

Green laid Anna on the carpet, unrolled her from the cloak and knelt to release her ankles and wrists. The woman stood above them. She was tall and looked powerful; boots emerged from beneath her ankle-length skirt. Her hair was dark and worn short. Her features matched her body, pronounced and forceful. She looked what she no doubt was, a born gaoler.

"She is very handsome," the woman remarked, as Anna sat up to rub herself.

"She is beautiful," Green commented.

The woman snorted. "Very well. You can leave her now."

"You are sure you can cope?"

"Of course. Can you speak German, girl?"

"She can," Green said. "Although she likes to pretend that she cannot."

"Get up," the woman said.

Anna stood up.

"I am sure we are going to get on very well," the woman said. "My name is Hannah. And you are . . ."

"I am Anna."

"Anna and Hannah. How nice. Yes, we will be friends. As long as you obey me in everything. Do you understand this?"

Anna nodded.

"If you do not, I will beat you. Do you understand?"

Anna nodded again. She had already determined that she could not take on this woman in straightforward physical combat; Hannah was taller, bigger and undoubtedly stronger. On the other hand, she was obviously arrogantly aware of those facts, and that was a weakness.

"Very good," Hannah said. "You can go now; there will be no trouble."

Green still looked as if he would have preferred to stay, but he obeyed, closing the doors behind himself.

"Now," Hannah said. "The first thing I wish you to do is have a bath. The good doctor does like his women to be clean. Through there."

"I am very thirsty," Anna said. "And hungry."

Actually, she was, but she also felt that the kitchen was the best place to look for a weapon.

"I will make some coffee and something to eat," Hannah said. "After you have bathed. It is through there."

"What am I to wear? My suitcase . . ." Hannah had placed it against the wall.

"It is not necessary for you to wear anything. The doctor likes naked women."

Anna swallowed, then went through the indicated doorway. Here there was a bedroom, with the bathroom beyond. The décor was in rich reds and purples, which she supposed was indicative of Goebbels' personality.

Hannah followed her and switched on the taps, adding a liberal dollop of salts. Then she opened a drawer and took out a toothbrush still wrapped in cellophane and a tube of toothpaste. Anna cleaned her teeth, and felt considerably better.

By the time she was finished the bath was quite full. Hannah tested the temperature with her elbow, then switched off the taps. "In you get."

"You are staying?"

"Of course. I am not to let you out of my sight. Besides, I like looking at you; you are a very beautiful woman."

Anna had already determined that there was no worthwhile weapon in the bathroom. She lifted her nightdress over her head, let it fall to the floor, and sank into the water. It felt delightful. She looked up at Hannah, who was gazing at her and almost licking her lips . . .

"Would you like me to help you?" Hannah asked.

Anna knew she had to make a hasty and irrevocable decision. She would probably never have a better opportunity than this. But to attempt and fail . . . On the other hand, what did she have to lose? The woman had threatened to beat her, but she couldn't actually damage her until Goebbels arrived.

"That would be very nice," she said.

Hannah undressed. Her figure, large and strong, was in keeping with her face, but it was well-shaped. She picked up a bar of soap and knelt behind Anna. "Just relax and enjoy it," she suggested.

Anna waited, every muscle tensed. Hannah's soapy hands slid over her back and shoulders. "I doubt that Herr Goebbels will be here much before this evening," she said. "We can have an enjoyable day together."

Her hands slid down from Anna's shoulders to caress her breasts. Anna drew up her legs and put up her own hands to hold Hannah's wrists, and Hannah gave a grunt of pleasure. Anna drew a deep breath, closed her hands as tightly as she could, and at the same time threw herself forward, generating all the power she could from her thighs down into her legs. Hannah gave a startled exclamation as she was dragged into the bath with an enormous splash, water scattering in every direction, her slippery hands unable to grasp Anna's flesh. For a moment her weight smothered Anna, but the girl twisted round, propelling herself backwards, reaching the end of the bath. Hannah had fallen between her legs, and was now attempting to push herself up, hands slipping on the porcelain tub. Anna closed her hands together and struck down on the back of the woman's neck. Hannah gasped, making a ghastly gurgling sound as her lungs filled with water. Anna unclasped her hands and placed them on the back of Hannah's head, holding it beneath the water. Hannah twisted desperately and managed to roll right over, legs kicking and arms flailing. Anna thrust Hannah's head back under again, even as she gave a little shriek of agony as the woman's teeth closed on her flesh. But she would not let go, and a few seconds later Hannah subsided, the frothing bubbles that had been escaping from her nostrils finally ceasing.

Still Anna pressed down, while the blood from her bitten hand spread in the water.

The End of the Journey

Anna remained sitting in the bath for several seconds, Hannah's body now quiet between her legs. Then she grasped the edges of the bath and pushed herself up. She was still breathing hard from her exertions, but her brain was, as always in moments of crisis, ice-cold.

She was again guilty of murder, and this time identifiably so. This was Goebbels' flat and he had sent her here. Should he arrive to claim her and find only the dead body of his housekeeper, he would simply go to the police. Once she was arrested, even if they believed her story that she had been resisting a lesbian rape, she would still be charged and probably sent to prison . . . if the Nazis did not get her first.

Well then, get out of here, contact the Cohns, and with their help make for Poland? The Cohns had not bargained on having to aid a wanted murderess, nor could they be asked to.

Then make for Poland on her own? Presumably by train. But it would be several hours before she could reach the border, by which time Goebbels would have arrived and alerted the police.

Her mission would have been a total failure, save that it would give the Nazis an added motive for seeking her father's death. And then again there did not seem much doubt that Goebbels was Himmler's boss, from the conversation she had overheard between him and Green. Thus if she executed Goebbels she would be striking at the very heart of the enemy.

If she executed Goebbels! How was she to do that? She got out of the bath, dried herself, and sucked at her bite. She hunted through the flat, opening drawers and wardrobes. Hannah's clothes were in the spare room and various items of men's clothing in the master bedroom; she presumed they were Goebbels'. But there was nothing remotely like a weapon. Even the knives in the kitchen drawers were too small to be of much use save at very close quarters. If there was one thing she had learned during her chaotic life it was that men were usually stronger than women when it came to wrestling. She would only succeed if she could get him at a disadvantage. But if he was coming here to have sex with her, then she would definitely have him at a disadvantage at some time during the coming afternoon or night. There was even the chance that he might be carrying a gun; he looked the sort of man who would.

So . . . She stood above the tub, looking down at Hannah, feeling no revulsion or even distaste for what she had to do. She reached down between Hannah's legs and pulled out the plug. While the water drained away she opened various cupboards and found a large towel.

Now the tub was empty. Anna grasped Hannah's armpits and dragged her out. Hannah's body hit the floor with a thump and Anna checked, listening. If there was anyone in the flat below . . . But there was no reaction. She knelt beside Hannah and dried her, then dragged her across the floor into the corridor and on into her room. There was a large wardrobe, and Anna heaved the body into that and closed the door. She did not think the housekeeper would become a nuisance for perhaps twenty-four hours, and her business would be completed long before then.

Green had left her suitcase in the lounge. She checked it to make sure her passport was there and gave a sigh of relief when she found it. She contemplated dressing, then decided against it. The sooner she got to Goebbels, and let Goebbels get to her, the better. She went into the kitchen, ate some bread and cheese, washed it down with a bottle of lager, and then got into bed to wait. She took with her the largest of the kitchen knives, placing it beneath the pillow.

"Heinrich," Goebbels said over the telephone, "I would like you to come to Berlin."

"About the girl?"

"Yes. I have her. But before I proceed I need to know about her."

"I have told you," Himmler said. "I know nothing about her. Green acted entirely without authority. He is the one who knows about her. Anyway, I cannot come to Berlin. The Führer wishes you here in Munich. Have you not heard the news?"

"What news?"

"About the financial crisis? There has been a crash on the New York Stock Exchange. Millions have been wiped out."

"And a good thing too," Goebbels said.

"You do not understand, Josef. The possible ramifications are endless."

"My dear Heinrich, how can what happens in New York affect us in Germany?"

"Schacht has been explaining it to us. Germany's entire economy is based upon American loans. If their banks run out of money at home and decide they cannot lend us any more, or worse yet, decide to call in the money outstanding, we would have a most severe economic crisis. It could bring down the government."

"Is that not what we all fervently desire?"

"Exactly. The Führer wishes us to be fully prepared for every eventuality. That is why he is calling this meeting."

Goebbels frowned. He could see this was important. But the thought of that girl; so much beauty waiting not only to be raped but to be "questioned" as well. . . . On the other hand, she wasn't going anywhere.

"Josef?" Himmler was anxious.

"I will come to Munich," Goebbels said. "But it will have to be a brief visit. We must clear up this matter here as quickly as possible."

"Yes, yes," Himmler agreed. "I will come back with you. Just let us get this American business done first."

Goebbels replaced the phone. It was his opinion that the Americans were always being a nuisance. But of course, this event might present great opportunities for embarrassing and perhaps even overthrowing the government. Again he thought of the girl. He knew Hannah well enough to be sure she would be unable to keep her hands off such a dainty morsel. He had no objection to that, but he also knew that Hannah had an unstable temper and was quite capable of hurting those who attempted to resist her; and that was a pleasure he wished to reserve for himself.

He picked up the telephone, gave the number and waited while it rang several times without being answered, a frown slowly gathering between his eyes. Then he hung up and rang his bell.

His secretary hurried in. "Get me a ticket on the next train to Munich," he said, "returning tomorrow morning."

"Yes, Herr Goebbels."

"And is the man Gerber still in the building?"

"I believe so, Herr Goebbels."

"Send him to me."

He waited, drumming his fingers on the desk, until Gerber arrived. "You delivered the young woman to the address I gave you?"

"Yes, Herr Goebbels."

"Did she attempt to resist you?"

"No, sir."

"And you gave her into the care of Frau Vesta?"

"Yes, sir." Gerber's expression spoke volumes.

"Well, I wish you to return there and make sure everything is all right," Goebbels said. "It would be a good idea for you to stay there overnight; I will not be able to attend to the matter until tomorrow. Now Gerber," he pointed, "I do not wish the young woman harmed in any way. Not the slightest blemish. Understand that, and make sure Frau Vesta understands that too."

"Yes, sir. Am I not to return to England?"

"Not until the young lady has told us what she is up to. We will find that out tomorrow. You can help me find out."

Gerber's tongue circled his lips. "Yes, Herr Goebbels."

"But until then, Gerber, not a blemish. Remember that."

The compartment was crowded on the way to London, but once Martina and Druce boarded the Folkestone train they were alone and able to talk for the first time.

"Are you nervous?" Martina asked.

"I suppose I am. This is really a little out of my experience."

"Well, do not be afraid. I will take care of you."

He snorted. "I did not say I was afraid, except for Anna. I assume you are armed?"

"Of course. But you are not?"

"I would hope we can accomplish our purpose without resorting to guns."

Her turn to snort. "In this business, only guns matter."

"Are we not going to the Berlin police?"

"We will act on the advice of the Cohns. They know what is going on."

"I doubt that. The police are our best bet. Failing that, the British embassy."

"What good will they be? Berkeley is *persona non grata* with his own government. They will not lift a finger to help his daughter."

"I think they might," Druce said.

"We will do what the Cohns recommend," Martina said. "All we really need is an address where these people may be holding Anna." She glanced at him. "If she is alive. You do understand this."

"I do understand this. And if she is dead?"

"We will avenge her."

Hans Gerber whistled a little tune as he unlocked the flat door. It was relief that his over-enthusiasm had not landed him in hot water. It was the fact that he was being allowed to spend the night with that gorgeous creature – of course he would not be able actually to touch her, well, not more than a stroke or two, and undoubtedly the dragon of a housekeeper would be a nuisance. But, most of all it was the fact that he had been admitted into Herr Goebbels' inner sanctum, as it were. The doctor was an important member of the party; anyone who was his protégé was going places. Look at Himmler, nothing more than a chicken farmer, now suddenly commanding the *Schutzstaffel*!

The door swung in, and he stepped through, carefully closing and locking it behind him. There was a not a sound in the apartment. "Hello!" Gerber called. "Frau Vesta?"

"She went out," Anna said.

Gerber's turned sharply. She was framed in the master-bedroom doorway, naked, her red-gold hair clouding past her shoulders. For a moment he couldn't speak, then he licked his lips.

"What do you want?" Anna asked. "Why are you here?"

"Herr Goebbels sent me to make sure everything is all right. He telephoned but could not get a reply."

"I heard the phone ring," Anna said. "But I decided against answering it. I did not know if my presence here was supposed to be secret."

"Where is Frau Vesta?"

"I told you; she went out."

"Leaving you alone, here? Why did you not leave?"

Anna shrugged. "Have I anywhere to go?"

Gerber smiled. "That is a very sensible attitude."

"When is Dr Goebbels coming?"

"He cannot come until tomorrow. He has been called away." Gerber took a step forward, staring at her, committing every contour of that perfect body to memory. Oddly enough, he got the impression that she was doing the same thing to him, although of course he was fully dressed. "He told me I could spend the night here. With you."

"That would be very nice," Anna said. "Let me take your coat."

Now she came towards him, holding out her arms. He stepped inside them, brought her against him, kissed her mouth while his hands slid over the satin of her skin. She made no objection but allowed her hands to wander as well, inside his jacket.

"Oh," she said. "You have a gun."

He pulled his head back. "Do you object?"

"I find it exciting. Tell me, Herr Gerber, are we alone in the building? All the other flats . . ."

"They belong to members of the party. But there is no one here at the moment. Why, are you going to scream?"

"Only if you make me."

Her body was still pressed against his, her arms round his chest, inside his jacket. He grinned down at her. "I would like to make you scream."

"I know," she said, stepping away from him.

Gerber stared at the Luger automatic pistol she held in her right hand.

"You little bitch," he said. "Maybe I will make you scream after all. You'd better put that down before it goes off."

"Yes," Anna said, and shot him through the heart.

* * *

"This is very nice," Martina said, surveying the sleeping compartment as the train pulled out of Boulogne Station. "Very cosy."

"Yes," Druce agreed. He thought it was too cosy by half; they could hardly move without squeezing against each other.

"Very intimate," Martina added. "Now, you will take me to the dining car and we will have dinner, and then we can go to bed. And wake up in Germany?"

"Yes," Druce said, more doubtfully yet.

But the meal and the wine were good, the waiters attentive.

"Tell me," Martina asked the waiter serving the main course. "Are you on this run every night?"

"Not every night, madame," the waiter said. "We have time off."

"But were you on last night?"

"Yes, madame."

"A cousin of mine made this journey last night. I'm sure you will remember her: a very beautiful girl, twenty years old, with reddish-brown hair."

"Oh, indeed, madame, I remember the young lady. I thought it odd that she should be travelling alone."

"She has an independent spirit," Martina said. "Can you tell me where she left the train?"

"Mademoiselle Townsend was booked through to Berlin, madame."

"How do you know her name?" Druce asked.

"It is our custom to collect all the passengers' passports before we reach the border, monsieur. We change crews at the frontier, you see, and also there is a customs check. We give the passports to the border police, who inspect them and return them. This way we do not have to wake the passengers."

"Very helpful of you. Will you be asking for our passports as well?" Martina enquired.

"Certainly, madame. One of my colleagues will do so when you retire."

"You say Miss Townsend was booked through to Berlin, but could she have left the train before then?" Druce asked.

"That is not possible, sir. This is an express train. Its only stop is at the border, and that is not for either the embarkation or disembarkation of passengers."

"Thank you," Martina said. "You have been most helpful." She waited until they had regained the privacy of the sleeper, then said, "We shall have to make inquiries on the German side."

"It looks like it. How long do you need?"

"To do what?"

"To undress yourself and get into bed."

"I have no idea. I do not hurry over these things."

"I will give you half an hour," Druce said, opening the door.

"Where are you going?"

"To the smoking car."

"Do you smoke?"

"No, I don't. But I have to go somewhere while you undress."

Martina gave a shriek of laughter. "That is absurd. You are a prude."

"I hope I am a gentleman."

Martina shrugged. "Then be a gentleman. I will take the upper bunk."

When Druce returned, she was in bed and could have been asleep, the sheet pulled to her shoulder, her hair scattered about her, but he didn't trust her. He switched off the light before undressing himself, slid into the bunk, but had not been there more than five minutes when he saw, in the gloom, a pair of long, white, perfectly shaped legs dropping past his face.

"You've nothing on!" he accused as the rest of her followed.

"I never wear anything to bed," she explained. "And those pyjamas of yours are ridiculous. Move over."

"Whatever for?"

"I wish to get in with you. You do not have to fuck me. Just a kiss and a cuddle and a bit of a feel."

"You are engaged to be married," he pointed out.

"Berkeley knows all about me," she said.

"I am also engaged to be married."

"And I am sure Anna knows all about you."

"Martina," he said. "We came here to do a job of work. Go back to bed."

She surveyed him for several seconds. "You do not wish to have sex with me?"

"No. I mean, not right now."

"There may not be another opportunity. You will be sorry." She climbed back into her bunk. "At least you should have pleasant dreams."

The train rumbled into Tiergarten Station at eight o'clock. Druce had been up and dressed at six, Martina a few minutes later. Again he insisted on leaving the compartment while she dressed, and then they had an early breakfast.

"Well?" Martina enquire wickedly. "Did you dream?"

"No," Druce lied.

"I shall have to try harder. The train is stopping."

They collected their bags and stepped on to the platform; Martina gave one of her squeals of pleasure. "David! Judith!"

The Cohns came forward to be embraced. They were in their middle thirties now, handsome and prosperous thanks to the success of their catering business.

"Martina! It is good to see you," David said. "I only wish it was in happier circumstances."

"We shall make the circumstances happier," Martina said. "This is Harry Druce, Anna's fiancé."

The Cohns shook hands. "We have arranged the meeting you requested, with Commissioner Schuler," David said. "But it is not until ten o'clock."

"Then let us have a cup of coffee and you can bring us up to date."

Druce looked around with interest as they walked from the station to a coffee shop; it was his first visit to Berlin. The city looked busy and prosperous, but the faces were anxious.

"It is the news from America," Judith explained. "The Wall Street crash. No one knows how it will affect us here in Germany."

"There have been crashes before," Martina said. They sat down and ordered coffee. "Now," she said. "You met the train, this same train, yesterday morning. But you say that Anna was not on it."

"That is correct," David said. "We met the next one as

well, just in case she had been delayed. But she was not on that either."

"They told us it was not possible for her to have left the train before Berlin."

"That is correct, normally."

"What do you mean?" Druce asked.

"Simply that it is extremely likely the Nazis, if they were responsible, bribed the driver and the night guard. Then, if Anna had already been made prisoner, it would be simply a matter of stopping the train for a few seconds at some isolated station. I should not think anyone else on the train would even have woken up, and the schedule could be regained by the slightest increase in speed."

"My God," Druce said. "You mean she could have been taken off the train and now be anywhere in Germany?"

"I'm afraid that is a possibility, yes."

"Just who are these Nazi people, anyway? I had never even heard of them until a few days ago."

"They call themselves a political party, but they've never had much of an impact on the political scene."

"They may do, if unemployment rises because of this American crisis," Judith said.

"That is a worrying point," her husband agreed. "The fact is, however, at the moment they are just an extreme right-wing group who pander to everything that is evil in society. They oppose the communists, violently wherever possible, and they blame the Jews for all of Germany's ills."

"And the government does nothing about this?"

"Much of what the Nazis say appeals to the government, or certain elements in it. They are opposed to the Versailles Treaty, claim that Germany should be allowed to rearm, say that the refusal of the Allies to allow us to regain control of the Rhineland and the Ruhr is iniquitous . . . These are all things the government would like to see happen, but of course they dare not say so themselves."

"One of the big problems," Judith said, "is that no one knows who is a Nazi and who is not. So, as we said, several of the staff on the train may have been party members. But there is no way of finding out."

"Is Schuler a Nazi?"

"As far as we know, he is not. But it is certain that quite a few of his policemen are."

"Then it would appear that we are on a hiding to nothing," Druce remarked.

"Not necessarily," Martina said. "Don't forget that I worked for a police commissioner for several years. Alexandros knew everything that was going on in Serbia. Much of it he did not like but was unable to do anything about because of political pressure. But when someone came along like Berkeley, who did wish to do something, he was very happy to assist him, clandestinely of course. That is how their friendship began."

"It's worth a go," Druce agreed.

Commissioner Schuler surveyed the four people seated in front of his desk. The Cohns he already knew; they were typical of the many young entrepreneurs who had done well out of the *laissez-faire* Weimar years. He wished them well; he had no personal antagonism to the Jews. But he wondered how well they were going to do in the future as political opinions in Germany hardened into race hatreds.

Nor did he much like what they, and their English friends, had just told him.

"If I had a mark," he said, "for every young girl who came to Berlin and then disappeared, I would be a wealthy man."

Martina translated for Druce's benefit.

"But Anna came here specifically to see you," she explained. "And she was abducted from the Boulogne Express."

"You mean she left the Boulogne Express before it reached Berlin."

"She was abducted, Herr Commissioner," David said. "That train does not stop. An English citizen, Herr Commissioner. If the newspapers in England get hold of this story, they will make life very difficult for you."

Schuler surveyed the young man and decided not to take offence. "Very well, Herr Cohn. Give me her full name and I will have some inquiries made. You say she was very good-looking? If she was abducted, with respect ladies, it was probably for sexual purposes."

"We do not believe it was for sexual purposes," David said. "At least not in the first instance. Her name is Anna Townsend."

Schuler frowned.

"You have heard this name?" Martina asked.

"I have heard the name," Schuler said carefully, "in connection with an officer in the British army."

"Colonel Berkeley Townsend," Martina said.

"That is correct."

"Anna is his daughter."

Schuler's head jerked.

"You may not be aware of it," Martina went on, "but there have been several attempts on Colonel Townsend's life over the past year. The last attempt came very close to succeeding. These attempts were made by the Nazi Party."

"You have proof of this?"

"Yes," Martina said boldly. "Anna was coming to Berlin to place this proof before you. Obviously these people found out her intention, and determined to prevent her seeing you."

Schuler stroked his chin. He had no doubt at all that next year's elections were going to be conducted in an atmosphere of violence, with the Nazis to the fore. It would be quite a *coup* for the forces of law and order to embroil the party in a criminal case which, whatever the outcome, would carry a large whiff of scandal. But if the plan misfired . . . He was well aware that a number of his officers, including some in senior positions, were sympathetic to the Nazi cause. Were he to move against the party and his case prove to be inadequate, there might well be a call for his removal from office on the grounds of prejudice.

"You have no proof that Fräulein Townsend was kidnapped by the Nazis," he pointed out.

"We were hoping that you might cooperate," David said.

"How? Do you suppose I have the resources to deal with wild and unsubstantiated accusations against people of standing? Proof, Herr Cohn, if you could obtain proof . . ."

"What sort of proof?"

"Well, if you could find out where she is being held . . . If she is being held anywhere, of course."

"It could be anywhere in Germany," Martina protested.

"I do not think so," Schuler said. "You say a man called

Himmler is behind this? Himmler has recently left Berlin for Munich. However, he has never, until now, been a man of any importance in the party, certainly not to the extent of being able to order international assassinations. I would say he has been carrying out the orders of his immediate superior, Dr Goebbels, who is the party boss in Berlin. If I am right, the young lady will be here in Berlin. Dr Goebbels is well known for his interest in the female sex."

"And you know where we can find this Dr Goebbels?"

"Certainly. But he is not likely to be holding the girl at his home. The party owns certain houses in the city, which it rents out to its people. I happen to know that Dr Goebbels maintains a *pied-à-terre* in Three Amhasser . . ."

"Well, then," Martina said, "can you not raid this place?"

"Me? My dear Frau . . ." he glanced at the pad on which he had noted their names, "Savos, I have no reason for doing so, no reason for asking for a warrant. I have no proof that any crime has been committed. Now, if you were able to provide me with such proof . . ." He looked from face to face.

"Three Amhasser," David said.

"That is where Dr Goebbels has an apartment, yes," Schuler said.

"And have you any objection if we pay this flat a visit?"

"My dear Herr Cohn, Germany is a free country. You may do whatever you wish. However, I should warn you that should you break any laws, I will have to arrest you."

"But equally," Martina said, "if we bring you proof that Fräulein Townsend is being held there, you will act."

"Depending on the nature of the proof, I shall reconsider the situation," Schuler said.

He watched them file from the office, then pressed the buzzer on his intercom.

"Will you come in here, please, Studt."

His assistant appeared a moment later.

"I wish you to stake out Three Amhasser," Schuler said.

"Is that not the address where—"

"Yes," Schuler said. "I wish this to be done with the utmost discretion, Studt."

"And the instructions to be given to my men?"

"They are to observe the apartment building for the next twenty-four hours. They are only to interfere if any law is broken. And Studt, this does not include suspicious loitering. There has to be a definite breach of the peace before our people become involved. Understood?"

"Understood," Studt said.

"Then put out your men. Now."

"Three Amhasser," David Cohn mused over another cup of coffee. "That is not a very good neighbourhood. What do you plan to do?"

Martina had explained the conversation with Commissioner Schuler to Druce.

"We intend to visit this flat," she said, "and bring Anna out."

"And if she is not there?"

"We shall find out where she is."

"You understand that these people, these Nazis, are highly dangerous."

"So am I," Martina said

David clearly found this hard to believe.

"However," Martina said, "I know that Berkeley would not wish you and Judith to be involved. The only help we would ask is if you could get us out of Berlin afterwards."

"Of course," David said. "You intend to go there alone?"

"I shall be with her," Druce said.

David looked more doubtful yet. But he said, "We will get you out of Germany afterwards."

"That was a complete waste of time," Josef Goebbels remarked as he and Himmler stepped down from the Munich train. "Talk, talk, talk. I had supposed we were a dynamic party, one that made things happen rather than waited on events."

"At least the Führer has put you in charge of organising our strategy for the election," Himmler said placatingly.

"Yes," Goebbels said. "That is satisfactory. Ah, Bruckner."

Bruckner stood to attention.

"We will go directly to Amhasser," Goebbels said.

"Yes, Herr Doctor." Bruckner escorted them from the station to the waiting car. "I have heard nothing from Gerber."

Goebbels nodded. "That is correct. I told him to spend the night at the flat, just to make sure nothing goes wrong with our arrangements."

"I have, however, been able to ascertain from one of our people at Police headquarters, that this young woman had an appointment with Commissioner Schuler for yesterday morning," Bruckner said.

"Oh, my God!" Himmler said, getting into the back of the car.

"There is no need to be concerned," Goebbels said, sitting beside him. "She cannot have told him anything for the simple reason that she did not keep the appointment. Does your informant know if Commissioner Schuler was concerned at her non-appearance?"

"I do not believe he was, Herr Doctor. The commissioner is a busy man."

"Quite," Goebbels agreed.

The car turned down several side streets.

"Do you know," Goebbels said, "I am quite excited. More excited than I have been for a very long time, at least about a woman."

"She is still just a woman," Himmler remarked.

"You have never seen her, have you?"

"No."

"Well, let me tell you, she is exceptional. Before I have sex with her, before we interrogate her, I am going to photograph her and have the print blown up, to remind me of what she was, what I possessed."

"But you still mean to execute her?"

"I don't see that there is any alternative. Do not worry. I will let you have her also, before we deal with her."

Himmler shuddered.

"How do we get in?" Himmler asked, as they stepped down from the car. "Do you have a key?"

"I gave mine to Gerber," Goebbels said. "We will simply ring the bell and let him admit us."

He did so, and waited.

"Yes?"

Goebbels frowned. "Anna? Is that you, Anna?"

"Why, Dr Goebbels," Anna said, "I thought you were never coming. I will open the door."

The phone clicked off.

"Isn't she a treasure?" Goebbels asked his companions. "So utterly innocent."

"Can she really be of any value to us?" Himmler asked.

"She is of value to me," Goebbels said.

The door clicked open and they climbed the stairs. The apartment door was closed, but responded to Goebbels' push. It swung in, and he stepped through, nostrils dilating.

"What is that smell?"

"I am afraid it is your housekeeper," Anna said. "Very unpleasant, isn't it? But I had expected you long before now."

He turned to look at her, standing naked in the bedroom doorway, her hands behind her back.

"My God," he said. "Where is Gerber?"

"Come in," she said. "Close the door, and I will show you."

Goebbels hesitated then stepped into the room, and Anna for the first time saw the two men behind him.

"Bastard!" she snapped, and brought her hands round in front, the pistol held between them.

"Look out!" Bruckner shouted unnecessarily. Goebbels was already diving to the floor while Himmler was taking shelter behind the door. Bruckner alone continued to advance.

Anna hesitated for a fatal second, then determined to go for Goebbels. She squeezed the trigger and the bullet smacked into the floor behind him. Before she could fire again, Bruckner was upon her, his shoulder charge spinning her round and throwing her against the doorway, the chop of his right hand forcing her to release the Luger, which clattered to the floor. He reared over her, fists clenched.

"Don't harm her!" Goebbels was scrambling to his feet. "That was well done, Bruckner. Heinrich, stop cowering back there and come in. And close the door."

Himmler slunk into the room.

Anna was on her knees, panting, for the moment unable to comprehend how she had failed in her mission but able to understand that she had virtually committed suicide.

"You are quite a handful," Goebbels remarked. "Search the

apartment," he told Bruckner. "Find that smell. You may get up," he told Anna.

Slowly Anna got to her feet, looking from Goebbels to Himmler. She did not know who Himmler was; that he was one of Goebbels' henchmen was sufficient.

"Herr Doctor!" Bruckner's voice was urgent.

Goebbels handed the Luger to Himmler. "Keep her covered."

Himmler licked his lips as he took the gun. "Please do not do anything stupid. Have you no clothes?"

"You wish me to dress?"

"Oh, do not be a fool," Goebbels said. "Admire her, Heinrich. It will do you good."

He went into the housekeeper's room, paused, and held his hand to his nostrils.

Bruckner was looking a little green as he stood by the open cupboard door. "She has been here at least twenty-four hours."

"How did she die?"

"There are no wounds. It is difficult to say. Perhaps the girl can tell us."

"I am sure she will. And Gerber?"

Bruckner gestured at the corner of the room, where Gerber's body lay in a crumpled heap. "He is still in rigor mortis. This is a police matter, Herr Doctor."

"Under no circumstances," Goebbels said.

"Gerber has been shot in the chest at close range."

"You think that girl did this? Did them both?"

"It looks like it, Herr Doctor. And if she did, well . . . I do not think we can any longer describe her as a girl. She is a monster."

"Then we will deal with her as a monster. But the police must not be involved. That would be to reveal the kidnapping, and would cause problems."

"And the bodies?"

"Have them disposed of. Secretly. It will be necessary to do this with the girl, anyway."

Bruckner looked doubtful, but he nodded.

"Now," Goebbels said. "Let us have a chat with this monster."

*   *   *

"It looks empty." Martina studied the apartment building from across the street.

The street was also empty, Druce reflected, thankfully. "The house isn't empty," he said, pointing at the parked car.

"You think the driver is inside?"

"And whoever he was driving. What do you intend to do?"

"Knock on the street door. Ring the bell, if there is one. These people do not know who we are. And when the door is opened, we will force our way in. I expect your total support in this, Harry."

"You shall have it," he promised, wondering if he was telling the truth.

They crossed the road and checked the list of names.

"Goebbels, first floor," Martina said with satisfaction, and pressed the bell.

"Now," Goebbels said, returning to the lounge, where Anna had seated herself on the settee, watched by a clearly embarrassed Himmler, "tell me what happened here."

"The woman attempted to rape me," Anna said, "so I drowned her in the bath."

"Just like that. And no doubt Gerber attempted to rape you as well."

"Yes."

"So you shot him. Just like that. Did you not spend some years as a prostitute?"

"Yes. That does not mean that I must allow myself to be raped."

"It's a point of view. So tell me, why did you come back to Berlin?"

"I came here to deal with the man who has been attempting to kill my father. A certain Himmler."

"Then you have failed. That is Herr Himmler holding the gun on you."

Anna's breath hissed through her nostrils as she looked at Himmler but her expression did not change. Himmler looked terrified. "I had already worked out that he was but an underling," she said. "That it was you I should be dealing with."

"So you waited, patiently, for me to come to you, disposing of any other people who got in your way. You are really an amazing creature, and an amazingly dangerous creature, it seems. But now your career is at an end, my dear. Do you know what we are going to do to you?"

"I am sure you will tell me," Anna said.

"We are going to rape you, and rape you, and rape you," Goebbels said, "until each of us is satisfied. Then I personally am going to to strangle you, and smile at you while you die. But first, as you have been a naughty girl, I am going to cane you until I draw blood. Go into the bedroom and lie on the bed. On your face."

Anna licked her lips as she looked from face to face. But there was no pity to be seen, even if Himmler continued to look apprehensive.

She stood up. "At least I know I shall be avenged," she said.

"By whom?" Goebbels sneered,

"My father will take care of it."

"Your father?" Goebbels looked at Himmler.

"Your father is already dead," Himmler said.

Anna stared at him. "You—"

The street-door bell buzzed. All four people in the room stared at the phone. "Answer it," Goebbels snapped.

Himmler picked up the phone. "Yes?"

"I have an urgent message for Dr Goebbels," a woman said.

Anna took a quick breath as she recognised Martina's voice.

As Goebbels noticed.

"No one of that name lives here," Himmler was saying.

"I know the apartment belongs to Dr Goebbels," Martina said. "Will you let me in or shall I call the police?"

"Let her in," Goebbels said, and moved with great speed to stand behind Anna, throwing one arm round her waist and clutching her throat with his other hand. "Who is this woman?"

"I do not know," Anna gasped.

"I think you do. But no matter. She may be armed. Heinrich, stand by the door and disarm her as she enters."

"Dis— Me?"

"For God's sake, are you a man or a mouse? Bruckner will cover you. But I wish her taken alive. And you, miss, keep quiet, or I will skin you."

Anna knew she was helpless; he was far stronger than he looked. But the mere touch of his hands made her skin crawl, and she did not intend to go out without a fight.

And Martina was coming up the stairs. Martina had come to get her! Martina! One against three; but if anyone could do it, Martina could.

There was a tap on the door.

"It is open," Goebbels called.

Himmler was standing against the wall, next to the opening edge of the door, hands poised to strike downwards. Bruckner was in the middle of the room, facing the door, gun in hand. But Goebbels had told him not to shoot unless it became necessary. That might be vital.

The door swung in.

"Martina!" Anna screamed. "It's a trap!"

Goebbels' hand closed so tightly on her throat she thought she was about to die, but she got her foot up against the door jamb and pushed with all her strength, so that they both fell over, hitting the floor with a crash. Dimly she was aware of what was happening in the rest of the room. Martina had entered, gun hand thrust forward as Goebbels had anticipated. Himmler's hand chopped down and she gave a little scream of pain as it landed on her wrist. The revolver fell to the floor with a clatter, and Himmler gave a shout of triumph and jerked Martina from her feet so that she landed on her hands and knees, while Bruckner moved forward.

Then Anna, still wrestling with Goebbels who was trying to regain his grip on her throat, saw Druce behind Martina, bending to pick up the revolver. As he straightened, Bruckner fired. The bullet hit the wall above Druce's head. But now he had the revolver in his grasp, straightening and firing in the same instant. Struck in the chest, Bruckner fell backwards and hit the floor with a crash.

The sounds of the shots had not died when there came the blast of a whistle from the street, followed by several more. Goebbels released Anna and rolled across the floor into the bedroom, kicking the door shut. She got to her feet, and Druce threw his arm round her shoulders. Martina tried to restrain Himmler, but he threw her hand off and fled through the front door.

"Oh, my darling."

"Harry! You killed a man. For me."

Druce looked down at the revolver he still held, realising what he had done.

The blasts were now outside the house, and they could hear Himmler shouting.

"We must get out of here," Martina said. "Otherwise we will be arrested and charged with murder. Hurry."

Anna looked at the closed bedroom door. "That man is behind it all. We must deal with him."

"Some other time," Martina snapped. "Come *on*! Is this yours?"

She indicated the suitcase.

"Yes."

"You can dress outside."

Anna looked at the bedroom door again.

"She's right," Druce said. "That man's life is not worth yours."

Anna sighed, then suddenly remembered what Himmler had said about Papa's business being completed. She had to get home as quickly as possible . . .

She allowed herself to be led from the apartment.

"Be careful," Himmler warned, as the policemen climbed the stairs. "They have guns. They are killers. They . . ." He gazed at the open door of the flat, in which Goebbels was framed.

"Heinrich?" Goebbels asked. "Whatever are you up to now?"

"Those people . . ."

"We heard shots, Herr Doctor," the sergeant said.

"And you were conveniently close by," Goebbels remarked sarcastically. "How gratifying it is to be protected by such an efficient police force. I'm afraid I fired those shots, Sergeant. I have just bought a new automatic pistol; I was inspecting it, and it went off. Why, I almost shot poor Heinrich."

Himmler gulped.

"But . . ." The sergeant was totally confused. "He said—"

"Heinrich is inclined to be hysterical," Goebbels said. "Come inside, do, Heinrich, and cease terrifying the neighbourhood."

Shoulders bowed, Himmler went into the flat, Goebbels stepping aside to let him through. He clearly had no intention of letting anyone else through, however.

"Now," he said, "if you'll excuse me, Sergeant . . ."

"With respect, Herr Doctor," the sergeant said, "I would like to look inside your flat."

"And with respect, Sergeant, I will not permit that unless you have a warrant. Do you have a warrant?"

"I can obtain one."

"Then I suggest you do so, if you can."

The sergeant gulped; he was as aware as anyone that the district magistrate was a Nazi sympathiser.

"Permit me to ask you a question, Herr Doctor."

"Certainly," Gobbels said courteously.

"That peculiar smell . . . It is not very pleasant, is it?"

"It is very unpleasant," Goebbels agreed. "It is some meat that my housekeeper forgot to refrigerate and which has gone off. I am now going to do something about it. You'll excuse me."

He closed the door, leaned against it and gazed at Himmler.

"Those people have got away," Himmler said. "You let them get away."

"Is it relevant? We know who they are and thus where they live. In any event, did you not say that the Townsend matter has finally been solved?"

"Yes, yes," Himmler said. "I sent Hassler. Our very best. It is done."

"Well, then . . ."

"But that girl . . . that monster . . . Now she will want to avenge her father."

Goebbels smiled. "But now we not only know what she looks like, but of what she is capable. I intend to deal with her personally, Heinrich. It will be a great pleasure. But it must be done when it cannot harm the party. To allow the police in here, for them to find the bodies and discover what had happened, that would be front-page news in every newspaper in the country. In Europe. With us looking very bad. Can you imagine what that girl might say if she were brought to trial? Schuler would have a field day. What do you think those policemen were doing, so close by, at such an inconvenient moment? Schuler knew that something was going to happen. Thus we must make sure that nothing did happen. Now, telephone central office and tell them we require a squad up here, to deal with this mess."

"Are you awake, sir?" Mary Lockwood was still somewhat overawed by her new duties, not that she would have wanted anything better.

Berkeley stirred. "I'm awake."

"I have your breakfast."

She placed the tray beside his bed and sidled from the room. Berkeley looked at his watch. It was nine in the morning, which made it just over twenty-four hours since Martina and Druce should have arrived in Berlin. Which meant that if they had succeeded in their mission, they should be on their way to Poland. If they had succeeded. Not knowing, not knowing if Anna was alive or dead, was almost unbearable.

The doorbell rang, and Mary hurried through from the kitchen.

"Just a moment," Berkeley said.

"There's someone at the door."

"It sounds like it. Is there a car in the yard?"

Mary frowned. "No, sir."

"A bicycle?"

"I didn't see one, sir."

"Did you see anyone?"

The kitchen overlooked the drive.

"Just this man, sir. He suddenly appeared."

"Having walked here," Berkeley mused. "From where, do you suppose?"

"Oh, sir!"

"I think we won't answer the door," Berkeley said. "You go back to your kitchen and tell me if he attempts to go round the house. But under no circumstances must you let him see you, or become involved in what may happen."

"Oh, sir," Mary said again, but she left the room.

The door bell jangled again, for longer than before.

Berkeley reached into his bedside drawer and took out the Browning. He checked that it was loaded, then slipped it beneath the covers, resting against his thigh. He experienced a surge of elation. He would show them there was life in the old dog yet.

The doorbell rang a third time.

The telephone had been placed by the bed. Berkeley picked it up, gave the number of Northampton Police Station. "Chief Inspector Watt, please."

The bell had stopped ringing, and the sound had been replaced by a scratching noise.

Mary appeared in the doorway. "I think he's trying to break in, sir. What cheek."

"He probably thinks there's nobody at home. Now go to the kitchen and stay there."

"Shall I close this door, sir? Keep him out. If he gets in."

"I think we'll leave the door open, Mary. If he gets in I'll need to deal with him as quickly as possible. Ah, Peter. Good morning to you."

"And to you, Colonel," Watt said. "Is there anything we can do for you?"

"Yes, there is. There is a man attempting to force his way into my house. I would say he intends to kill me."

"What did you say?"

"You know the score, Peter. Now, I shall defend myself to the best of my ability, but there is only me and a single, very young, maidservant. I do think it would be very helpful were you to send some people, or better yet, come yourself."

"Yes," Watt said. "Yes. We'll be right out. It may take half an hour. If you can keep him talking . . ."

"If I can think of anything to say, certainly. However, Peter, I think you and your people should be armed."

Berkeley replaced the phone and put his hand under the covers to rest on the gun. His position was a strong one: the assassin could not possibly suspect that he was downstairs. The only information he would have would be that his victim was badly wounded and crippled. That indicated bed and an inability to move. The drawback of his situation was that he could not see the front door. His line of vision through the open door ended at the foot of the stairs leading up.

But it would be to those stairs that the man would go.

The noises from the front door had been growing louder. Now they suddenly ceased. He had picked, or broken, the lock.

Berkeley brought the Browning out from beneath the covers and levelled it at the door.

He heard no footfalls; the man was tip-toeing. Then he appeared at the foot of the stairs. As Berkeley had expected, he was nondescript in appearance, with a little moustache. One hand was in the pocket of his light overcoat, and his hat was pushed back on his head.

"In here," Berkeley said.

Hassler turned sharply, drawing his Luger as he did so. Berkeley fired as the gun came up, saw the man buckle beneath the impact of the bullet, and then was aware of pain. Briefly.

"Perhaps I should not say this, Miss Anna," Peter Watt said, "but I cannot escape the feeling that your father died as he would have liked to die."

"Gun in hand, facing his enemy," Martina said softly.

They stood round the graveside; the brief service of interment had just concluded.

"My men and I came as quickly as we could," Watt said anxiously. "But it happened too quickly."

"It was terrible," Mary sobbed. "Terrible."

"I know you all did everything possible," Anna said. "And I am grateful. The fault is mine. I should have been here."

"We must all thank God you were not, Miss Anna. Otherwise . . . well . . ."

"I might have died along with Papa," Anna said, softly.

Druce squeezed her hand.

"*I* should have been here," Johnnie said fiercely. He and Alicia had come home for the funeral; neither of them as yet knew of the Berlin adventure, or the truth of the Shrimpton affair.

"Again, I think we should be grateful that you were not," Watt said.

"What about the assassin?" Druce asked. "Have you identified him?"

"No, we have not, sir. And I don't think we will. He carried nothing on his person save the gun with which he killed the colonel, and some money. The gun was German-made, to be sure, but his suit was made in England. We should be able to trace where it was bought, but I don't think we'll be much ahead, if, as seems obvious, he was a foreigner."

"But he got in and out of the country, and had to be helped to get here."

"I agree, sir. But then, the Karlovys were also helped, and we have never been able to find out who looked after them. I would say this man came from the same source. At any rate, the business would now appear to be finished. The feud was between the colonel and these people, and with the colonel dead, well, there'd be no point in it."

"I am sure you are right," Martina said.

"What will you do, Mrs Savos?"

"It was Papa's wish to marry Martina," Anna said. "I therefore regard her as my stepmother, and hope she will remain so."

Martina embraced her.

"And you, Miss Anna? Will you . . ." Watt looked at Druce.

"We will be married, yes, Chief Inspector," Druce said. "Just as soon as is practical."

"Then I will wish you every happiness." Watt touched his cap and went to his car.

"Well, then," Anna said. "It is just us, now." She looked at Mary and Harry Lockwood.

"We are with you, Miss Anna," Harry said. "Always."

"It isn't really over, is it?" Johnnie asked.

"No," Anna said. "Papa's death had absolutely nothing to do with the Karlovy feud."

"Then we will avenge it."

"Yes," Anna said. "However long it takes, we will avenge his death."

"Do you understand this, Mr Druce?" Johnnie asked. "That it is something we have to do?"

Anna put her arm round Druce's waist to give him a hug. "Of course he does. Harry is one of us, now."